"Superb." —*Publishers Weekly* (starred review)

"Poignant and terrifying . . . Take a deep breath before diving into this one." —*Entertainment Weekly*

"Alex North weaves a stunningly captivating narrative that's a nuanced and grounded exploration of father-son relationships. . . . A master class in genre exploration. An incredible read." —Joe and Anthony Russo, directors of *Captain America: Winter Soldier, Captain America: Civil War, Avengers: Infinity War*, and *Avengers: Endgame*

"*The Whisper Man* is the most unsettling thriller I have read since Jo Nesbø's *The Snowman*. Much more than the sum of its parts, it is nightmarish and disturbing and, at the same time, a moving and life-affirming novel about fathers and sons, grief, loss, and recovery." —Alex Michaelides, author of the #1 *New York Times* bestseller *The Silent Patient*

"Brilliant . . . An affirmation of the power of the father-son relationship . . . Will satisfy readers of Thomas Harris and Stephen King." —*Booklist* (starred review)

"A terrifying page-turner with the complexities of fatherhood at its core." —*Kirkus Reviews*

"A powerful and scary story that will haunt readers long after the final page is turned." —*Library Journal*

"First it's spooky. Then it's scary. Then it's terrifying. And then . . . Well, dear reader, proceed at your own risk. An ambitious, deeply satisfying thriller—a seamless blend of Harlan Coben, Stephen King, and Thomas Harris. My flesh is still crawling." —A. J. Finn, author of the #1 *New York Times* bestseller *The Woman in the Window*

ALSO BY ALEX NORTH

*The Whisper Man*

# THE
# SHADOWS

ALEX NORTH

CELADON
BOOKS
NEW YORK

This is a work of fiction. All of the characters, organizations, and events portrayed in this novel are either products of the author's imagination or are used fictitiously.

Published in the United States by Celadon Books, a Division of Macmillan Publishers.

THE SHADOWS

For information, address Celadon Books, a Division of Macmillan Publishers, 120 Broadway, New York, NY 10271.

www.celadonbooks.com

ISBN: 978-1-250-87630-0

Our books may be purchased in bulk for promotional, educational, or business use. Please contact your local bookseller or the Macmillan Corporate and Premium Sales Department at 1-800-221-7945, ext. 5442, or by email at MacmillanSpecialMarkets@macmillan.com.

Printed in the United States of America

Celadon Books hardcover edition / July 2020
Celadon Books trade paperback edition / October 2021
Celadon Books mass market edition / December 2022

10  9  8  7  6  5  4  3  2  1

For Lynn and Zack

# PROLOGUE

It was my mother who took me to the police station.

The officers had wanted to drive me in the back of their squad car, but she told them no. It's the only time I can remember her losing her temper. I was fifteen years old, standing in the kitchen, flanked by two huge policemen. My mother was in the doorway. I remember her expression changing as they told her why they were there and what they wanted to talk to me about. At first she seemed confused by what she was hearing, but then her face shifted to fear as she looked at me and saw how lost and scared I was right at that moment.

And, while my mother was a small woman, something in the quiet ferocity of her voice and the strength of her posture caused both of those huge policemen to take a step back from me. On the way to the police station, I sat in the passenger seat beside my mother, feeling numb as we followed the car that was escorting us through the town.

It slowed as we reached the old playground.

"Don't look," my mother told me.

But I did. I saw the cordons that had been put in place. The officers lining the street, their faces grim. All the vehicles that were parked along the roadside, their lights rotating silently in the late afternoon sun. And I saw the old jungle gym. The ground beside it had always been dull and gray before, but right now I could see it was patterned in red. It all seemed so quiet and solemn, the atmosphere almost reverential.

And then the car ahead of us came to a stop.

The officers were making sure I got a good look at a scene they were certain I was responsible for.

*You have to do something about Charlie.*

It was a thought I'd had a great deal in the months leading up to that day, and I still remember the frustration it always brought. I was fifteen years old, and it wasn't fair. Back then, it felt like my entire life was constrained and controlled by the adults around me, and yet none of them appeared to have noticed the black flower rotting in the middle of the yard. Or else they had decided it was easier to leave it alone—that the grass it was poisoning didn't matter.

It should not have been left to me to deal with Charlie.

I understand that now.

And yet, as I sat in the car right then, the guilt they wanted me to feel overwhelmed me. Earlier that day, I had been walking through the dusty streets, squinting against the sun and sweating in the simmering heat, and I had spotted James right there in the playground. My oldest friend. A small, lonely figure in the distance, perched awkwardly on the jungle gym. And while it had been weeks by then since he and I had spoken, I had known full well what he was doing. That he was waiting there for Charlie and Billy.

A number of the officers at the scene turned to look at us, and for a moment I felt trapped in a pocket of absolute silence. Stared at and judged.

Then I flinched as a sudden noise filled the air.

It took me a second to realize that my mother was leaning on the car horn. The blaring volume of the sound seemed jarring and profane in the setting—a scream at a funeral—but when I looked at her I saw my mother's jaw was clenched and her gaze directed furiously at the police car ahead. She kept her hand pressed down, and the sound continued, echoing around the town.

Five seconds.

"Mom."

Ten seconds.

"*Mom.*"

Then the police car in front of us began moving slowly away again. My mother lifted her hand from the horn and the world fell quiet. When she turned to me, her expression was somehow both helpless and resolute at the same time, as though my hurt were her own and she was determined to bear the weight of it for me as much as she could.

Because I was her son, and she was going to look after me.

"It's going to be okay," she said.

I did not reply. I just stared back, recognizing the seriousness in her voice and the conviction on her face, and feeling grateful that there was someone there to look after me, even if I would never have admitted it. Grateful there was someone with me who cared about me. Someone who had such faith in my innocence that the words themselves didn't need to be spoken out loud.

Someone who would do anything to protect me.

After what felt like an age, she nodded to herself, and began driving. We followed the car out of the town and left the parked police vans, the staring officers, and the bloodstained playground behind us. And my mother's words were still echoing in my head as we reached the main road.

*It's going to be okay.*

Twenty-five years have passed, but I still think about that a lot. It's what all good parents tell their children. And yet what does it really amount to? It's a hope, a wish. A hostage to fortune. It's a promise you have to make, and one you must do your best to believe in, because what else is there?

*It's going to be okay.*

Yes, I think about that a lot.

How every good parent says it, and how often they're wrong.

# PART ONE

# ONE

--·--·—·--·--

## NOW

On the day it began, Detective Amanda Beck was technically off work. She slept late. Having been woken in the early hours by the familiar nightmare, she clung to the thin threads of sleep for as long as possible, and it was approaching noon by the time she was up and showered and making coffee. A boy was being killed right then, but nobody knew it yet.

In the middle of the afternoon, Amanda started out on the short drive to visit her father. When she arrived at Rosewood Gardens, there were a few other cars parked in the lot, but she saw nobody. A profound silence settled over the world as she walked up the winding path between the flower beds that led to the gated entrance, and then took the turns she had committed to memory over the last two and a half years, passing gravestones that had become familiar markers.

Was it strange to think of the dead as friends?

Perhaps, but a part of her did. She visited the cemetery at least once a week, which meant she saw more of the people lying here than the handful of living friends she had. She ticked them off as she walked. Here was the grave that was always well attended by fresh flowers. There, the one with the old, empty whiskey bottle balanced against the stone. And then the plot covered with stuffed toys: a child's grave, that one, Amanda guessed, the presents left by grieving parents who couldn't quite allow their child to leave them yet.

And then, around a final corner, her father's grave.

She stopped and pushed her hands into the pockets of her coat. The plot was marked by a rectangular stone, broad and strong, the way she remembered her father from growing up. There was something pleasingly implacable in the simplicity of it—the way there was just his name and a pair of dates that bookmarked his life. No fuss, exactly the way he would have wanted. Her father had been loving and caring at home, but his life had been spent on the force, where he had done his duty and left his work in the office at the end of the day. It had felt right to reflect that aspect of his character in her choice of headstone. She had found something that did the job required of it—and did it well—but kept emotion separate.

*No bloody flowers on my grave, Amanda.*

*When I'm gone, I'm gone.*

One of the many orders she had followed.

But, God, it still felt odd and jarring to her that he was no longer in the world. As a child, she had been scared of the dark, and it had always been her father who came to her when she called out. Whenever he was out on a night shift, she remembered being anxious, as though a safety net had been taken away and if she fell there would be nothing there to catch her. That was the way life seemed these days too. There was a constant sensation in the back of her mind that something was wrong, something missing, but that it wouldn't last. Then she would remember her father was dead, and the stark realization would come. If she called out now, there was nobody to find her in the night.

She pulled her coat a little tighter around her.

*No talking to me after I'm gone either.*

Another order, so all she ever did when she visited the grave was stand and think. Her father was right, of course. Like him, she wasn't religious, and so she didn't see much point in saying anything out loud. There was nobody to hear now, after all; the opportunity for interrogation had passed. She had been left with the short lifetime of experience and wisdom her father had gifted her, and it was down to her to sift through that. To hold parts up to the light, blow dust from them, and see what worked and what she could use.

*Dispassionate.*

*Aloof.*

*Practical.*

That was how he had been when it came to his job. She thought often of the advice he had given her: When you saw something awful, you had to put it away in a box. The box was something you kept locked in your head, and you only ever opened it to throw something else inside. The work, and the sights it brought you, had to be kept separate from your life at all costs. It had sounded so simple, so neat.

He had been so proud of her joining the police, and while she missed him with all her heart, there was also a small part of her that was glad he wasn't around to see how she'd dealt with the last two years. The box of horrors in her head that would not stay closed. The nightmares she had. The fact that it had turned out she wasn't the kind of officer he had been, and that she wondered whether she ever could be.

And although she followed her father's instructions, it didn't stop her from thinking about him. Today, as always, she wondered how disappointed he would be.

She was on the way back to the car when her phone rang.

Half an hour later, Amanda was back in Featherbank, walking across the waste ground.

She hated this place. She hated its coarse, sunscorched bushes. The silence and seclusion. The way the air always felt *sick* here, as though the land itself had gone sour and you could sense the rot and poison in the ground on some primal level.

"That's where they found him, right?"

Detective John Dyson, walking beside her, was gesturing toward a skeletal bush. Like everything else that managed to grow here, it was tough and dry and sharp.

"Yeah," she said. "It is."

*Where they found him.*

But it was where they had lost him first. Two years ago, a little boy had disappeared while walking home here, and then, a few weeks afterward, his body had been dumped in the same location. It had been her case.

The events that followed had sent her career into a free fall. Before the dead boy, she had imagined herself rising steadily up the ranks over the years, the box in her head sealed safely shut, but it turned out she hadn't known herself at all.

Dyson nodded to himself.

"They should fence this place off. Nuke it from orbit."

"It's people who do bad things," she said. "If they didn't do them in one place, they'd just do them somewhere else instead."

"Maybe."

He didn't sound convinced, but nor did he really seem to care. Dyson, Amanda thought, was pretty stupid. In his defense, he at least seemed to realize that, and his entire career had been marked by a singular lack of ambition. In his early fifties now, he did the work, collected the pay, and went home evenings without so much as a backward glance. She envied him.

The thick tree line that marked the top of the quarry was just ahead of them now. She glanced back. The cordon she'd ordered to be set up around the waste ground was obscured by the undergrowth, but she could sense it there. And beyond that, of course, the invisible gears of a major investigation already beginning to turn.

They reached the trees.

"Watch your step here," Dyson said.

"Watch your own."

She stepped deliberately in front of him, bending the fence that separated the waste ground from the quarry and then ducking under. There was a faded warning sign attached a little way along, which did nothing to stop local children from exploring the terrain. Perhaps it was even an incentive; it probably would have been to her as a kid. But Dyson was right. The ground here was steep and treacherous, and she concentrated on her footing as she led the way. If she slipped in front of him now she would have to fucking kill him to save face.

The sides of the quarry were dangerously steep, and she made her way down cautiously. Roots and branches, baked pale by the oppressive summer heat, hung out from the rock like tendons, and she gripped the rough coils of them for balance. It was about a hundred and fifty feet down, and she was relieved when she reached solid ground.

A moment later, Dyson's feet scuffed the stone beside her.

And then there was no sound at all.

The quarry had an eerie, otherworldly quality. It felt self-contained and desolate, and while the sun was still strong on the waste ground above, the temperature was much cooler here. She looked around at the fallen rocks and the clusters of yellowing bushes that grew down here. The place was a maze.

A maze that Elliot Hick had given them directions through.

"This way," she said.

Earlier that afternoon, two teenage boys had been taken into custody outside a nearby house. One of them, Elliot Hick, had been borderline hysterical; the other, Robbie Foster, empty and calm. Each was holding a knife and a book, and both were soaked almost head to toe in blood. They were being held for questioning at the station, but Hick had already told the attending officer what the two of them had done, and where they would find the results of it.

It wasn't far, he'd said.

Three hundred feet or so.

Amanda headed between the rocks, taking her time, moving slowly and carefully. There was a pressure to the silence here that felt like being underwater, and her chest was tightening with apprehension at the thought of what they were about to see. Assuming Hick was telling the truth, of course. There was always a chance there was nothing to be found here at all. That this was some kind of bizarre prank.

Amanda reached out and moved a curtain of sharp branches to one side. The notion that this was a practical joke seemed absurd, but it was infinitely preferable to the idea that she was about to step out into a clearing and see—

She stopped in her tracks.

And see that.

Dyson stepped out and stood next to her. He was breathing a little faster, although it wasn't clear if that was from the physical exertion of the climb and the walk, or the sight that lay before them now.

"Jesus Christ," Dyson said.

The clearing ahead of them was roughly hexagonal, the ground jagged but basically flat, and it was bordered on all sides by trees and tangles of bushes. There was something almost occult about the setting, a first impression that was only enhanced by the tableau laid out there.

The body was about fifteen feet away, directly in the center. It had been posed in a kneeling position, bent over almost in prayer, the thin arms folded backward along the ground like broken wings. It appeared to be that of a teenage boy. He was dressed in shorts and a T-shirt that had ridden up to his armpits, but the blood made it difficult to tell what color the clothing had been. Amanda's gaze moved over the body. There were numerous dark stab wounds on the boy's exposed torso, the blood around them pale brown smears on the skin. There was a deeper pool beneath his head, which was tilted awkwardly to one side, barely attached, and facing mercifully away from her.

*Dispassionate,* Amanda reminded herself.

*Aloof.*

*Practical.*

For a moment, the world was completely still. Then she saw something else and frowned.

"What's that on the ground?" she said.

"It's a kid's fucking body, Amanda."

She ignored Dyson, and took a couple of careful steps farther into the clearing, anxious not to disturb the scene but needing to make sense of what she was seeing. There was more blood on the stone floor, stretching out in a circle on all sides around the body. The pattern seemed too uniform to be accidental, but it was only when she reached the edge of the bloodstains themselves that she realized what they were.

She stared down, her gaze moving here and there.

"What is it?" Dyson said.

Again, she didn't reply, but this time it was because

she didn't quite know how. Dyson walked across to join her. She was expecting another exclamation, more bluster, but he remained silent and she could tell he was just as disturbed as she was.

She counted the stains as best she could, but it was hard to keep track of them. They were a storm on the ground.

Hundreds of blood-red handprints pressed carefully against the stone.

# TWO

The hospice in which my mother was dying was on the grounds of Gritten Hospital.

It seemed a slightly melancholy arrangement to me. On the long drive cross-country, I had wondered why they didn't go for the hat trick and install a cemetery and a conveyer belt while they were at it. But the grounds turned out to be pleasant. Once past the hospital, the driveway curled leisurely between carefully trimmed lawns dotted with brightly colored flower beds and apple trees, and then over a small bridge with a stream burbling underneath. It was a hot day, and I'd rolled the car window down. The air outside was saturated with the rich smell of freshly cut grass, and the sound of the water on the rocks below seemed threaded through with a child's laughter.

Tranquil surroundings for the end of a life.

After a minute, I reached a two-story building with lush swathes of ivy covering its blackened walls. The car tires crackled over a sea of neatly turned pebbles.

When I killed the engine, the only noise was the gentle trill of birdsong, the silence behind it heavy and profound.

I lit a cigarette and sat for a moment.

Even now, it wasn't too late to go back.

It had taken four hours to drive here, and I'd felt the presence of Gritten growing closer the whole time, and the dread inside me had increased with every passing mile. The sky might have been bright and clear, but it had felt as though I were driving toward a thunderstorm, and I had half expected to hear rumbling in the distance and see crackles of lightning at the horizon. By the time I was driving through the ramshackle streets and flat industrial estates, past the rows of weathered shops and factories and the forecourts scattered with litter and broken glass, I was feeling so sick that it had been an effort not to turn the car around.

I smoked now, my hand shaking.

Twenty-five years since I'd been here in Gritten.

*It's going to be okay,* I told myself.

I stubbed out the cigarette, then got out and walked across to the hospice. The glass doors at the entrance slid open to reveal a clean and minimalist reception area, with a polished black-and-white floor. I gave my name at the desk and waited, smelling polish and disinfectant. Aside from the sound of cutlery clinking somewhere away to one side, the building was as quiet as a library, and I felt an urge to cough, simply because it felt like I shouldn't.

"Mr. Adams? Daphne's son?"

I looked up. A woman was approaching me. She was

in her mid-twenties, short, with pale blue hair, numerous ear piercings, and she was dressed in casual clothes. Not an orderly here.

"Yes," I said. "Sally, right?"

"That's me."

I shook her hand. "Call me Paul."

"Will do."

Sally led me up a set of stairs, and then down a warren of quiet corridors, making small talk along the way.

"How was your journey?"

"Fine."

"How long has it been since you've been back to Gritten?"

I told her. She looked shocked.

"*Actual* wow. Do you still have friends locally?"

The question made me think of Jenny, and my heart leaped slightly. I wondered what it would be like to see her again after all these years.

"I don't know," I said.

"I guess the distance makes it difficult?" Sally said.

"Yeah, it does."

She meant geography, but distance worked in other ways too. The car journey today might have taken four hours, but this short walk inside the hospice seemed longer. And while a quarter of a century should be a span of history with heft and weight, I was shivering inside. It felt like the years had dropped dangerously away, and that what had happened here in Gritten all those years ago might as well have occurred yesterday.

*It's going to be okay.*

"Well, I'm glad you could come," Sally said.

"Work's always quiet over the summer."

"You're a professor, right?"

"I teach English, but I'm not that high up."

"Creative writing?"

"That's one of the classes."

"Daphne was proud of you, you know? She always told me you'd be a great writer one day."

"I don't write." I hesitated. "She actually said that?"

"Yeah, totally."

"I didn't know."

But then, there was a lot about my mother's life I hadn't known. We might have spoken on the phone every month or so, but they were always short, casual conversations in which she had asked after me, and I had lied, and I had not asked after her, so she hadn't needed to. She had never given me a hint that anything was wrong.

And then three days ago I had received a phone call from Sally, my mother's care worker. I hadn't known about Sally. I also hadn't known that my mother had been suffering from steadily advancing dementia for years now, and that over the last six months her cancer had become untreatable. That in recent weeks my mother had become so frail that the stairs were difficult for her to climb, and so she had been living almost entirely on the ground floor of the house. That she had refused to be moved. That one evening earlier in the week, Sally had entered the house to find her unconscious at the bottom of the stairs.

Because, either out of frustration or confusion, it seemed my mother had made an attempt to reach the landing above and her body had betrayed her. The head injury she suffered was serious rather than fatal, but the fall had goaded the rest of her afflictions into attacking more swiftly.

There was so much I hadn't known.

Time was short, Sally had told me. Could I come?

"Daphne's mostly sleeping," she said now. "She's receiving palliative care and pain relief, and she's doing as well as she can. But what will happen over the next few days is that she'll sleep more often, for more prolonged periods of time. And then, eventually, she'll . . ."

"Not wake up?"

"That's right. Just pass away peacefully."

I nodded. That sounded like a good death. Given there has to be an end, maybe that's all any of us can hope for—to drift steadily off. Some people believed there were dreams or nightmares to come afterward, but I've never really understood why. As I know better than most, those things happen in the shallow stages of sleep, and I've always hoped that death would be a much deeper state than that.

We stopped outside a door.

"Is she lucid?" I said.

"It varies. Sometimes she recognizes people and seems to understand vaguely where she is. But more often it's like she's in a different place and time." She pushed open the door and spoke more softly. "Ah— here's our girl."

I followed her into the room, bracing myself for what I was about to see. But the sight was still a shock. A hospital bed rested against the nearest wall, with wheels on the legs and controls to elevate and change its position. To the side of it, there was more machinery than I'd been expecting: a cart with a bank of monitors, and a stand of clear bags with tubes looping out, connected to the figure lying beneath the covers.

My mother.

I faltered. I had not seen her in twenty-five years, and, as I stood in the doorway now, it looked like someone had made a model of her from wax, but one far smaller and frailer than the old memories I had. My heart fluttered. Her head was bandaged on one side, and what I could see of her face was yellow and motionless, her lips slightly parted. The thin covers were barely disturbed enough to suggest a body beneath, and for a moment I wasn't sure she was even alive.

Sally seemed unperturbed. She walked across and then bent over slightly, checking the monitors. I caught the faint scent of the flowers on the table beside the machinery, but the smell was corrupted by a hint of something sweeter and more sickly.

"You're free to sit with her, of course." Sally finished her examination and straightened up. "But it's probably best not to disturb her."

"I won't."

"There's water on the table if she wakes and wants it." She pointed to the bed rail. "And if there are any problems, there's a call button there."

"Thank you," I said.

She closed the door behind her as she left.

And then silence.

Except not quite. The window nearest the bed was

half open, and I could hear the peaceful, soporific buzz of a lawn mower coming from somewhere in the distance. And then, beneath that, the slow, shallow breaths my mother was taking. There were long stretches of empty seconds between them. Looking down at her, I noticed the pink floral pattern of the bedsheets for the first time, and the sight of them delivered a ghost of memory. They weren't identical to the ones I recalled from childhood, but close enough. Sally must have brought them from the house to make my mother feel more at home here.

I looked around. The room reminded me of the one in the residence halls during my first year at college: small but comfortable, with an en suite bathroom built into one corner and a desk and cabinets along the wall opposite the bed. There were a handful of objects spread out on the desk. Some of them were clearly medical—empty bottles, popped pill cases, and torn strips of cotton wool—but others looked more ordinary, more familiar. There was a pile of carefully folded clothes. Eyeglasses in an open case. The old photograph of my parents' wedding I remembered sitting on the mantelpiece when I was a child: here now, and angled so my mother could see it from the bed if she woke.

I walked over to the desk. The photo should have been a record of a happy occasion, but, while my mother was smiling and hopeful, my father's face looked as stern as always. It was the only expression of his I could remember from childhood, whether illuminated by the constant fires he would build in the backyard or shadowed in the hallway as we passed each other without speaking. He had always been serious and sour—a man let down by everything in his life—and we had both been glad to be rid of each other when I left here. None of the phone calls from my mother over the years had featured him. And when he died six years ago, I had not returned to Gritten for the funeral.

I glanced along the desk and saw something I hadn't noticed before. A thick book, placed cover-down. It was old and weathered, and the spine was slightly twisted, as though it had been soaked in water at some point and then left to dry crooked. My mother had never been much of a reader; my father had always been sneeringly dismissive of fiction, and of me and my love for it. Perhaps my mother had discovered a passion for it after his death, and this was what she had been reading before the accident. A nice gesture on Sally's part, although it seemed fairly optimistic to imagine my mother was going to finish it now.

I turned the book over, and saw the red, leering devil's face on the cover—and then pulled my hand away quickly, my fingertips tingling as if they'd been burned.

*The Nightmare People*.

"Paul?"

I jumped and turned around. My mother was awake. She had moved onto her side and was propped up on one elbow, staring at me almost suspiciously with the one eye I could see, her hair hanging down to the pillow in a thin gray stream.

My heart was beating too quickly.

"Yes." I spoke quietly, trying to calm myself. "It's me, Mom."

She frowned.

"You . . . shouldn't be here."

There was a chair by the bed. I walked slowly across and sat down. Her gaze followed me, as wary as that of an animal primed to flee.

"You shouldn't be here," she said again.

"I kind of *had* to be. You fell. Do you remember?"

She continued staring at me for a moment. Then her expression softened and she leaned toward me and whispered conspiratorially.

"*I hope Eileen's not here.*"

I looked around the room helplessly. "She isn't, Mom."

"I shouldn't say that, really. But we both know what a *bitch* that woman is. Poor Carl." She looked sad. "And poor little James too. We're only doing this for him, aren't we? You know that, I think. We don't need to say so, but you understand."

*It's like she's in a different place, a different time.*

This was a place and time I recognized.

"Yes, Mom," I said. "I did understand."

She lay down carefully again and closed her eyes, whispering.

"You shouldn't be here."

"Do you want some water?" I said.

For a moment, my mother did nothing. She just lay there breathing steadily, as though the question were taking time to work its way through the confusing labyrinth of her mind. I had no faith that it would reach its destination, but I couldn't think of anything else to say right now. And then suddenly my mother lurched awake again, jolting upright at the waist, and reached —

out and grabbed my wrist so fast there was no time for me to recoil.

"*You shouldn't be here!*" she shouted.

"Mom—"

"Red hands, Paul! There are red hands everywhere."

Her eyes were wide and unblinking, staring at me in absolute horror.

"Mom—"

"Red hands, Paul."

She let go of me and collapsed back on the bed. I stood up and staggered backward a little, the white imprint of her grip on my skin. I pictured a jungle gym and a ground patterned in crimson, and her words repeated over and over in my head in time with my heartbeat.

*Red hands, red hands, red hands everywhere*—

"Oh God, it's in the house, Paul!"

And then my mother's face contorted in anguish, and she screamed at the ceiling, or perhaps at something out of sight above.

"*It's in the fucking house!*"

And with panic lighting up my whole body, I scrabbled for the alarm button.

# THREE

--·-----·--·

During the summer break when I was fourteen, my mother took me and my friend James to see Gritten Park, our new school. We arrived at James's house first thing that morning, and I remember my mother whispering to me as we walked up the path.

"I hope Eileen's not here."

I nodded. I hoped that too. Eileen was James's mother, but you wouldn't have known that from the way she treated him. James could never do anything right in her eyes, assuming she noticed him at all. I'd always found her frightening. She smelled of sherry, and seemed to smoke constantly with one hand cupping her elbow, watching you suspiciously, as though she thought you might have stolen something from her.

But it was Carl who answered the door that morning.

Carl was James's stepfather, and I liked him a great deal. James's natural father had abandoned Eileen when she was pregnant, and Carl had raised him as though he were his own son. He was a humble man, quiet and kind, but while I was glad he was good to James, it also baffled me how he'd ended up with a woman like Eileen. Carl and my mother had been close friends since childhood, and I suspected it was a mystery to her too. Years earlier, I'd overheard a conversation between the two of them. *You can do so much better, you know,* my mother had told him. And there had been a long silence before Carl replied. *I really don't think I can.*

Carl looked tired that day, but he smiled warmly at us both before calling back into the house for James, who then emerged a few moments later. James was wearing old tracksuit bottoms, a grubby T-shirt, and an awkward smile. He was a timid boy: shy and sweet and defenseless; always desperate to please the whole world, but never sure what it wanted.

And my best friend.

"Come on, then, urchins," my mother said.

The three of us walked away from the house toward the main road that connected our town to the rest of Gritten. It was a warm morning, and the air was close and full of dust and flies. The metal of the overpass clanked beneath our feet as we made our way across to the dirty bus stop on the far side. Below us, a steady stream of vans and semi trucks shot past indifferently. Our town saw little traffic, and while it was technically a suburb of Gritten, it barely existed on maps. Even its name— Gritten Wood—gave more prominence to the enormous nearby forest than to the idea that anybody still lived here.

Eventually a bus appeared in the distance.

"Have you got your tickets?" my mother said.

We both nodded, but I rolled my eyes at James and he smiled back. We were both fine on buses, and had visited Gritten Park the previous term, after learning the small school we had attended up until now was closing. But while James might not have admitted it, he was scared about starting a new school, and so my mother had come up with a way to help without embarrassing him, and I was happy to go along with it.

It was a half-hour journey. Most of Gritten was saturated with poverty, and the view through the bus window was so drab that it was sometimes difficult to tell the empty premises from the occupied. I wanted nothing more than to escape from here—to move away and never return—but it was hard to imagine it ever happening. The place had a gravity that held whatever was dropped where it fell. That included the people.

Off the bus, the three of us took the five-minute walk to Gritten Park.

The school was much bigger and more intimidating than I recalled. The gymnasiums were about three hundred feet back from the main road, their vast windows reflecting the bland sky and trapping it in the glass. Beyond, the main building was visible: four stories of murky, monotonous corridors, the classroom doors thick and heavy, the way I imagined doors in a prison. The angles of the two buildings were slightly off, so that from the street the school looked like something that was pulling itself out of the ground, with one shoulder hunched up behind it, awkward and broken. I looked to the right of the gyms. The area there was being renovated, and I could hear the tapping of a pneumatic drill from somewhere behind the stretched tarps. An inter-mittent, staccato sound, like distant gunfire.

We stood for a while.

And I remember feeling uneasy. There was some-thing malevolent about the school—in its stillness, and the way it seemed to be looking back at me. Before then, I'd understood James being nervous about starting here. The school was huge—home, if you could call it that, to over a thousand students—and James had always been a natural target for bullies. He was my best friend, though. I'd always looked after him in the past, I'd told myself, and I always would. And yet there was something omi-nous about the school before me right then that made me doubt myself.

The silence stretched out.

I remember looking at my mother and recognizing the confusion she was feeling, as though she had tried to do a good thing, a caring thing, but had somehow gotten it wrong.

And I remember the look on James's face. He was staring at the school with absolute dread. For all my mother's good intentions, this expedition hadn't helped him at all.

It was more like we had brought him to his place of execution.

The quickest route from the hospice to the town would have taken me along that same road outside the school. I went a different way. I wanted to avoid any contact with the awful things from my past for as long as I could.

But that became impossible as I drove into Gritten

Wood itself. The town I had grown up in appeared untouched by the intervening years. Its spiderweb of quiet, desolate streets was immediately familiar, and the dark wall of the woods still dominated the landscape ahead, looming over the dilapidated two-story houses sitting in their own separate plots of scratchy land. I had the sensation that the faint sand misting up beneath the car's tires was the same dust that had been here when I was a kid. Picked up and put down again in slightly different places, but never really moving.

The foreboding I'd been experiencing all day intensified. It wasn't just the sight of this place, but the *feel* of it. Memories kept threatening to surface—ripples of history beginning to blur the surface of the present—and it was all I could do to push them down. As I drove, the steering wheel beneath my hands was slick with a sweat that had little to do with the temperature.

I was still shaken from seeing my mother at the hospice. Sally had arrived within a minute of my pressing the alarm, but by then my mother had collapsed back into sleep. Sally had checked the machines and looked a little alarmed.

"What happened?"

"She woke up. She spoke."

"What did she say?"

I hadn't answered immediately, because I didn't know what to say. My mother had recognized me, I told her eventually, but had seemed to be somewhere else, reliving a memory she clearly found distressing. But I didn't tell Sally what that time and place had been—or what she'd said next, and how badly it had thrown me.

*Red hands everywhere.*

Despite the heat, the words brought a shiver. I was still trying to rationalize them. My mother was confused and dying; it made sense that she was retreating into her own past, and that some of that would be upsetting for her. And yet whatever I told myself, the sick feeling inside me—the sense of foreboding—kept growing stronger.

*You shouldn't be here.*

But I was.

I parked outside my mother's house. Like almost all the buildings in the town, it was a ramshackle two-story structure, separated from the neighbors by stretches of dirt and hedges comprised mainly of brambles. The wooden front was weathered and the windows were dark and empty. The yard was massively overgrown. The drainpipes and guttering were rusted and almost falling away in places.

The house didn't seem to have really changed over the years; it had just gotten old. The sight of it now brought a wave of emotions. This was the place I'd grown up in. It was the place where, twenty-five years ago, two policemen had waited with me for my mother to return home.

I'd left it behind, and yet it had been here the whole time.

I got out of the car. Inside the house, it was the scent that hit me first—like unsealing a trunk full of your childhood belongings, leaning over, and breathing in deeply. But other smells kicked in almost immediately. I looked at the wall by the side of the stairs and saw it was covered with fingerprints of black and gray mold. The trace of cleaning products in the air couldn't mask the dust and dampness. I smelled ammonia. And something else too. The same sweetly sick air I'd breathed in back at the hospice.

That last smell turned out to be stronger in the front room, where it was clear my mother had spent most of her time. Sally appeared to have tidied up a little, but the pile of soft blankets on the arm of the couch, however neat, only made it easier for me to picture it as a makeshift bed. A small table had been moved across beside it. There was nothing on it now, but I could imagine things there.

A glass of water. My mother's eyeglasses.

The book, perhaps. The one I was holding now.

*The Nightmare People.*

Back out in the hallway, I followed the smell of ammonia to the pantry beneath the stairs. A couple of flies were buzzing against the murky green glass of the window, and the carpet had been untacked, then rolled up and bagged. It took a few seconds for me to understand. Because she had been unable to get upstairs in recent weeks, this bleak space must have served as my mother's bathroom.

At that, I pictured my mother—her body diminished, her faculties failing her, shuffling awkwardly about in a world that was closing in around her—and a wave of guilt hit me.

*You shouldn't be here.*

Despite everything, I should have been.

The stairs creaked beneath my feet, and I went up

carefully, as though wary of disturbing someone. Halfway up to the landing above, I looked back down. An angle of sunlight was coming through the glass in the front door. It revealed a swath of the floorboards there that had been cleaned and polished, and again, it took me a moment to recognize what I was seeing. It must have been where my mother had been lying after she fell.

Upstairs, I stood for what seemed like an age outside what had once been my bedroom, and then the hinges creaked as I opened the door. The space revealed itself slowly. Nothing had changed in here. My parents obviously hadn't used the room for anything in the years since, and the only real difference now was that it seemed so much smaller than I remembered. The remains of my old bed were still by the wall—just a metal frame with a bare mattress on top—while my old wooden desk remained under the window across from it. The room had always been as spare as this. I had never had much. My clothes had been kept in piles on the floor by the radiator; my books stacked up in teetering columns against the walls.

I might have moved out yesterday. A part of me could almost sense the ghost of a boy sitting hunched over at the desk late at night, working on the stories he liked to write back then.

I walked across the room and opened the curtains above the desk, flooding the room with light. Below me was the tangled mess of the backyard, leading off to the fence at the far end and then the wall of trees beyond.

The town might have been named after the woods, but like everyone else here I knew them as the Shadows. For as long as I could remember, that was what everyone called them. Despite the sun, the spaces between the trees had always seemed full of darkness and secrets, and as I stared at them now, a memory fluttered out of them, black and unwanted.

How Charlie used to take us in there.

Every weekend that year, we would meet in the old playground, then head up to James's house and go into the woods through his backyard. We walked for miles. Charlie always led the way. He claimed the Shadows were haunted—that a ghost lived there—but, while I often had the sensation of being watched by something between the trees, I was usually more worried about getting lost. Those woods had always seemed alive and dangerous to me. The deeper you went, the more it began to feel as though you were actually staying still— that the illusion of movement was caused by the land rearranging itself around you, like the squares on a chessboard shifting around the pieces.

And yet Charlie always brought us out safely.

But then I remembered the last time I ever went in there with them. Deep between the trees, miles away from another living soul, Charlie pointing a loaded slingshot at my face.

I closed the curtains.

And I was about to leave the room when I noticed that it wasn't entirely bare—that there was an old cardboard box on the floor beside the desk. At some point, the top had been sealed with layers of brown packing tape, but it had been cut open now, and the folds had been pulled back. I knelt down carefully, spreading them a little wider.

There was a scattering of my old possessions inside. The first thing I found was a yellowing magazine. *The Writing Life*. As with the book at the hospice, my fingertips tingled as I touched it, and I quickly put it on the floor to one side. Beneath that, there was a slim hardback book. I knew what that was, and I didn't want to look at it right now, never mind touch it.

And then, below, there were several of my notebooks. The ones I'd used to write down my faltering attempts at stories as a teenager.

Among other things.

I picked up the notebook nearest the top, then opened it and read the beginning of the first entry.

*I am in the dark market.*

A flurry of memories erupted suddenly, like birds startled from a tree.

James, sitting on the jungle gym that day.

The knock on the door later.

The thought I'd had so often:

*You have to do something about Charlie.*

I put the notebook down, shivering slightly despite the heat of the day. When Sally had called me earlier that week, told me about my mother's accident, and asked if I was able to come back here, I had not answered immediately, because the idea of returning to Gritten filled me with horror. But I had done my best to persuade myself the past was gone. That there was no need to think about what had happened here. That I would be safe after all these years.

And I had been wrong.

Because more memories were arriving now, dark and angry, and I realized that however much I wanted to be done with the past, what mattered was whether the past was done with me. And as I listened to the ominous thud of silence in the house behind me, the foreboding I'd had all day moved closer to the dread I remembered feeling twenty-five years ago.

Something awful was going to happen.

# FOUR

## BEFORE

It was early October, a few weeks into our first term at Gritten Park School. That day we had rugby. James and I got changed at the main building with the rest of the class, and then trooped off through the cobbled streets to the playing field. I remember the air was icy on my thighs, and the way my breath misted the air. All around us, the *click* of cleats on the road was harsh and sharp.

I glanced at James, who was walking beside me with the air of a condemned man. He was watching the larger boys ahead with a wary eye. While the two of us had assimilated as quietly into the background of our new school as possible, James had been a target for bullies from day one. I did my best to protect him when we were together, but I couldn't be with him all the time, and the rugby field felt like open season. A place where violence was not only tolerated but actively encouraged.

The teacher—Mr. Goodbold—was swaggering among the boys ahead, bantering with the favored. The man seemed little more than an older, larger version of the school bullies. There was the same angrily shaved head and solid physicality, the same resentment at the world and barely concealed contempt for the softer, more sensitive kids. On a few occasions I had seen him walking his bulldog around Gritten, both of them moving with the same hunched, muscular rhythm.

We reached the road and had to wait at the traffic lights as cars hurtled dangerously around the corner. I winced at the blasts of air as they shot past. From the speed some of them went, there was no guarantee they'd stop for a red light in time.

I leaned in to whisper to James.

"It's like every part of this experience is designed to kill us."

He didn't smile.

Once we were safely across the road, Goodbold led us down the field. At the far end, a teaching assistant was wrestling with a tangled net of rugby balls. The sky stretching overhead seemed gray and endless.

"Two groups!"

Goodbold spread his arms, somehow managing to separate his favorite pupils from the rest of us.

"You lot along this line. Organize yourselves by height."

He led the larger boys across the field, and we all looked at each other and began shuffling around. I was a good head taller than James, and so ended up a distance away along the line. The assistant handed me a ball. Across the field, Goodbold organized the other side so that the tallest boy in that group was opposite the smallest of ours.

"When I blow this," he bellowed, holding up a whistle, "you will attempt to get your ball to the other side. Your opponent will try to stop you. Simple as that. Do we all understand?"

There were a few murmured *Yes, sirs,* but not from me. I could see how the boys across the field were conspiring and rearranging themselves behind Goodbold's back. A boy named David Hague swapped places with the one beside him so that he could be directly opposite James. *Bastard,* I thought. Hague was the worst of the bullies. He came from a difficult family; his elder brother was in prison, and it seemed likely he would end up the same. The first day at Gritten, Hague had shoved me for some perceived slight, and I'd thrown a punch without hesitation. The fight got broken up, and after that he had pretty much left me alone. But James was an easier victim.

I told myself there was nothing I could do about it. James was on his own for now. Instead, I focused on my own opponent. The success of my team didn't matter to me, but I was determined to win if only for my own sake, and I gritted my teeth as I clutched the ball to my side and put my right foot back. My heart began to beat faster.

The whistle sounded.

I set off as fast as I could, only dimly aware of the boy coming at me from the opposite side. When it came, the tackle was brutal. He smacked into me around the waist, the collision knocking the breath out of me and sending the field whirling, but I kept struggling forward, twisting against him angrily, stamping down, focusing on the line in the distance. A moment later, he lost whatever grip he had and I was plunging forward again. Another second, and the ball was on the line, my hand pressing down on it.

The whistle blew again.

Breathing hard, I looked down the line. Only a handful of us had made it across, and the middle of the field was scattered with kids, some of them standing, some still grappling on the hard ground. It was Hague I saw first. He was standing a distance away, laughing. James was lying at his feet, curled up and crying.

Apparently oblivious, Goodbold simply meandered along the line, counting the winners. I looked back and saw Hague, still laughing, spit on James.

The anger overtook me.

He looked up as I approached, but not in time to avoid the hard shove I gave him, knocking him away from James. The impact was a shock to both of us—I hadn't known I was going to do that. Hague looked equally surprised for a second, but then his face darkened with anger. As if from nowhere, two of his friends were standing beside him.

"What the fuck is wrong with you?" I said quietly.

Hague spread his arms.

"What? So it's my fault your friend's a fucking gayboy?"

I swallowed. Even if Goodbold was watching, he wasn't going to intervene—not until it got serious, at least. But other kids would be watching us, and I knew I couldn't afford to back down. Which meant I was going to have to take a few punches. The best I could really hope for was to give a few back in return, and so I clenched my fists at my sides and forced myself to stare back at Hague.

"What the fuck is *wrong* with you?" I said again.

Hague took a step toward me.

"Going to do something about it?"

Talking was useless—it would be better just to swing and hope. And I was about to do just that when I became aware of a presence beside me. I looked to my right and saw that two other boys had joined us.

Charlie Crabtree.

Billy Roberts.

I didn't know them beyond their names, and barely even those. They were in the same year, and shared a few of the same classes as me and James, but they'd never spoken to either of us. In fact, I'd never seen them speaking to anyone. As far as I knew, they'd been at Gritten Park for years, but it felt like they were as separate from the rest of the school as James and I were. At breaks and lunchtimes, they seemed to disappear.

And yet it was obvious from their body language that they were backing me up here for some reason. Neither of them were obvious fighters: Billy was tall and gangly, too skinny to be a real threat; Charlie was only the same height as James. But there was strength in numbers, however unexpected it was to have them, and right then I was grateful.

Or at least I was until Charlie spoke.

"I dreamed about you last night, Hague," he said.

He sounded so serious that it took a second for the words to sink in. Whatever I had been expecting him to come out with, it hadn't been that. Hague was taken aback too. He shook his head.

"What the fuck are you talking about, Crabtree?"

"Just what I said." Charlie smiled patiently, as though he were talking to a slow child. "You were lying on the ground, and you were badly hurt. Your skull was smashed open, and I could see your brain pulsing—your heartbeat in it. You only had one eye left, and it kept blinking at me. You weren't dead, but you were going to be. You knew it too. You knew that you were dying, and you were terrified."

Despite the disparity in their sizes, Charlie didn't seem remotely afraid of Hague, and there was a buzz to the air, as though he were channeling something terrible—some inner power he could unleash if he wanted to. Hague was more used to physical confrontations. He had no idea how to respond to something as alien as what he'd just heard.

He shook his head again.

"You—"

The whistle blew behind us.

All of us instinctively took a step back—all of us except for Charlie. He remained standing exactly where he was. Still smiling. Still staring intently at Hague.

"Six of you made it." Goodbold's voice echoed across the field. "It would have been nine if Crabtree and his friends hadn't left the line. Think about that next time, lads."

Hague and his two friends headed off toward their line, Hague glaring back over his shoulder at us. I reached down to give James a hand, pulling him to his feet.

"You all right, mate?"

"Yeah."

But although it was me who was helping James up, it was Charlie he was looking at right now. Charlie, who was still smiling to himself. Beside him, Billy met my eyes for a second, his expression blank and unreadable.

"Let's try that again," Goodbold shouted.

After gym class, the four of us ended up traipsing back up the field together. It didn't feel like an accident to me, but I also wasn't quite sure how it had happened; none of us seemed to seek each other out, and yet somehow we found ourselves walking side by side. It felt like, even then, there was already a design to what happened.

Hague and his friends were a little way ahead, and Hague kept glancing back at us. The effect of what Charlie had said had faded by now, and he had regained his usual angry swagger.

Charlie seemed indifferent to the attention.

"I wonder," he said idly, "how many times Mr. Goodbold will come into the changing rooms on the pretense of making sure we all shower."

I checked quickly behind to make sure Goodbold was out of hearing range. It wasn't clear that he was.

I turned back. "At least we're not too muddy."

Billy kicked at the hard ground. "Only good thing about winter."

"It's not winter yet," Charlie said.

Billy looked a bit hurt. "It feels like it, though. It's as cold as winter."

"Yes," Charlie conceded. "That's true."

"I don't want to hear about you dreaming about me, you fucking gayboy."

Up ahead, Hague had turned around and was walking backward now, staring at Charlie. He was talking a lot more loudly than Charlie had been, so this time I was convinced Goodbold could hear. But, of course, he wasn't going to intervene.

Hague made kissing noises. "I know you can't help it, though."

Charlie smiled at him. "Who says I can't help it?"

"What?"

"Who says I can't help it?" Charlie repeated. "Maybe I *choose* to dream about you dying, with your eye burst and your brain hanging out of your head. I mean, who *wouldn't* choose to dream that? It was a wonderful sight."

Despite the recovered bravado, a little of the color drained from Hague's face.

"You're a fucking *freak,* Crabtree."

"Yes." Charlie laughed. "Yes, I am."

Hague pulled a disgusted expression, then turned back around. I could see James was still riveted by Charlie. He was staring at him, as though he were a question he'd never encountered before and needed an answer to.

"A fucking freak," Charlie said.

It was loud enough for Hague to hear, deliberately provocative. And as we reached the sidewalk, Hague turned around and started walking backward again, furious at being goaded. But whatever his response was going to be, I never heard it, because, as he stepped thoughtlessly into the road, a van smashed into him, and he disappeared.

There was a screech of brakes. I looked numbly to the left and saw the vehicle skewing across the road, spinning now, leaving smoke in the air and a swirl of tire prints on the road. It came to rest about a hundred feet down the street, a spread of blood smeared up its cracked windshield like an enormous handprint on the glass.

Everything was silent for a moment.

Then people started screaming.

"Out of the way!"

As Goodbold barged past us, I looked at Charlie. I was still too shocked to blink, never mind process what had just happened, but I remember that Charlie seemed entirely calm. He had that same smile on his lips.

James was staring at him, his mouth open in horror and something a little like awe.

*Your skull was smashed open,* I thought.

*I could see your brain pulsing.*

And I remember Charlie looked back at James and winked.

# FIVE

----------

"I really liked it."

I looked up. The lunchtime creative writing club had finished, and I was busy cramming stuff back into my backpack. I'd thought that everyone else had already left, but a girl had hung back and was standing by the classroom doorway now.

"Your story," she said more slowly. "I really liked it."

"Oh—thanks."

The compliment made me feel awkward, not least because it came from a girl. She was small, with jet-black hair that looked like it had been cropped short with scissors in a kitchen, and she was wearing a T-shirt under her school blouse.

*Jenny . . . Chambers?*

Her name was all I really knew about her. To the extent I'd noticed her at all, it seemed she existed on the periphery of the school the same way James and I did.

"Thanks." I finished stuffing my bag. "I thought it was shit."

"That's a nice way to respond to a compliment."

She seemed more amused than insulted.

"Sorry," I said. "It's nice of you to say. You know what it's like, though. You're never happy with what you do."

"It's the only way to get better."

"I suppose so. I liked yours a lot too."

"Really?"

She looked slightly skeptical. It must have been obvious I'd said it out of politeness and couldn't actually remember her story. Our English teacher, Ms. Horobin, ran a creative writing club for half an hour one lunchtime a week. We'd write stories in advance, and two of us would read them out each session. It had been Jenny's turn last week. Or had it been the week before?

Her story came back to me just in time.

"The one about the man and his dog," I said. "I loved it."

"Thanks. Although it was more about the dog and his man."

"That's true."

Her story had been about a man who mistreated his dog. Dragging it around everywhere; hitting it; forgetting to feed it. But the dog, being a dog, had loved the guy anyway. Then the man died of a heart attack at home, and because he had no friends, nobody found the body for ages. So the dog—almost apologetically—was forced to eat the corpse. Jenny had written it from the point of view of the dog and called it "Good Boy."

There had been a couple of seconds of silence when she finished reading, and then Ms. Horobin had coughed and described the story as *evocative*.

"I don't think Ms. Horobin was quite expecting it," I said.

Jenny laughed.

"Yeah, but those are the best kind of stories, right? I like ones that take you by surprise."

"Me too."

"And it *was* based on a true story."

"Really?"

"Yeah. It happened not far from here. Obviously, I wasn't *there*. So I made a lot of it up. But the police really did find what was left of the guy when they went to his house."

"Wow. I didn't hear about that."

"A friend told me." Jenny nodded at the door. "You heading out?"

"Yeah."

I zipped my bag shut and we left together.

"Where did you get the idea for your story?" she said.

And again, I felt embarrassed. My story was about a man walking through the town he'd grown up in, making his way back to his childhood home. In my head, he was being hunted for something, and wanted to revisit the past one last time—go back to a place where the world had still felt open and full of possibilities. It wasn't clear whether he made it home or not; I ended it just as he was arriving at his old street, with sirens in the distance. I'd pretended to myself that it was clever and *literary* to be ambiguous like that, but in truth, I hadn't been able to think of a better way to finish it.

"Have you read *The Stand*?" I said.

I wasn't expecting her to have, but her eyes widened.

"Oh God, yeah. I love Stephen King! And I get it now. The Walkin' Dude, right?"

"Yeah, yeah." Her enthusiasm fired my own a little. "That guy really stuck with me . . . even though, you know, he turns out to be the Devil or whatever. But at the beginning, when he's just walking, and you don't really know why? I liked that a lot."

"I did too."

"Have you read any other Stephen King books?"

"All of them."

"*All of them?*"

"Yeah, of course." She looked at me as if the idea of not reading all of them was insane. "He's my favorite author. I've read most of them two or three times. *At least,* I mean."

"Wow."

Later, I would learn how true this was. Jenny was a voracious reader. Partly that was because her family was poor and books were a cheap form of escapism, but it was also just the way she was. Right then, I was just amazed that she'd read more King than I had.

"I've read most of them," I said. "*Some* of them more than once."

"Favorite?"

"*The Shining.*" I thought about it. "Maybe."

"Yeah, it's difficult to pick, isn't it? They're all so good."

"What about you?"

"*Pet Sematary.*"

"Oh God, that one's *horrible.*"

"I know—I love it." She grinned. "The ending! Bleak. As. Fuck."

"And you *like* that?"

"Sure. They're meant to be horror stories, right? And obviously they are, but look at *The Stand.* Lots of bad things happen, but in the end the good guys basically win. And in *The Shining,* yeah, it's sad and everything what happens to the dad, but the kid's okay. *Pet Sematary,* though. There's just no hope there at all."

I nodded, but also recognized the sad resignation in the way she said it. A part of me wanted to tell her that not all endings had to be hopeless. But then we walked out into the main playground, and faced the sea of children and the gray landscape around us, and the words wouldn't come. On good days, it was possible to believe I was going to escape Gritten when I grew up, but the truth was that very few people around here were going to have anything but difficult, miserable lives. There was no reason to think Jenny or I were special, or that our endings would be any happier than most were.

I looked to the right. James was waiting for me at the far end of the gymnasiums.

I hitched my bag up on my shoulder. "I'm off this way."

"And I'm off the other. That's the way it works."

Which seemed an odd thing to say. But then I remembered how I never saw her at breaks and lunchtimes—how she seemed to disappear in the same way as James and I did. I wondered where she went: what forgotten part of the school she had made her own, and what she did there.

"Have you read 'The Monkey's Paw'?" she said.

"I don't think so. That's not Stephen King, is it?"

"No. It's a short story—an older one. It's quite similar to *Pet Sematary,* though. You might like it."

"It sounds good."

"It is. I've got it at home. I could bring it in for you to borrow? I mean, only if you like."

Some people might have added the qualification at the end to avoid the embarrassment of being turned down, but Jenny sounded relaxed about it—like it genuinely didn't matter to her one way or the other. She'd come across as a loner before now, but it was remarkable from talking to her how self-assured and at ease in her own skin she seemed. It was as though the world were something she could take or leave, and it felt like some weird kind of privilege that she'd chosen to connect with me.

"Yeah," I said. "I'd really like that."

Then I went to meet James.

And Charlie and Billy, of course.


In the weeks and months that followed Hague's accident, the four of us had started hanging out together.

I was never sure how it happened. It was a little like how we'd found ourselves walking back from the field together that day—as though it only appeared to be accidental. But I know it was mostly because of James. He became fascinated by Charlie after what happened that day, Charlie encouraged the attention, and it was the attraction between the two of them that gradually brought the four of us into closer orbit. We began spending more of our time together. On weekends, Charlie would take us on treks into the woods talking about ghosts, and at school we spent our lunchtimes in Room C5b.

The room was in the basement of the school, down a secluded flight of stairs at the end of the main corridor. I remember there was a dark alcove at the bottom, with an ancient elevator that looked like the doors would screech if they ever opened. As far as I could work out, there were no corresponding doors above, so I assumed it must run to a floor below even the basement. A boiler room, perhaps. Some dank, wet place full of rusted, clanking pipes.

The only other door down there was to Room C5b, which I imagined had been a classroom once. There were skewed rows of dusty desks at the front, but also comfy chairs at the back of the room, giving it a ramshackle, piecemeal feel, as though the furniture had been gathered from different secondhand shops over a period of years. The room was like a part of the school that had been forgotten, and I suppose on that level it was an appropriate place for the four of us. We would meet there and lounge around. Eat lunch. Chat. Sometimes we'd use the old stubs of chalk to write song lyrics on the blackboard at the front. Nirvana. Pearl Jam.

Faith No More. Whatever we wrote stayed there until we rubbed the words off and wrote something else.

Charlie and Billy were already there when James and I arrived one day. Billy was slouched in an armchair, reading one of the guns-and-ammo magazines he was obsessed with. He looked up briefly, to make sure we weren't a teacher finally coming to evict us all, then continued reading. Charlie was in his usual seat at the far end of the room, high up behind a solitary oak desk. He didn't acknowledge us at all. His attention was focused on a notebook on the desk in front of him. He was holding a pen above the page, as though poised to make a decisive mark.

I led the way through the maze of furniture.

"Hey, guys. What's up?"

Billy shrugged, a sullen look on his face, as though he'd been told off for something. Since he often looked that way, it was impossible to say for sure. Charlie still didn't respond. But as we reached the back of the room, he frowned to himself, and then carefully wrote something in the notebook.

I sat down in one of the armchairs across from Billy, got out the packed lunch I'd made for myself that morning, and ignored Charlie right back. I'd become accustomed to this sort of behavior. Every now and then, we'd arrive to find Charlie very conspicuously doing something mysterious. As I ate, I noticed the curiosity in James's expression, and had to suppress the irritation it brought. He had become a little too impressed with Charlie for my liking. While I was prepared to entertain Charlie's eccentricities, I made sure there was always a little mental eye roll there, whereas it was obvious James often thought Charlie was exactly as important as Charlie did himself. For reasons I found hard to articulate, that annoyed me.

"What are you doing, Charlie?" James said eventually.

"I already asked him that." Billy pulled a face but didn't look up from his magazine. "It's a *secret,* apparently."

Charlie sighed, then put his pen down on the desk.

"It's not a *secret,*" he said. "I was concentrating. When you're thinking about something important, you want to carry on without being interrupted."

"Jesus," Billy muttered. "Sorry."

"The same way you wouldn't want me to interrupt . . . whatever it is you're reading."

Billy glanced down at the magazine. He closed it.

Charlie smiled at James.

"I was writing in my dream diary."

"What's a dream diary?"

Charlie held up the notebook.

"Every morning, I write down what I dreamed the night before."

I took a mouthful of sandwich. "It's not the morning."

"I didn't say that's what I was doing *right now.*"

I swallowed. Annoyingly true.

"I never remember my dreams," James said.

"Most people can't." Charlie put the notebook down. "I used to be the same. Dreams are stored in the short-term memory, which is why it's important to write them down as soon as you wake up, before you forget. If you don't, they vanish forever."

I resisted the urge to do an actual eye roll. I had become used to Charlie's fascination with arcane bullshit. He'd bring books on magic and demonology in to school, but I always thought it was more to be seen reading them than out of any genuine interest—that it was part of a persona he liked to cultivate. Charlie would have been more than happy for people to believe he spent his evenings cross-legged in a chalk pentagram surrounded by candles. But he usually liked his reputation to have more of an edge to it than talking about dreams.

"So what were you doing?" I said.

"Searching for patterns." He looked at me. "Making notes on what I've discovered. Once you start doing that, you begin to notice the same dreams crop up time and time again. The same themes. The same places. The same people."

"And so what?"

"It helps with *incubation*." Charlie smiled.

And I hesitated for a moment, the sandwich halfway to my mouth. It felt a little like when he had spoken to Hague on the day of the accident—saying something unexpected and odd enough to pull you up.

*Incubation.*

I didn't like the word. It made me think of something awful being cultivated in a jar. And, of course, I realized I had been wrong just then—after what had happened to Hague, dreams actually did have an edge when it came to Charlie.

James seemed uneasy too.

"What does *incubation* mean?"

"Influencing what you dream about," Charlie told him. "Which helps to waken lucidity. Do you know what a lucid dream is?"

James shook his head.

"It's when you become aware that you're dreaming while you're in a dream. Almost as if you're waking up inside your dream but staying asleep. Once you do that, you're in control of what happens. You can do anything you want, live any experience you want, make your dream world exactly how you want it to be. Anything you can think of can be real."

I looked at James and I could see he was considering that, and I wondered what he would choose to do if he could do anything at all. Get back at the bullies who tormented him? Envision a happier home life? Escape from Gritten altogether? I imagined the idea must appeal to him, and I didn't like the way he was staring at Charlie as though he'd just been offered something magical.

"They're still just *dreams*," I said. "When you wake up, it's not like it matters. It hasn't changed anything."

Charlie looked at me. For a moment his expression seemed completely blank, but there was an undercurrent to it that set me on edge, as though I'd committed some kind of transgression by challenging him.

"What do you mean?" he said.

I shrugged. "Just that. They're only dreams. They don't make any difference."

Charlie smiled then, and for some reason it unnerved

me more than the blankness had. It was the same smile he'd shown to Hague that day, one that suggested he was way ahead of me, and that I'd said something simplistic and childish that he himself had gotten past a long time ago.

*They're only dreams.*

A smile that said he knew a secret I didn't.

# SIX

-----·-----

## NOW

Amanda worked late that night.

She drew the blinds in her office and turned off the light, so that the only illumination in the room came from the computer screen on her desk and an angled lamp beside it. The arrangement was probably not great for her eyesight, but she liked working this way when she could. It concentrated her attention and made the rest of the world go away. It allowed her to think.

What she was thinking about right now was dream diaries.

The concept seemed ridiculous to her. Everyday diaries were alien enough—if something happened that wasn't important enough to remember *in your actual head*, what was the point in writing it down? The idea of going one step further and recording your dreams as well was so far off-planet she needed a telescope to see it. But that appeared to be what she was looking at now.

While Robbie Foster was not cooperating, and Elliot Hick was borderline hysterical, the police had managed to establish a rough timeline of events, and Amanda now knew a little more about what had happened. Close to midday, Hick and Foster had gone to the quarry with a friend of theirs named Michael Price, and they had murdered him there. Afterward, they had taken sleeping pills. When they eventually woke up, they had wandered out across the waste ground, bloodstained and lost, at which point they had been spotted by a concerned member of the public. Each of the boys was carrying a knife and a book. Neither had denied the killing, and while the forensics would take time, Amanda had no doubt the two teenagers were guilty. She had the *what* and she had the *who*.

What she didn't understand yet was *why*.

She'd had a meeting with her boss, Detective Chief Inspector Colin Lyons, an hour ago. Lyons was a notorious bastard, and she had known full well the calculations that had been going through his head at the time. There had been a murder on his patch, which looked bad, but the killers were already in custody and there appeared to be no risk to the wider community. The convictions were going to be iron clad, and the department would look good as a result. A boy was dead, basically, but things could have been worse.

That was how Lyons's mind worked—and while her father had certainly not been a bastard, Amanda imagined the two men would at least have understood each other. *Why* was not necessarily a question that mattered. Motivations, causes, reasons—they almost always turned out to be mundane and disappointing. What explanation could there possibly be for the horror she had seen in the quarry that afternoon that would make sense of it? Asking why was like diving into a black hole. The deeper you went, the less light you found.

But she had been compelled to look.

And she had found darkness that was difficult to understand. Foster and Hick had taken their dream diaries with them to the murder scene, and on the desk before her now were printed scans of the last few entries. She read what the boys had written down that morning.

Robbie Foster's first:

I am in the quarry. The light is strange. I perform nose trick and environment technique to stabilize then walk to the stage. Elliot is waiting for me. He's vague but I can tell he's really there. (We both place hands on the ground.) RH is in the bushes watching us and I almost see his face. Elliot sees him too, and we both know it's time.

And then Elliot Hick's:

I am at the stage in the quarry. The air is an odd color. Robbie arrives a moment later, and we stabilize each other by placing our hands on the ground. It takes a while, but then I feel RH. I still can't see his face, but he's in the bushes to one side. Robbie smiles at me. We have prepared everything carefully and know exactly what to do, just like Charlie told us. We both know tomorrow is the time.

Amanda leaned back in her chair.

Taking the entries at face value, it appeared that both boys had dreamed the same thing. Except the accounts were not identical. It was more like an event being described from two different perspectives. As though Hick and Foster had been in the same dream together.

Which was obviously not possible.

Of course, the boys had to be delusional to have done what they had, and what interested her most were the other details there. What did RH mean?

And who was Charlie?

Whoever he was, Hick's entry in particular implied the pair of them had been following instructions from him. And that in turn suggested the killing might not be quite as contained as Lyons had hoped.

Amanda put the printouts to one side and turned her attention to her computer, opening the case file that was building online. Hick's and Foster's laptops had been seized earlier. Both were awaiting full analysis, but she did have a list of their browsing activities. The pair had frequented various sites online. But, scanning through the details now, it seemed that one specific forum had commanded the majority of their attention.

The Unsolved and the Unknown.

Amanda typed the address into her own browser.

She was met by a schlocky-looking true crime website.

The title was scrawled at the top in red, as though by a fingertip dipped in blood, and below it there was a dizzying number of sub-forums. The folders were arranged chronologically by the most recent post, and the one at the top of the page caught her attention immediately.

Crabtree/Roberts—"RH"

The use of RH could hardly be a coincidence. She clicked through, and was then faced by another wall of posts, each of which had numerous replies of their own. The top few were in italics—old, pinned threads, she assumed—but her heart sank as she clicked on the most recent post below and began reading the thread.

LP242: Guys, just got word of a murder in Featherbank. It's not far from where I live which is how I know. No details on the victim yet but local rumor is a teenager and police have two boys in custody. Close to @RF532 and @EH808 I think? They've not been online today as far as I can tell. Hope they've not done something stupid? Trying to find out more.

KH854: No recent posts I can find either. The murder itself is on the news, but no connection to RH I can find so far?? Let's not jump to conclusions. Copying @RF532 and @EH808. Check in with us, guys!

SR483: Thoughts with the poor parents regardless. My reservations about @RF532 and @EH808 are a matter of record. Also perhaps the Mods might reflect on whether this is finally time to ban @CC666? Because if this is true then @CC666 has blood on his/her fucking hands.

LP242: Okay, spoken to law enforcement source I trust. Victim and perps being widely named locally. Being told victim was nearly beheaded, dream diaries found, handprints on the ground. 100% RH, but police either being coy or haven't made the link. God damn it, @RF532 and @EH808. We all shitpost on here, but I never thought you'd go through with it. RIP to the poor kid you killed and I hope you guys rot in hell.

Amanda read the whole thread again.

*@CC666 has blood on his/her fucking hands.*

She checked the time and picked up the phone.

Detective Theo Rowan worked in the basement of the department. His office was commonly referred to as the "dark room," and the reason for that nomenclature was twofold. It came from the lack of windows and natural light down there, and also the work Theo and his team did within it. Amanda knew many officers in the department thought Theo was creepy. She figured that was fair enough. If some people kept sealed boxes of horror in their heads, Theo's probably held a fucking trunk.

But he was efficient. Within twenty minutes of her call to him, her email pinged and a complete download of all of Hick's and Foster's posts and messages on The Unsolved and the Unknown arrived in her in-box. She blinked as she took in the volume of material: the messages had been pasted into a Word document that was close to a hundred pages long. The pair of them had clearly been active participants on the forum.

Amanda scrolled down and started reading at random.

RF532: Limited success with lucid dreaming so far. Some experience of RH but @EH808 and I still struggling to connect. Advice?

PT109: Difficult to say. Sounds like you're making progress. But don't run before you can walk. Keep up the diaries and incubation and you and @EH808 will get there! Have faith brother.

She read several similar messages that were equally oblique, but which all pointed toward the same conclusion. Foster and Hick had been engaged in some kind of experiment, and they were seeking advice and help in doing so on this forum. But it was difficult to make sense of what it was.

Further on, a post took a more sinister turn.

RF532: Can anyone confirm the precise make of knife that was used by CC and BR? Thanks in advance.

FG634: I can! It was an Ithaca S3 hunting knife. There were a handful of photographs in the news-

paper coverage at the time. Attaching some old scans
I made. Posted FOR INFO ONLY as always. All best.
[knife1.jpg]
[blackwidow1.jpg]

The images weren't included in the document. But
a few minutes later, in a post from a couple of months
ago, she found what she was searching for.

RF532: Advice folks. @EH808 and I now having constant success. Shared LDs every night. RH etc. Now
thinking of next level, but slightly nervous given failed
attempts in past. What do folks think went wrong
there? Why did it work for CC and not for BR and the
others? Theories welcome.

CC666: I was there. DM me.

Amanda peered at the screen. That was the only
contribution to the thread by the user known as CC666.
There were a handful of posts afterward, including a
comment from SR483 expressing reservations about
Foster's question and asking for advice from the mod-
erator. But nothing appeared to come of that, and neither Foster nor Hick replied to the thread again.

*I was there. DM me.*

The record of the two boys' direct messages on the
site was pasted in at the back of the file. Amanda scrolled
through to that, and quickly found the exchange between
Foster, Hick, and whoever was posting as CC666. The
thread took up several pages.

[Participants]: @RF532, @EH808, @CC666
RF532: Hey there CC666. When you say you were there, what do you mean?

CC666: You know what happened in Gritten. That's all I'm prepared to say, but here's a token. You can read between the lines and make up your own mind. Do you want the answer to your question or not?

There had been an attachment to that particular message: [entry.jpg]. Amanda couldn't open it directly from the document, but from the messages that followed, it seemed that Foster and Hick had been impressed by the contents.

RF532: Yes!

CC666: Good. It didn't work for Billy or the others because they didn't believe strongly enough. But it worked for me, and it can work for you. You just need to follow the instructions.

Amanda read on, feeling increasingly sick.
After a while, she closed down the transcripts and opened the national database, searching for details of a different crime in a different place. She had never heard of Gritten before now. It turned out to be an industrial town a hundred miles north of Featherbank. A quarter of a century ago, a murder had been committed there.
She opened the file.
And then leaned closer to the screen, unable to

believe what she was seeing. There was a photograph here. It had been taken years ago, but it might have come from Featherbank that very day. The image showed a playground. The body there had been rolled under one of the nearby hedges, perhaps in a half-hearted attempt to hide it, and the ground was patterned with hundreds of bloody handprints.

She read through what had happened.

On the afternoon of the killing, a teenager named Paul Adams had been taken into custody on suspicion of murder. But he had been released that evening, when a boy named Billy Roberts had wandered into the town, bloodstained and holding a book and a knife, and confessed to the crime. He and a boy called Charlie Crabtree had killed one of their classmates in the playground that day.

The police in Gritten had their *what* and *who* almost immediately, but the *why* had taken a little longer to emerge—a story that was gradually pieced together over the days and weeks that followed.

In the months leading up to the crime, Charlie Crabtree and Billy Roberts had become obsessed with lucid dreaming. They had kept diaries. They had believed they shared the same dreams while asleep. And over time, they had conjured up a shadowy figure that ruled over this fantasy kingdom, the killing an act of sacrifice to him. By doing so, they believed they would disappear from the real world and live—all-powerful—in the land of dreams forever.

After the murder, the two boys walked to the nearby woods with their knives and dream diaries, took sleeping pills, and fell asleep in the undergrowth. Billy Roberts woke up hours later and staggered back to the town, where he was immediately arrested.

But not Charlie Crabtree.

Because he had vanished off the face of the earth and was never seen again.

# PART TWO

# SEVEN

## NOW

In the first few days after returning to Gritten, I spent my time drifting between the house and the hospice.

My mother continued to deteriorate. She was asleep during most of my visits, and I felt guilty over the relief that came from that. While I told myself it was best for her to be resting, I knew I was also afraid of what she might say if she was awake. On the few occasions she was, I found myself holding my breath, waiting for her to say something else about a past I had made a conscious decision to seal away and avoid. She didn't. Most often, she was confused and didn't seem to recognize me at all. It was as though I were a stranger—and I supposed I might as well have been, a thought that delivered a parcel of guilt from a different direction, and which left me confused too. I didn't know what I wanted to happen. I didn't know what to say or what I wanted to hear.

After visiting her, I would go to a pub for a time.

It was a local place I remembered sneaking into as a teenager, and it had changed more than I had. Spit and sawdust back then, it was a sports bar now, slick and efficient, the décor dark wood and the lighting soft. It was never busy in the afternoon. I would sit at a table with a single beer, listening to the *clack* of pool balls from somewhere at the far end of the room, and for an hour or so I would try not to think of anything at all.

Because back at the house, the memories were everywhere.

I had put my old possessions back in the box, but I could always feel them inside—a constant throb of threat from across the room by the desk—and the ghost of the boy I'd imagined sitting there seemed to become more solid by the day.

I remembered the lunchtime when Charlie had first started talking to us about dreams—about *incubation*— and how midnight that day had found me sitting at the desk. That was always my favorite part of the day. Chores and homework done; the house silent; my parents asleep. I would sneak out of bed, click on the lamp, and work on my stories. I had so many notebooks back then. I kept them hidden away in the desk drawer, because my father wouldn't have hesitated to read them if he found them, and I could easily imagine the sneer on his face if he did.

But that night, the notebook before me had been new.

Events that lunchtime had panned out exactly the way I'd expected them to. Charlie had decided we were all going to do something, and so eventually we had agreed to go along with it. Even the process had been predictable. James had been interested, which meant that Billy—keen not to be replaced in Charlie's affections—had joined in too. That left me on my own, and eventually I'd given in.

*Lucid dreams.*

As much as I'd disparaged it at the time, the thought of it had intrigued me. Looking around my dusty, threadbare bedroom, and thinking about the misery of my home life and the flat, gray, beaten-down world around me, the idea of being able to escape it all and experience whatever I wanted was appealing. It had felt like it might be the only way I ever would.

Charlie had told us the first thing we needed to do was keep a dream diary. After a week, we should read through the entries and look for patterns. That way we would be more likely to recognize them in future, at which point we would realize we were dreaming and be able to take control.

Lying in bed that night, I had stared up at the bland ceiling for a while, then switched off the light with the cord that hung down by the headboard. Charlie had explained we needed to tell ourselves something before we went to sleep each night. It was *incubation*—a signal to the subconscious—and while it might feel as though the words were going nowhere, something deep inside us would hear them and respond.

*I will remember my dreams,* I had told myself.

And it had worked. When I'd woken up the next morning, I'd remembered far more than usual. When I sat at my desk with the notebook first thing, images came tumbling out, each one leading to an earlier one, as though I were pulling myself back along the rope of the night.

In the dream I remembered most vividly, I had been in a strange outdoor market. It was night there, and I was running down narrow aisles, past stalls that were too dark to see properly. There were people bustling around me, as gray and indistinct as ghosts, and I knew that I needed to get out—that there was *something else* in there with me. I could hear it stampeding angrily and randomly along pathways close by, hunting me like a minotaur in a labyrinth. And yet every passage looked the same, and whatever turns I took there seemed to be no way out.

And I knew I couldn't escape from this place by myself.

*I was in the dark market.*

But it wasn't just twenty-five-year-old memories that filled the house now. There was also the silence hanging in every room, which seemed heavier and more judgmental by the day. What had my mother meant by what she'd said? *What* was in the house?

I tried to tell myself it didn't matter—that the past was something that could be left alone—but there were moments when it seemed like the house and I were engaged in a war of attrition, and I couldn't help but feel that on some level it was winning. And that something bad was going to happen when I found out what.

*Red hands everywhere.*

It was on the fourth day that I saw her.

I was sitting in the pub at the time, a half-finished beer on the table in front of me. I reached out to pick up the bottle, running my finger over the cool condensation on the glass, and I saw the door across from me open.

A woman walked in, framed by a wedge of warm afternoon sunshine. I only caught a sideways glimpse of her face, and the half jolt of recognition was left unfulfilled when she immediately turned her back to me and walked to the bar.

*Is that . . . ?*

She was wearing blue jeans and a smart, black leather jacket, her brown hair hanging halfway down her back. I watched her fumble with her handbag and purse. I waited, telling myself to keep calm, that it couldn't really be her. The barmaid brought a white wine I hadn't noticed being ordered, and then the woman clipped her handbag shut and turned around, scanning the pub for somewhere to sit.

For a few seconds it was hard to believe my eyes.

Jenny looked different now, of course, and yet somehow the same. I could still see the outline of the fifteen-year-old girl I'd known: forty now, her face sketched over by life, but still immediately recognizable.

The years fell away.

*Perhaps it would be better if she doesn't see you.*

But then Jenny's gaze met mine, and moved briefly over before returning again. She frowned. I could see her having the same thought I had.

*Is that . . . ?*

And then she smiled.

God, her smile hadn't changed at all.

I felt a spread of warmth in my chest at the sight of it, and any fear or reservation about seeing her again disappeared as she walked over, the heels of what looked like expensive boots clicking against the wooden floor.

"Good God," she said. "Hello, there, stranger."

"Hello. Wow."

"Wow indeed. How long has it been?"

I tried to work it out. She had visited me at college a few times, but it had started to feel awkward, and at some point we'd lost contact.

"Twenty years?" I said.

"That's outright *madness*."

She evaluated me quietly for a moment. I wondered what she saw. My own appearance—shabby clothes; disheveled hair; tired eyes—must surely have provided a stark contrast to her own.

"Okay to join you?" she said.

"Of course."

She sat down across from me and put her wine on the table.

"I suppose it isn't *actually* a surprise to see you," she said. "I'd heard you were visiting."

I raised an eyebrow. "Oh?"

"Yeah. Small community, news travels fast—that kind of thing. Always has done, always will. You know what this place is like."

"I do."

"I would have gotten in touch, but, well . . . you know."

Yes. I remembered how things had ended between us.

"I know that too," I said.

She smiled sadly. There was a moment of silence,

and then she looked at her glass and rubbed her fingertip slowly around the rim.

"Listen, I was very sorry to hear about your mother."

"Thank you."

The response came automatically, but I realized how unqualified I was to give it. Another thing I'd been suppressing these past few days was the guilt, but with Jenny it felt safe to let a little of it out.

"I don't know how I feel," I said. "I should have been here, but my mother and I hadn't spoken much recently. I didn't even know how ill she was. I've not been back to Gritten since I left."

Jenny sipped her wine.

"It feels like I'm here all the time," she said. "I come back to see Mom pretty often. You remember my mom, right?"

"Of course. How is she?"

Jenny nodded to herself. "She's good, yeah. Old, but good."

"Better than the alternative."

"That's true. God, you've really not been back here?"

"No," I said. "I went away to college and that was it."

"How come?"

"Too many bad memories here."

"I get that." She was silent for a moment. "But some good ones too, right?"

She risked a smile, and despite myself I returned it. It was difficult to think of it like that, but yes, there were good memories here too. Moments that, looking back on them objectively, had been filled with light.

The problem was that what happened later cast such a shadow they were hard to see.

"It turns out I still have your book, by the way," I said.

"My book?" It took her a second. "Oh—*The Nightmare People*?"

"That's the one."

She had brought it in to school for me the day after we'd met: a worn anthology of classic horror stories. The spine was as weathered as tree bark, and the price— 50¢—was written in faded pencil on the top corner of the first page. Not a lot of money, of course, and she gave it to me with the same apparent lack of concern she'd exhibited the day before, but I felt the book was important to her, and I had determined there and then to take care of it. If it was in danger of falling apart, then it wasn't going to happen on my watch.

And I supposed I had done that.

"I think my mother was reading it," I said.

"Yeah, but more importantly, have *you* finished it yet?"

I smiled. "Many times."

"Do you still write?"

"Nah. You know what they say. Those who can't, teach."

I picked up my beer and told her a little about my work at the college and the classes I taught.

"What about you?" I said.

"Yeah," she said. "I still do all of that. Art and music too. But mostly writing. I've had a few books published."

"Wow."

I was pleased for her; it was good that one of us had kept hold of that particular dream. And as I leaned back in my chair, I realized how good it was to speak to her again, even after all this time. She looked great, and I was amazed by how *happy* she seemed. I was glad that things had turned out well for her—that she had gotten away from Gritten in the end and was living a good life.

"Wow," I said again. "I hadn't seen. I'll have to look you up."

She tapped her nose secretively. "I publish under a pseudonym."

"Which you're not going to tell me?"

"No. Anyway, that's work stuff taken care of. What about family? Wife and kids?"

I shook my head. I'd had a string of relationships over the years, several serious, but none of them had worked out in the end. It would be too dramatic to say the women involved had sensed some kind of darkness in my past, but the shadow of what had happened did fall over me from time to time. I didn't let people in; at my worst, I pushed them away. The need to avoid addressing it was always more urgent, more important, than the relationships I found myself in, and I knew deep down that was no basis for anything long-term.

"Never got around to it," I said.

And for some reason, I resisted asking the question in return. Jenny wasn't wearing a wedding ring. But that didn't mean anything, and right then I decided I didn't want to know.

We sat in silence for a few seconds.

"Is your mother comfortable?" Jenny said.

"She's sleeping, mostly. When she's awake, she doesn't recognize me. . . ."

I frowned. Jenny prompted me.

"Except?"

"Except for the first time I saw her."

And because, once again, it felt safe to talk to Jenny, I told her what my mother had said on that first visit. How I shouldn't be here. About there being *red hands* everywhere. That there was something in the house.

Jenny shook her head.

"*What* was in the house?"

"I don't know," I said. "Nothing, I guess. There was a box of my old stuff she'd been looking through, so maybe she was just feeling guilty about me seeing that. But she's confused. It probably doesn't mean anything at all."

"Yeah, but you mentioned it. It's clearly been bothering you."

I hesitated.

"Because I've been doing my best not to think about it. I've done some cleaning, some tidying. I've sat with her." I gestured at nothing. "I just want to do whatever I need to and then get out of this place. Go back home. Leave the past where it belongs."

Jenny had started shaking her head before I finished.

"But that's bullshit, Paul. You don't have to worry about any of that. I mean, look at the pair of us now. Is it weird to see me again?"

"No. It's nice."

"Exactly. And I'm the past, aren't I? The past was a long time ago. It can't hurt you anymore."

"Maybe."

She checked her watch, then drained her wine.

"I need to go." She stood up. "But if you're worried about what your mother said, just . . . *do something* about it? You might be right—it might be nothing. But there's nothing to be scared of here."

"Maybe."

"Listen to you: Captain Maybe." She hitched her bag onto her shoulder. "*Maybe* I'll see you around?"

"I hope so," I said.

And I felt that warm feeling in my chest again as I watched her walk to the door. A small light in the shadows. It was like a candle flame I wanted to cup with my hands, blow on gently, and bring to brighter life. But, of course, there was always a danger when you did that.

Always a risk you would blow it out instead.

# EIGHT

*Do something about it.*

Jenny's words remained with me the next morning, and as I showered in the small beige stall in the old bathroom, I decided she was right.

*Oh God, it's in the house, Paul.*

*It's in the fucking house!*

Whatever my mother meant when she said it was in the house, it was probably nothing. There was nothing to be afraid of here, and I thought that before I finally did leave this place forever, I needed to find out for certain. When I turned the shower off and began drying myself, it felt like the silence in the house was humming.

Expecting.

I had been attempting to do some work in my old bedroom, and my laptop was set up on the desk there. After I was dressed, I walked in and moved it to one side. Then I picked up the box of my teenage belongings and emptied the contents methodically onto the desk, one item at a time.

The notebooks and dream diary.

The writing magazine.

The slim hardback book. *Young Writers*.

Each item brought a flash of recognition. They felt like magical artifacts that, together, told a kind of story. I picked up the magazine, the old pages coarse and stiff against my fingers, and saw the cover—*The Writing Life*—then turned it over and read the back, feeling the years slipping away from me. I put it down again. Despite my fresh resolve, the narrative told by these things was not one I was prepared to follow through from beginning to end just yet. And despite what I'd suggested to Jenny, while my mother had clearly been looking through the box, I wasn't convinced it was this she had been referring to.

So what was it?

Until now, I'd spent much of my time in the house tidying: wiping down the surfaces in the kitchen; removing the blankets from the front room and storing them in the wardrobe; sweeping and polishing. But rather than being productive, it had felt like procrastination. Now I steeled myself and set about trying to answer the question my mother's words had set for me. I opened drawers and cabinets, rattling through the contents. I pulled out clothes and scattered them, and lifted cushions and piled them on the floor. After days of approaching the house with care, I dedicated myself to the opposite now: grabbing it and pulling out its stuffing, searching for anything that might explain what she'd said.

Nothing.

Or at least, nothing that helped. But there were memories here, fluttering out of the seams of the house like dust. Working through my mother's clothes, I recognized items I remembered her wearing: old jeans, worn through over the years and patched at the knees and the side of the hips; the flimsy black coat she'd always managed with in winter; a bag full of shoes, paired upside down and pressed so flat they seemed glued together.

And alongside the memories were mysteries: artifacts of a life I knew little of. In a small jewelry box I discovered rings and bracelets, and a locket on a chain that, when I clipped it open, revealed an oval black-and-white photo of a woman I didn't recognize. My grandmother, perhaps, but it was impossible to tell, as even the parts of my past I hadn't chosen to forget were shrouded in mist. It occurred to me that, when my mother died, I would be all that was left of a family I hadn't known, and for a moment all my adult confidence evaporated and I was left feeling lost and unmoored.

But the strangest thing was the photographs, which I found gathered haphazardly in a shoebox, filling it to the brim. I emptied it onto the bed and then spread the photos out, forming an overlapping mosaic on the sheets. There was no order to it. Different points in the past mingled freely, resting above and below each other; people and places from separate ages sat side by side.

I was there.

I picked up a photograph of me as a baby, cradled in my mother's arms. I was crying, but while she looked exhausted, she was smiling. There was one of me on the driveway, maybe about three or four years old, toddling along and grinning happily at someone outside of the frame. Six years old, riding a bike with training wheels. A school photo at eight or nine, my home-cut hair slightly ragged and my cheeks dotted with freckles. My eleventh birthday, with my hands thrust in my pockets, my thin shoulders a coat hanger for my clothes, standing awkwardly beside the cake she had made for me.

And she was there too.

It wasn't the ones with me in them that caught my eye so much as the older photographs: images so faded it was like the paper they were printed on was forgetting them. There was a black-and-white photo of my mother as a little girl, lying down in the grass and smiling shyly at the camera, a book splayed open before her. In another, she was a little older, standing outside a house I didn't know, shielding her eyes against the sun.

But it was the shots of her as a teenager that struck me the most. She had been beautiful, and the photographs caught her in unguarded moments, her face unlined, a whole life ahead of her, her eyes sparkling as she laughed. I found a staged group shot of five people sitting on steps. I didn't recognize three of them, but my mother was on the right, next to a teenage boy I realized with a jolt was a young Carl Dawson—a boy who would eventually grow up to marry Eileen and become James's stepfather.

In the photo, he was turned to her. My mother's hands were on her knees and her face was frozen in an expression of wild delight, halfway between shock and laughter, as though he'd deliberately said something outrageous just as the picture was taken.

*You can do so much better, you know?*

I blinked, then gathered the photographs together and put them back in the box. When I thought of my mother, it was always as a presence—a role, almost—and it was strange to be faced with a truth that should have been obvious: that she had been someone with her own dreams and aspirations, who had felt the same as I had, and who had once had a life that existed entirely outside of her relationship to me.

None of which got me any closer to what I needed to know.

*It's in the house.*

I walked out into the hallway and rubbed my forehead. Perhaps there should have been a sense of relief that I hadn't found anything, but having committed to the enterprise, I felt frustrated. Absence of evidence was not evidence of absence. The fact that I hadn't found anything didn't mean there was nothing to find, only that I would never be sure.

The silence was still humming.

*Come on, house,* I thought. *I'm trying here. Meet me halfway.*

But of course the house said nothing.

The window here faced out onto the backyard and the face of the Shadows. I stared out for a time, looking at the trees that stretched upward, forming a wall of fractured foliage that seemed to go halfway to the sky.

And then I looked up a little farther. Directly above me, I saw the thin outline of a hatch in the ceiling.

The attic.

The humming in the house intensified a little.

In my mother's present condition, there was obviously no way she could have gotten up there, but I had no idea when her physical health had started to fail, or how quickly it had deteriorated. And while I didn't relish the prospect, the attic was the one area of the house I hadn't searched.

So I reached up and pressed the edge of the hatch.

It lifted a little. There was a faint click, and when I moved my hand down, the hatch came with it. I expected to be showered with dust and cobwebs, but there was nothing. The space above was pitch-black, but I could hear a faint rush of air.

The ladder was built into the edge. I reached up again and rolled it out over the gap, then unfolded it down with a clatter, wedging its feet into the carpet. I'd been up in the attic a few times as a child, but as I climbed now, the metal seemed flimsy and far more insubstantial than I remembered. As I moved up into the darkness by increments, each rung bent precariously beneath my weight.

The air in the attic was musty and cool—full of the smell of old clothes and luggage and dampness. I put my hands on the rough wood of the first beam, then levered myself up. Once I was standing, I stepped forward, teetering slightly, suddenly conscious of height and distance. The hatch behind me looked tiny, and the sunlit hallway down there seemed to be miles below me rather than feet. It felt like I was in a different world from the rest of the house.

I reached out to the right and found the cord for the light.

*Click.*

"Shit."

I was surrounded by a flock of bright red birds.

The sight was so overwhelming that I took a step back, my heart leaping, and I almost fell through the hatch. But then the vision around me resolved into what it really was. Not birds at all. Instead, the eaves of the attic were covered with crimson handprints. There were hundreds of them, pressed onto the wood at angles, the red paint overlapping in places, the splayed thumbs and fingers giving an approximation of wings.

They were all the same size. All small enough to be my mother's. I pictured her coming up here, back when she was still able, flitting across the beams like a ghost, pressing her dripping palms against the eaves. And I noticed a different smell to the air up here, and a different feeling too.

It was like I was standing inside madness.

With my heart beating too rapidly, I looked away from the handprints, toward the far end of the attic. When I saw what was there, the world seemed to freeze.

*It's in the house, Paul.*

Because I thought I'd found it.

# NINE

‒‒•‒‒‒‒‒‒‒•‒‒

## BEFORE

A week after the experiment with dream diaries began, I remember heading down the stairs to Room C5b, with James following behind me. He was dragging his heels a little, and I could tell he was nervous.

"You okay?"

"Yeah."

It was obvious he wasn't. Even if he didn't want to admit it, I could guess the most likely reason why. That lunchtime, we were supposed to be going over our efforts with the dream diaries, and it was clear from James's anxious manner that he was worried about disappointing Charlie. The realization brought a pang of irritation. It shouldn't have mattered to him so much.

"The whole thing's fucking stupid," I said.

"Did it work for you?"

"Who cares?"

The thing was, it had worked for me—at least to an extent. Each morning that week, I'd had increasing success recalling my dreams from the night before, and last night I'd had a dream I recognized. I hadn't been in the dark market, but somewhere roughly equivalent: a cramped, maze-like place where I was lost, unable to find my way out, with the sensation of being hunted by something.

The fear from the dream had lingered upon waking. But there had also been a thrill of recognition. It felt as though I'd been given a strange kind of insight into myself: a glance at the cogs turning below the surface of my mind.

Charlie had been right.

Not that I would admit it to him, of course.

"Don't worry about it," I said. "None of this matters."

When we walked into the room, Charlie was in his usual seat at the far end. Billy was sitting in one of the comfier chairs nearby, holding an old year planner, presumably repurposed for the experiment. When James got his diary out, I saw it was just a bunch of sheets of paper, folded in half and stapled at the crease. Charlie's dream diary was on the table in front of him. It was a black notebook, exactly the same as the ones I used for my stories and the one I had started to use to record my own dreams. For some reason, this made it feel as though there were some kind of unspoken battle going on between the two of us.

"Okay," Charlie said. "Who wants to start? James?"

James shuffled awkwardly in his seat.

*Jesus,* I thought. *Pull yourself together, mate.* I didn't know whether I wanted to reassure him or shake him. But it turned out I didn't need to worry about doing either, because there was no way Billy was going to let James steal his rightful position as Charlie's second-in-command.

"I had a lucid dream." Billy smiled, pleased with himself. "It really worked—it was just like you said. One night, I dreamed I was in my dad's workshop, and then I dreamed the same thing the night after. And that time, it was like a switch flicked or something. I totally woke up in my dream. It was amazing. I used the nose trick and everything."

"What's the nose trick?" I said.

"We'll come to that." Charlie didn't look at me. "Billy, I'm so pleased."

Billy beamed quietly.

"How long did you dream lucidly for?" Charlie said.

"Not long. I woke up almost straightaway. It was the shock of it."

"So you didn't use the environment technique?"

"No, I didn't remember."

Charlie looked disappointed, and Billy stopped smiling, looking sheepish now instead. For my own part, I was just trying to keep up. Glancing to one side, I could tell that James was feeling as bewildered as I was. The way Charlie was talking, it was like we'd been set a test without being given the classes to prepare for it.

"What the fuck is *the environment technique*?" I said.

"I said I'd explain." Charlie turned to me. "What about you, Paul? How did you do?"

I hadn't actually decided for certain whether I was going to talk about the success I'd had, but I didn't like the way Charlie phrased that right then. *How did you do?* As though I had to prove myself to him.

"Nothing at all," I said.

"No?"

"Maybe if I'd have known about *the nose trick*."

Charlie ignored the jibe and simply nodded, as though it was what he'd been expecting. With me, there was none of the disappointment there had been with Billy. He moved on.

"What about you, James?"

James pressed the stapled papers down onto his lap and looked awkward.

*For fuck's sake,* I wanted to tell him. *It doesn't matter.*

"Nothing," James said miserably. "Just like Paul."

The words stung a little, but it was the tone of his voice that hurt the most. He made it sound as though being like me was such a failure.

"You didn't notice any patterns?" Charlie said.

"Nothing at all. It was all just a random jumble."

"That's fine. It just takes practice and experience. Give it another week or so, and you'll get there. You've done well just for trying."

James gave Charlie a nervous smile.

Billy looked at him. "So what *did* you dream?"

James glanced down at what passed for his note-book. "Nothing interesting."

"No, go on." Billy leaned forward and made to take the dream diary away from James. "Maybe we can find some patterns there even if you can't."

James leaned away from him. "Don't."

"Just tell us, then."

"Well . . . last night, I dreamed about the woods."
James glanced at me. "The ones behind our town. The
Shadows."

He looked slightly guilty. Perhaps that was because,
after all of the weekend expeditions the four of us had
done, the town and the woods no longer felt like *ours*
anymore. It might have been where James and I had
grown up, but it was Charlie who had started taking
us into the woods and making up stories about ghosts.

"Go on," Charlie said.

"It was dark in the dream. I was standing in my yard,
at the edge of the trees, looking out into the woods."

"Was anyone else there?"

"There were a lot of people in the yard behind me—
like there was a party going on. I think some of them
had hoods and masks on. But it wasn't scary. It was more
like some kind of gathering I hadn't been invited to."

Charlie leaned forward, intrigued now.

"But what about the woods?"

James fell silent for a moment. "Yeah, there was . . .
someone in the woods, I think."

"One person?"

"I couldn't tell. It was more like a *presence*. But it felt
like whoever was there could see me. Like they were
staring right at me. Because it was all lit up in the yard
behind me, right? But they were out in the trees—in the
darkness—so I couldn't see them."

"Did *that* scare you?" Charlie spoke more quietly
now. "Did the people in the woods frighten you?"

James hesitated.

"A little."

"That makes sense." Charlie settled back. "There was no need to be scared, but you didn't know that at the time. Did you think they might have been about to call out to you? Or come toward you?"

"I don't know."

"So what did happen?"

"The dream shifted. I just went somewhere else."

Even after only a week, I was familiar with that sensation by now—the way dreams melted seamlessly into one other—but the way James phrased it still made me feel uneasy. *I just went somewhere else.* He made it sound as though the dream were real somehow. And Charlie was staring at him with fascination now, as though something important had happened and he couldn't quite believe it.

"You *saw* him," Charlie said, his voice full of wonder.

A beat of silence in the room.

"Saw who?" I said.

"He *didn't* see him." Billy sounded sullen. "He never said he *saw* him."

"Felt him, then." Charlie gave Billy the briefest of glances before his attention returned to James. "Do you know what I dreamed last night?"

"No."

"I dreamed I was in the same place as you. I was in the woods with him, and I could see you, looking back at us. It was very dark where we were standing, so I wasn't sure if you could see us. But you did." He smiled proudly. "It happened much sooner than I was expecting."

"What are you talking about?" I said.

Charlie looked at me. "James and I were in the same dream last night."

"*What*?"

"James and I shared a dream."

"Oh, don't be fucking *ridiculous*."

The words came out without me thinking, and the atmosphere in the room changed with them. While I might have rolled my eyes in the past, I'd never challenged Charlie as directly or aggressively as that before now. His smile vanished and his eyes emptied, and I knew I'd overstepped a line.

But I pressed it anyway.

"That's not possible, Charlie."

"I understand, Paul," he said. "You haven't tried as hard as the rest of us. You haven't achieved anything. But believe me. It really did happen."

"Yeah, well. It really *didn't*."

Charlie opened his dream diary and held it out over the desk to James.

"James, can you read this for me, please?"

James hesitated. The sudden edge to the conversation had made him nervous. But I could tell he was also intrigued, and after a second he stepped across and took Charlie's diary, then stood there, reading the page that was open in front of him.

His eyes widened.

"What?" I said.

But James didn't reply. When he was done reading, he lowered the book, and looked at Charlie with something like awe on his face.

"This is . . . this can't be right."

"But it is." Charlie nodded in my direction. "Show Paul."

James handed me the dream diary. Even though he was obviously spooked, I still thought this whole thing was absurd. People couldn't share dreams. I looked down at the book. Charlie's most recent entry started on the left-hand page, and his small, spidery handwriting filled both. The date at the top was that morning.

I started reading.

*I am sitting with him in the woods.*

*It is very dark here, but I can tell he is wearing that old army jacket, the one with the weathered fabric on the shoulders that looks like feathers, like an angel that's had his wings clipped down to stumps. There's a bit of moonlight. His hair is black and tangled, wild like the undergrowth around us, and his face is a black hole, just like always. But he is sitting cross-legged with his hands resting on his thighs, and for some reason I can see his hands clearly. They are bright red.*

*The man stands up, and towers over me, as big as a mountain. He shambles away into the forest, and the trees part for him, and I understand that I am to follow. There is something he wants to show me, something he needs me to see.*

*I trail after him through the wood. He's like a bear, a monster, blotting out the view ahead. I struggle to keep up, but I don't want to get lost and let him down. The forest closes up behind me*

*as quickly as it opens up for him ahead, and I'm
amazed by the control he has here.*

*He stops suddenly and holds one red hand
out, with the fingers splayed. I stop and move
to his side. He rests his huge red hand on my
shoulder, and my skin tingles where he touches
me. This close, he smells of earth and meat, and
I can feel his enormous chest expanding slowly
beside me, and his breath rattles in his throat as
he breathes. I want to lean into the weight and
strength and protection of him. I want to see his
face, but I know I'm not worthy yet.*

*The woods go on a short distance in front of
us. Then there is what looks like a yard, and
it's far more brightly illuminated than the place
where we are standing. Someone is there. He
won't be able to see us because of the darkness,
but I can see him.*

*It's James.*

*My heart starts beating harder then, because
I know it's finally working. What he's taught me
and told me is coming true. One by one, I will
lead us to him.*

*I am about to call out to James when I wake up.*

After I finished, I checked the date again. And then
scanned through the entry for a second time, giving
myself time to think. The room had gone silent, and I
was aware of the others staring at me, waiting for my
reaction—wondering whether it was going to be me or

Charlie who won this particular exchange. Everything felt balanced on a knife edge.

I glanced up at Charlie. He was watching me curiously, and I could hold his gaze for only a second before looking back down at the book again.

Because I had no idea what to say.

What I had just read—what was still in front of me right now—was impossible. Two people could not share a dream. And yet I was equally sure there had been no collusion between James and Charlie. The shock I'd seen on James's face had been genuine.

I felt the seconds ticking by, and with each one the frustration built up inside me. Try as I might, I couldn't work out how to unravel the magic Charlie had performed here. But I had to say something, and my stubborn desire to stand up to him was stronger than ever. There was something wrong here, I knew. Something dangerous, even. What I didn't know was how to deal with it.

I closed the diary and dropped it casually on the desk in front of Charlie, and then tried to sound as dismissive as I could.

"So who's *Mister Red Hands,* then?"

# TEN

--------

## NOW

"Michael practically lived down here."

Mary Price spoke softly, as though the air in the front room were delicate and she was worried her voice might bruise it.

Amanda looked around. It was true that remnants of Michael Price's life were still casually scattered about. There was a glass table over by the window with what looked like the boy's homework laid out on the surface; a pile of hoodies was slumped awkwardly over the back of one of the wooden chairs. A set of black headphones was stretched over the arm of the couch, and by the television, Amanda saw game cases spread across the floor beside a PlayStation. The room looked as though Michael had been here only moments earlier and would be back again shortly.

But when Amanda's gaze moved back to the boy's parents, it was immediately obvious he would not. Mary Price looked pale and shocked. Her husband, Dean, was sitting beside her on the couch, his face blank, with one hand tightly clenching his knee. Talking to relatives of victims was the part of the job Amanda found the most difficult. Especially recently, she found it hard not to take on their pain as her own, to imagine them standing beside her at the crime scene and to absorb the impact of their grief. The feeling of loss and absence in the room right now was almost unbearable for her.

*Lock it away,* she imagined her father telling her. *You need to keep yourself detached.*

But she couldn't.

"That's partly our fault, I know," Mary was saying. "We could never afford much. Michael's had the same room since he was eight. It's too small for a teenager— just space for a bed and some drawers, really. God, I've been such a terrible mother."

Amanda looked at Dean Price, waiting for him to comfort his wife. But the man seemed so far away right then that she wasn't sure he'd even heard.

"You shouldn't say that. I'm sure you both did your best."

"Do you have children?" Mary said.

*God, no.* Amanda still vividly remembered a pregnancy scare in her early twenties; it had genuinely been one of the worst things that had ever happened to her.

"No, not yet."

"It's worthwhile, but it can be so hard. Michael was always a quiet boy, but he got so *silent* when he was older. Didn't want to talk to his mom, of course." Mary looked at her husband, who was still staring off into the distance. "You two got on better recently, though, didn't you? That was nice for you both. Made him feel a bit less lonely, I think."

Mary patted his knee.

Dean didn't respond, and Mary turned back to Amanda.

"That's why I didn't mind him gaming so much. He let his guard down a bit then, you see. Forgot I was here. It was good to hear him interacting with people."

"Most of his friends were online?"

"Well, they weren't friends, really. Just strangers he was playing against. That's . . . that's why I was so pleased when he seemed to have met some friends in the real world."

Mary fell silent and Amanda shifted uncomfortably in her seat. This was going to be difficult. But it needed to be done. Apart from anything else, the two of them deserved to know what had happened.

"As you may be aware," she said, "two boys have now been charged with your son's murder. They're due to appear in court early next week."

Dean Price came to life.

"Elliot Hick," he said. "And Robbie Foster."

He spoke slowly and deliberately, but remained staring at the opposite wall. Amanda hesitated. The boys hadn't been named in the press, but there seemed little point in keeping this information from the parents. They already knew. Everybody did. That was the kind of community Featherbank was. It became that way after the Whisper Man all those years ago.

"Hick and Foster had been friends since childhood,"

Amanda said. "Am I right in thinking your son only started hanging around with them earlier this year?"

"That's right." Mary nodded. "They asked him to sit with them."

Which was what Hick had told them. The three boys started sitting together at school, and then on weekends they would go to the quarry. Michael Price had been eager for the company, Hick said. Almost painfully grateful for it. The way he had described it made it sound like the two of them had adopted a stray puppy. In the light of what had happened, the thought of that made Amanda feel sick.

On Saturday morning, Michael had met Hick and Foster at the waste ground as usual, and the three boys had walked to the quarry together. Presumably, Michael had been expecting more of the friendship and companionship he'd been looking for all his life and thought he'd now found. But this time his two supposed friends had brought their knives and dream diaries with them. Killing Michael had been their intention from the very beginning. And the user known as CC666 had told them everything they needed to know to replicate what Charlie Crabtree had done.

*I was there. DM me.*

"Did Michael ever mention a place called Gritten to you?"

Mary thought about it, her face blank. But after a moment, Dean leaned forward. He was a man made of hard angles, Amanda noticed, and there was something almost threatening about the way he had turned his attention to her now.

"No," he said. "Where's that?"

"A town a little way north of here." She hesitated. "What about Charlie Crabtree? Or someone called Red Hands?"

Dean just shook his head.

"Who's Red Hands?"

*A myth,* Amanda thought.

Except not even that, of course. *Myth* was too grand a term for a fantasy figure conjured up by a group of teenage boys from twenty-five years ago. But as absurd as it might be, and as sad and pointless as it felt to Amanda, it appeared that really *was* what lay behind Michael Price's murder that weekend. The original crime predated the modern internet, but the mystery of Charlie Crabtree's disappearance had been taken up and passed on like a baton over the years: researched, analyzed, discussed—and worse. Taken as inspiration.

Which on one level was hard to believe. Except that, even now, in her late thirties, she could still recall the inherent horror of her teenage years. The way she had struggled with negotiating a world that seemed to be constantly shifting; the confusion and doubts about the best way to behave in order to fit in; the web of competing tensions and pressures. Most of all, she remembered the desire to *escape* from it all—to be anywhere apart from where she was, and to find the person she was meant to be, as though the real *her* were already out there somewhere, and one day they would meet and shake hands. Teenagers were not rational, was the point, and the world was not always kind to them.

She did her best to explain to Mary and Dean Price

what had happened in Gritten twenty-five years ago. Dean listened intently now, his expression growing darker the whole time.

"I don't understand," he said. "Are you saying my son was murdered because of a ghost?"

"I'm not saying *it makes sense*. I'm saying that his killers appear to have really believed in all this. They genuinely imagined it would happen. They thought they would disappear."

"How did they even know about any of this?"

Amanda hesitated again. She didn't want to mention what CC666 had told Hick and Foster on that forum. That was one detail she really didn't want to get out to the public right now—especially as she'd now seen the content of the *proof* he or she had provided by direct message.

"There is a lot of information about the case online," she said.

But fortunately, Dean was still focused on everything she'd just told him. He seemed both furious and confused, and unsure how to negotiate his path between the two.

"But why would anyone believe such *rubbish*?"

"As I said, this murder occurred twenty-five years ago. And afterward, Charlie Crabtree really did disappear. He vanished into thin air."

"What do you mean, *vanished*?"

"Literally that," Amanda said. "From what I can gather, there was an extensive search, but he was never seen again. So some people—"

She was about to say *believe he really did it,* but Dean Price interrupted her again—this time simply holding his palm out to stop her. It was too much for him. He stood up and walked out of the room without another word. Amanda and Mary listened to the noise of his footsteps on the stairs, and then the sound of a door closing, surprisingly gently, in the hallway above.

A beat of silence.

"I'm sorry about my husband," Mary said.

"Neither of you have anything to apologize for."

Mary stood up slowly and walked over to the table. She started adjusting the precarious pile of hoodies over the back of the chair, neatening them out.

"It's just very hard for him," she said. "Dean used to be in the army, and Michael was always such a soft, quiet boy. They didn't understand each other. When Michael was younger, he used to be scared of the dark and he'd call out to us. Dean would get frustrated—tell him there was no such thing as ghosts or monsters. So in the end, it was always me that went."

"I was the same as a kid," Amanda said.

"Really?"

"Sure."

Except, of course, it had always been her father who came through to her: calm, kind, and patient when it came to looking after his daughter and reassuring her. Her father who would surely have been frowning at her right now, explaining that wasn't the kind of personal detail a police officer should be giving away in the course of their work.

"It's only since Dean left the army that the two of them started to bond," Mary said. "They were very close. And Dean's always been practical. A problem-solver."

"But this isn't a problem he can solve, right?" Amanda said.

Mary smiled sadly.

"No. It's not a problem *anybody* can solve, is it? It's just something you have to live with."

She finished adjusting the pile of clothes, and sighed to herself.

"What do you think happened to him? This boy, I mean."

"Charlie Crabtree?"

"Yes. Do you think he's still alive?"

Amanda considered that.

Over the last couple of days, she had researched as much as she could about the murder in Gritten, and she still didn't know what to think. On the one hand, the search for Crabtree had been exhaustive: hundreds of officers involved; local search-and-rescue teams; tracker dogs. These were individuals with tremendous experience in the land and terrain, and all of them had been focused on finding a teenager who surely couldn't have gotten that far.

But on the other hand, he had never been found.

And there was also CC666 to think about. Whoever was behind the account appeared to be implying they were Charlie Crabtree, and the information they had given to Foster and Hick had resulted in Michael Price's murder.

She thought about [entry.jpg], the file that had been

sent as proof of the user's identity. When she had opened it, the sight of what was on the screen had sent a shiver down her spine. A photograph of a notebook, held open at two pages dated from a quarter of a century ago and filled with lines of neat black writing.

*I am sitting with him in the woods.*

Charlie Crabtree's dream diary, which was supposed to have disappeared from the world when he did.

Amanda looked at Mary, but it was actually Dean's words that came back to her now, and his question that she answered instead.

*Are you saying my son was murdered because of a ghost?*

"I don't know," she said.

# ELEVEN

The attic was almost entirely empty apart from a stack of three cardboard boxes. They were piled neatly and were clearly the focus of the whole space, like a shrine. An open pot of congealed red paint rested beside them, and there were scrunches of rolled-up paper towels dotted about, so soaked in the paint they appeared drenched with blood.

My mother, I assumed, wiping her hands after creating what was plastered around me.

I approached the boxes tentatively, the corners of my vision filled with those mad red hands. I had the uncomfortable sensation they were moving when I wasn't looking at them—that the whole time I had been in the house the past few days, they had been up here, fluttering silently across the eaves in the darkness.

I took the first box down and sat on the floor.

It was sealed with tape, and I used one of my keys to cut it open along the seam. Inside, I saw a pile of weathered newspapers. I pulled the top one out. It was an old copy of the *Gritten Valley Times,* which had been the area's local paper when I was a child. I laid it out on the beams now and took in the stark headline across the middle of the yellowing front page.

### GRITTEN ROCKED BY TEEN SLAYING

The printed text below the headline had been smudged by thumbprints and faded by time, but the grainy photographs there were still visible. There was Billy, age fifteen, glowering sullenly at the camera. His thick brown hair was parted in the center and there was a smattering of acne on his cheeks. Below that photo was one of Charlie. He was smirking absently, his dyed black hair swept back, his eyes as empty and alien as a shark's.

I knew both of these photographs well. They had been taken from the class portrait we'd all posed for, early on in the year of the murder, and I knew the rest of us were there somewhere, outside of the frame. These were zoomed in, which explained the low quality of the images. There had been other, better photographs of Charlie and Billy, but these were the ones the media had generally run with at the time. I hadn't understood why back then, but I realized now they seemed to fit the story best—capturing not only the killers themselves but their roles in what unfolded.

Charlie, the leader.

Billy, the led.

I hadn't seen a photograph of either of them in years, and the sight of them now left me numb inside. I should have been feeling something, I thought, but for a moment nothing would come. I stared down at the blurry image of Charlie for a few empty seconds. And then— finally—something snapped inside me, as though a tendon in my mind had given way beneath a sudden strain, and the emotion came tumbling out, angry and sickening.

*I hate you.*

*I fucking* hate *you.*

My hands trembled as I took more newspapers out of the box. There were other copies of the *Gritten Valley Times,* but there were national papers as well, all of the stories about the murder here in Gritten and the subsequent investigation. There was coverage of Billy's arrest and trial. The search for Charlie. The grief of a community in shock at the pitch-black evil that had flowered in its midst.

My mother had kept it all.

But why? I remembered she had encouraged me not to follow the media at the time, trying to protect me from it. I had ignored her, of course, and each report I scanned now brought with it a jolt of memory. Here was a photograph of the playground, sealed away behind crime scene tape, a policeman standing guard by the bushes. There, yet another lurid sidebar detailing Charlie and Billy's obsession with lucid dreaming.

I turned one page to find a photograph of a knife, the blood on the blade dried to rusty-looking crumbs, and read the caption below.

*The weapon that Charles Crabtree and William
Roberts used to stab their classmate to death. A
total of fifty-seven wounds were recorded on the
body, leaving the victim's head all but severed.*

I put it quickly aside.

I felt hollow inside now: my whole body slightly
stunned, as though the impact of seeing all this again
were physical rather than mental. And the whole time,
the red hands flickered at the edges of my vision.

What was in the other boxes?

There was a sudden urgency to the question. I took
the second box down and opened it. There were newspapers inside this one too, but these appeared to be
more recent. The first I pulled out was dated only four
years ago.

And yet the headline was horribly familiar.

## BOY, 14, MURDERED BY CLASSMATES

Next to that, there was a photograph of a boy. He
had a mop of unruly blond hair and a scattering of
freckles, and the collar of his school uniform was visible at the bottom of the frame. He was smiling sweetly
for the camera. The caption told me his name had been
Andrew Brook. He looked far younger than fourteen,
and for a moment he reminded me so much of James at
that age that it took my breath away.

As I worked my way through the newspapers, everything felt strange and off-kilter around me, as though
the attic had rotated a few degrees and the world was

now resting at an odd, disorientating angle. The story of what had happened to Andrew Brook emerged piecemeal through headlines.

## TWO ARRESTED IN MURDER PROBE

## "OUTSIDERS" CHARGED WITH BRUTAL KILLING

## OCCULT CONNECTION "ONE LINE OF INQUIRY," CLAIM POLICE

The murderers weren't named in the reports, but it was clear from skimming the articles that Andrew Brook had been attacked by two boys from his school— boys he thought had been his friends—and that police believed they had killed him as part of some form of ritual. There was mention of diaries and other material being taken from their homes for analysis.

I pulled the third box across to me and opened it. Newspapers again. These were from only two years ago, and the reports were about another killing, this time of a fifteen-year-old boy named Ben Halsall. Two fellow students had been arrested and charged with his murder.

## DREAM CULT CONNECTION IN LOCAL MURDER

As with the previous box, the reports remained vague in terms of exact detail, but if you knew what you were looking for the link was even more overt here. There were references to the two suspects being withdrawn and isolated, and obsessed with dreams and internet mythology. The influence of the murder in Gritten was obvious. I knew exactly what I was looking at.

Copycat killings.

For twenty-five years, I'd done my best not to think about what Charlie and Billy had done, or my own role in the events leading up to it. Any guilt had been parceled away, and when I left for college I'd imagined the train I boarded that day had taken me away from it. To the extent I'd ever considered it, I'd assumed the rest of the world had done the same as I had, and that Charlie had been forgotten.

But he hadn't.

And my mother had known.

*Why did you keep all this, Mom?*

But of course there was no answer to that question here. I sat back on my heels and closed my eyes. The silence was ringing. And in the darkness around me, I felt a hundred blood-red hands slipping quietly over the eaves.

An hour later, I parked up outside the hospice. The surroundings were as tranquil as ever, with the day's hot sunshine filtering through the trees, but the world felt darker than it had before. It was as though a shadow were gradually falling over everything, and my chest was tight with nerves as I made my way inside to my mother's room.

She was sleeping. For the first time since arriving in Gritten, I wished that she wasn't. She looked smaller than ever today, the slow breaths her body was taking barely there. The machine that was monitoring her heart gave a soft beat every few seconds, and even that sound seemed quieter than usual.

"What are you dreaming?" I asked softly.

And then I sat in the chair beside the bed for a time, rubbing my hands together slowly. The window was open, and I could smell the trees and the cut grass out there, and hear a slight rush of breeze.

But although my body was here in the hospice, my mind kept returning to the attic and what I'd found there. And while I waited for my mother to wake up, I took out my phone and began searching online.

There were thousands of hits. It would have taken me hours to read it all, but I clicked onto a large forum devoted to the murder in Gritten, and then scanned through the hundreds of posts there. The amount of information surprised me; every aspect of the case was being discussed in detail. But what I found most fascinating were the threads devoted to Charlie's disappearance. The speculation there went on and on.

It seemed so pointless. If the police couldn't find Charlie a quarter of a century ago, what were a bunch of online amateurs going to achieve now? Regardless, they all had their own pet theory about how he had pulled off his vanishing act. Some thought his remains were out there in the depths of Gritten Wood, still waiting to be discovered. Others, that an accomplice had helped to spirit him away, and that he was still alive somewhere.

The thought of that made me shiver.

But even worse were the posts from people who appeared to believe the impossible. Charlie had thought a sacrifice would allow him to vanish into the dream world forever, and there were people online who genuinely believed he had managed it.

Which was ridiculous, of course. But at the same time, I remembered all too well the appeal that lucid dreams had had for me as a teenager, and how even though I hadn't bought into the outer reaches of Charlie's bullshit, that central idea of *escape* had still pulled at me. If I hadn't believed him, perhaps a part of me had wanted to. So yes, it was ridiculous. But I had seen it happen myself, hadn't I? I'd watched a belief take hold, and then the awful repercussions of that unfolding slowly and inexorably in real time.

The killers of Andrew Brook and Ben Halsall had believed.

It sickened me. What Charlie and Billy did that day had become a story, one that had grown and twisted over the years, and now at least two other children were dead because of him. It might have been absurd to believe Charlie had disappeared into a fantasy world, but in some ways he had achieved his wish. The murder had leaked out into the lives of so many others, and Charlie lived on in their dreams and nightmares, just as he'd wanted.

And because I had played my own role in what had

happened, it was impossible to shake the feeling that I was partly responsible for the murders that followed in its wake. That, whether I had known about them or not, in some way they were my fault.

After a time, my mother began stirring in her sleep. Her breathing changed, and while it was probably my imagination, the soft beep of her heart monitor beside me seemed a little louder.

She opened her eyes.

I waited as she stared at the ceiling for a few seconds. She turned her head and looked at me blankly. And then she looked as sad as I'd ever seen her. It was as though she wanted to reach out to someone—to touch them— but a window was keeping the two of them apart.

"You can do so much better, you know," she said.

I remembered the photographs I'd seen back at the house. My mother as a young woman full of hopes and dreams, laughing with such joy that it looked as though the whole world delighted her. The contrast right now was stark.

"Mom," I said. "It's me. Paul."

She stared at me. I was worried she might react the way she had on my first visit, but instead, after a moment, her expression changed, the sadness softening into something slightly happier, yet still tinged with melancholy and loss.

"You look so grown up," she said.

"I am."

"Oh, I know. Or at least you *think* you are. Everybody does at your age. But that doesn't stop me from worrying about you. My son, going out by himself into the big, wide world."

I swallowed.

She wasn't here with me right now, but I knew where her mind was and what it was seeing. I didn't need to close my eyes to picture that final day at the railway station as we waited for the train together. Me heading off to college, with my bags resting on the platform beside me. I remembered what she had said to me.

*It will be Christmas before you know it.*

My mother smiled sadly now.

"And I know you're not coming back," she said.

For a few seconds, I said nothing. Just as I had at the time.

Then I leaned forward.

"No, I'm not," I said quietly. "I'm sorry."

"You don't need to be."

"Are you sad about it?"

She shook her head gently, then looked up at the ceiling and smiled again, this time more to herself.

"I'll miss you so much," she said. "But I'm happy for you. I want you to go out and do great things. That's all I've ever wanted. For you to get away from this place, and everything that happened here. I want to throw you as far as possible, so you can grow big and strong somewhere better. So you can have a good life. I don't care if you ever think about me at all. I'll think about you instead."

I didn't reply. I hadn't known what was going through my mother's head that day, and I had never had a child of my own to help me understand the notion of unconditional sacrifice she was describing.

*That's all I've ever wanted.*

*For you to get away from this place, and everything that happened here.*

All these years, she had known about the copycat murders. She had kept newspapers detailing crimes connected to me, and which I had been blissfully unaware of. She had let me have my escape, and then carried a weight in my absence that should have been mine.

She had protected me.

"I went up into the attic, Mom," I said.

Her smile flickered at that. It was as though my words had interfered with her reception, interrupting the clarity of the signal she was receiving, like a burst of unpleasant static across the screen of her memories. I regretted it immediately. If she had done that for me over the years, surely it was my turn to shoulder the burden now. What mattered most was that her final days and hours were peaceful.

"What was that?" she said.

"Nothing, Mom."

She breathed slowly. The seconds passed.

Then she frowned slightly.

"There's something I need to tell you," she said.

"What?"

More silence. Just that quiet breathing.

"I just can't remember what it is," she said.

I waited. I had no idea what time or place my mother was speaking from right now, as my own words had clearly disrupted her. Was she still at the railway sta-

When she reached it, she knocked on the door and waited. Even though she didn't like it down here, it seemed easier to pay a personal call than to pick up the phone or send an email.

She heard movement from inside, and then the door opened a few seconds later. Detective Theo Rowan had a way of opening a door not quite as wide as you might expect; it reminded her of someone keeping the chain on at the arrival of an unwelcome visitor. But the reputation he had throughout the department was largely down to the work he did; in person, Amanda imagined he would be a surprise to people who had heard of but never met him. Theo was in his late twenties, with an athletic build and a mass of curly blond hair. And despite all the talk about him being creepy, he had a nice smile. It appeared now.

"Amanda."

"Hi, Theo."

While the smile remained, the door didn't open any wider.

"To what do I owe the pleasure?" he said.

"I need help finding someone."

Which was not, both of them knew, his job. But she had already tried the usual channels without success, and she figured Theo would recognize she was looking for a slightly different approach. Not outright illegal, but perhaps less conventional than the rule book strictly allowed for.

She also guessed he would be intrigued by the prospect of that. She was right. After a moment, the door opened properly.

"You should absolutely come in, then."

She followed Theo into the room, closing the door behind her. Despite the unofficial title that officers had given it, the dark room was in reality anything but. Although it lacked natural light, it was so brightly illuminated, and the surfaces so impeccably clean and polished, that it reminded her of a laboratory.

And in a way, there really were things growing in here.

Amanda looked to one side. While most of the room was white and swept clear, the desks covered with neatly arranged monitors, one of the walls was darker and messier. A huge library of black hard drives was slotted into an elaborate shelving system, the cables that emerged between them carefully looped and tied but still creating a mass of bristly texture from which a multitude of tiny green and red LED lights blinked out like spider eyes. Each of the hard drives was carefully marked with a thin white label. Many of them, she knew, were the names of children. Not real, living ones, but the fake online personas that Theo and his team had created. There were equally fabricated adult identities. Other drives simply listed the names of internet forums. Some of those were notorious, but others, mercifully, were well beneath the radar of the general public.

The work Theo did in the dark room was simultaneously straightforward and horrifying. He and his team spent their days in the depths of the internet, dredging its silt. If there was anybody who could help her track down a ghost online, it was Detective Theo Rowan.

He was the only one in right now, and he led her over to a desk at the far end of the room.

"This is to do with the Price murder?" he said.

"Yes. The Unsolved and—"

"The Unknown. Yes, I remember. Tell me what you need."

Amanda explained about the history of the case, and the user on the forum who had sent the photograph of what appeared to be Charlie Crabtree's dream diary. Using Foster's login, she had established that everybody registered on the site had a personal profile, but CC666's had been left entirely blank. The site was hosted outside of the country, and the registration was private. She had contacted the anonymous owner through a link on the forum but had been met with silence. He or she seemed to have no desire to cooperate with the police. All of which meant that, so far, the only lead she had on the user known as CC666 was their words on a screen. It seemed like there was nowhere else to go.

Theo listened carefully, but halfway through he had already turned his attention to a monitor in front of him and begun typing quickly.

"And you think this person might be Crabtree?" he said.

"I don't know," Amanda said. "It doesn't seem possible, but that's what they seem to be implying in their messages. And given the way they encouraged Hick and Foster, I'd very much like to find out who they are. I just can't see how."

Theo finished typing.

"I can maybe get you their IP address."

"You can?"

"Possibly. But you have to bear in mind that, even if I do, that might not be precise enough to identify them. IP addresses vary in their accuracy. I might not be able to pinpoint their exact house for you, but it might at least narrow it down to an area."

"That would be good," Amanda said. "How?"

Theo gestured across the room at his wall of hard drives.

"With a little help from my friends."

Or, in other words: set a ghost to catch a ghost.

Theo explained he would use one of his cultivated false identities to set up an account at the forum, providing enough information on the profile for someone looking at it to establish that they appeared to be a living, breathing person with no connection to the police. He would then send a direct message to CC666, including a link designed to pique their curiosity. The link itself would look generic and innocent—the two of them chose a newspaper article—but it would run through a spoof page first that the person who clicked on it would never see. That page would record extensive data about the user: their internet connection; the details of their computer; a location of sorts. And since CC666 was the only person who would ever visit that link, they could be confident any information they got would belong to their man or woman.

Theo made it sound simple.

"Of course, it depends on CC666 taking the bait," he said.

"Would you?"

He raised an eyebrow and laughed.

As Amanda took the elevator upstairs, she was still pondering the question she'd now been asked twice that day.

Did she think the user was Charlie Crabtree?

It was hard to imagine. Surely Crabtree must be dead by now. Or else someone would have found him. He had been fifteen years old at the time of the murder, and while what she had learned about the case had given her an idea of how cunning he had been and how carefully his plan had unfolded, it was difficult to believe he could have evaded capture all these years.

But not impossible.

The idea chilled her. If it really was him, then what was he doing?

What might his plan be now?

Back in her office, Amanda closed the blinds, switched off the light, and turned to her computer. She told herself to be sensible. Before she started thinking about ghosts, there were other avenues to explore.

*I was there. DM me.*

The police might not have found Charlie Crabtree twenty-five years ago, but the evidence against Billy Roberts had been overwhelming. Roberts had pled guilty to the murder. His lawyer had attempted to argue the boy was suffering from schizophrenia, but the diagnosis was contested by a second psychiatric examination, and the judge had ultimately rejected it. Implications of childhood abuse were taken into account, along with an acceptance that Crabtree had taken the lead in the crime. In the end, Roberts had been sentenced to twenty years in prison for the killing.

According to the online files she read through, he had responded well to the various initiatives and programs he had enrolled in over the course of his sentence. Evaluative reports repeatedly described him as thoughtful, repentant, and unlikely to present a further danger to society. He had been judged fit for release, and paroled over ten years ago.

Amanda leaned back in her chair.

Billy Roberts, a person who really *had* been there that day, was out there in the world somewhere right now.

The knowledge provoked mixed feelings. She had become familiar with the killing in Gritten, and the ferocity of what had been done there had lodged in her head. How could it not, she thought, when she had seen a reproduction of it with her own eyes in the quarry? The idea that one of the people responsible for such an atrocity was free in the community shook her a little.

But, of course, Billy Roberts had been little more than a child at the time of the murder. And she had to believe that people could change.

At the same time, she was reluctant to rely entirely on the judgments of strangers when it came to that. She read the reports on the screen again. Roberts may well have presented himself as thoughtful and repentant on the surface, but who knew what unseen damage the murder and subsequent incarceration had done to him on a deeper level?

Especially when he knew that Charlie had gotten away with it.

Amanda opened a new tab on the computer and started typing. She was prepared to attempt to trace Billy Roberts through the parole system—albeit gritting her teeth at the contortions that might involve—but it turned out that would not be necessary. As unbelievable as she found it, his address and phone number were publicly listed.

At least, she assumed it was him. It had to be. The address on the system was only a couple of miles away from the center of Gritten, and a quick sideways check to the original file told her it had been where Roberts's parents had lived at the time. Digging a little deeper, she found herself blinking at what she discovered. Roberts's mother had died while he was in prison. Upon his release, it seemed he had returned home and lived with his father, who had then died a couple of years afterward. Roberts had remained in the family home ever since.

*Jesus,* she thought.

Presumably, given his background, he'd had little choice, but it was still hard to imagine a man committing such a crime and then returning to the town where it had happened. Living there—or at least attempting to. She wondered how many of his neighbors had remembered or learned what Roberts had done, and whether his continuing presence in the area had been more difficult for them or for him.

Amanda picked up the phone.

It rang for a while.

"Hello?"

A man's voice. It somehow managed to sound both gruff and empty at the same time, as though he were annoyed to be disturbed by something he knew couldn't possibly matter. There were other voices in the background. She could hear swearing and shouting, but it was all distant, as though coming from another room.

"Hello," Amanda said. "Is this William Roberts?"

"Who are you?"

"My name is Detective Amanda Beck. I'm trying—"

Roberts hung up.

Amanda tried calling the number again. This time, as she had more or less expected, there was no answer.

She frowned.

*Why don't you want to talk to me, Billy?*

There were a million possible answers to the question, of course. But the fact remained that there was someone out there who claimed to have been present on the day of the killing in Gritten, who had access to what looked like Charlie Crabtree's missing dream diary, and who had helped to incite a murder. While the sting Theo had set up might give her a result, Roberts seemed a decent candidate to be looking at in the meantime.

She closed down the computer and went to see Lyons.

# THIRTEEN

I wanted to see Jenny again, and I had an idea of the best way to find her. The way the white wine had appeared without her ordering suggested she was a regular at the pub when she was in town, and I could imagine a routine that saw her escaping her mother's house to get some time by herself in the afternoons.

And sure enough, as I walked into the pub, I spotted her immediately, sitting at the same table as before, a glass of wine in front of her. I got a drink and made my way over. She looked up a little guiltily as I approached.

"You caught me," she said. "I don't have a problem, honestly."

"Hey—I'm here too. Mind if I sit?"

"By all means."

I sat down across from her, then began picking at a beer mat to give my hands something to do. The two of us sat in silence for a moment, until finally she leaned back in her chair.

"I was thinking about what you told me yesterday."

"What was that?"

"Stuff about your life. I always thought you'd be married with kids by now. Writing your stories. And also, the way you didn't want to look into what your mother said. It's just so different from how you used to be. Let's just say that I remember you being a little more . . . proactive."

She raised a knowing eyebrow. I realized that even after all this time she still had the ability to make me blush, and I ran my finger over the condensation on the bottle of beer to distract myself.

She was right, of course. But rather than thinking about me and her back then, I found myself remembering that day at rugby instead—the day Hague died— and how I'd been so determined to get through the boy opposite me on the field. About the way it had always been me who stuck up for James and protected him. And the focus I'd had back then, working on my ideas for stories late into the night, the house dark and silent around me.

"I guess so," I said.

"So what changed?"

I looked at her. "You know what changed."

"But it's been twenty-five years." She gave me a pointed look in return. "That seems a long time to be *dwelling*."

I didn't reply. Again, I supposed she was right. While I had spent most of my life trying not to think about what had happened in Gritten, the truth was you didn't need to think about something for it to affect you. I had been knocked off course, and by keeping my eyes closed, I had never been able to correct that trajectory.

"Well," I said finally. "I did look into what my mother said. I searched the house. You'd have been proud of me."

"So you searched. And?"

"And I found."

I told her about the boxes of newspapers my mother had collected—the coverage not only of what Charlie and Billy had done here in Gritten, but of the murders that had been committed since. How it appeared that, over the years, other teenagers had read about Charlie and sought to emulate what some of them believed he'd managed to achieve.

"Copycat cases," I said. "I checked online. All the details are there. Charlie thought a sacrifice to Red Hands would allow him to live in the dream world forever, and because he actually *did* vanish, there are some people who think he managed it."

Jenny shook her head. "But that's . . ."

"Ridiculous? Yeah, I know. But there are all these websites." I started to reach for my phone, but then thought better of it. "It's nuts. These websleuths—I mean, that's literally what they call themselves—they're poring over every little detail, trying to figure out how Charlie disappeared."

"People like a good mystery," Jenny said.

"But nobody's ever going to solve it. For all anybody knows, Charlie could even be alive."

Immediately I wished I could take the words back. The thought of him escaping justice after what he'd done was unbearable in itself, but it was also unnerving to imagine he might be somewhere out there. Even after all this time, the idea of him being close by scared me.

There was a beat of silence.

"I suppose he might as well be," I said. "Because people are still listening to him, aren't they? Still *learning* from him."

"Why do you think your mother kept it all?"

"I'm not sure," I said. "I think she didn't want me to know about it or have to deal with it. There's a whole lot of guilt there, and it feels like she was taking it on so I didn't have to."

"You don't have anything to feel guilty about," she said.

"Yeah, I do."

I looked at her, and a different memory came back to me. The first lucid dream I ever had happened a couple of weeks after Charlie and James appeared to have shared their first dream. It had started out as one of the recurring ones I kept having about the dark market— wandering along narrow aisles as something huge and dangerous hunted me—but this time had been different.

*I've been here before,* I thought.

*I recognize this.*

I had pinched the sides of my nose shut and tried to breathe. There were various ways to test whether you were dreaming or not, but Charlie had told us *the nose trick* was the most reliable. In real life, you wouldn't be able to breathe, but in a dream you always could. I was met with the startling, impossible sensation of my lungs filling with air.

*God,* I'd thought. *I'm dreaming right now.*

I had looked around at the gray stalls, the dimly illuminated crates, the rickety tables and dark, creaking
canopies, and they had all seemed completely real. The
world had been indistinguishable from the one around
me while I was awake, and I had felt a profound sense
of wonder. Everything was so intricate that it had been
ridiculous to think my brain was capable of construct-
ing something so elaborate.

*Show me the way out of here,* I thought.

"Paul."

Jenny's voice had come immediately from over to
my left.

"This way."

It was Jenny whom my subconscious had conjured
up to help me during that first lucid dream. If it hadn't,
things would have turned out very differently.

*You don't have anything to feel guilty about.*

"I do," I said again now.

Jenny frowned at me.

"Is that *really* how you've felt all this time?"

"No," I said. "That's a new thing. When I left here, I
made the decision to pack it away—to leave it all behind
me. Guilty is just how I *should* have been feeling."

"God, you should talk to someone."

"I am."

"Someone proper, I mean. Someone who can help."

"Yeah. Maybe."

"That word again. Like I said, you used to be more
decisive." She sighed and stood up. "I have to go."

"I know."

"But seriously. Think about what I said."

As I watched her walk away to the door, I did. *You don't have anything to feel guilty about.* I thought about it over and over, and tried to believe it, but it didn't feel true.

Later, I woke suddenly in the middle of the night, unsure what was happening. The bedroom around me was almost pitch-black. I was sure I had been pulled out of a state of deep sleep—jerked awake by something—but I didn't know what.

I lay there, my heart singing.

The bedroom revealed itself gradually, shadowy shapes emerging slowly, as though stepping forward out of the darkness toward me. My old room. The sight of it brought a disturbing sensation I had become used to in the days since I'd arrived back. I was not where I should be, and yet the room was so familiar that it felt like someplace where I had always been.

THUD.

THUD.

THUD.

I sat up quickly, my heart pounding now.

The sounds had come from downstairs—someone knocking at the front door. Except it had been more rhythmic than that: the noises spaced out, as though it took an effort for whoever was out there to lift their arm. From the weight of the blows, it seemed as though they were trying to hammer the door off its hinges.

I swung my legs out of bed, then scrabbled on the floor beside me. My phone came alive in my hand as I found it; it was just after three o'clock in the morning. Panicking slightly, I pulled on the jeans from last night and padded out onto the upstairs hallway.

Downstairs, the floor by the front door was illuminated by a wedge of weak light from the street outside. I stared down at it for a moment, expecting to hear the noises again and see the door rattle in its frame from the force of the impact.

Nothing.

I hesitated.

*You used to be more decisive.*

So I headed down carefully, the phone still in my hand. When I reached the front door, I swiped the phone open and flicked on the flashlight option. Bright light filled the hallway, then the beam flickered around as I unhooked the chain and opened the door.

There was nobody outside. The front path was empty and the street beyond was deserted.

The gate was open, though.

Had I left it like that?

I couldn't remember. I stepped outside, the night air cool on my skin and the stone path rough beneath my bare feet. I shone the flashlight left and right, flecking the overgrown yard with light and shadow. Nobody hiding there. Then I made my way down the path, and through that open gate onto the sidewalk. The street was bathed in a sickly sheen of amber, empty in both directions.

I listened.

The whole town was silent and still.

I closed the gate, and then headed back to the house.

As I reached the front door, the beam from the flash-light passed over it.

I froze, my heart beating quickly now.

Then I steadied the light, and my skin began to crawl as I shined the beam over the wood and thought about the knocking I'd just heard.

And as I took in the marks that had been left on the door.

# FOURTEEN

## BEFORE

After my first lucid dream, there were more and more in the weeks that followed. I never mentioned any of them to Charlie or the others. That was partly because they felt too personal to share, but also, as time passed, I found myself resentful of the way the experiment began taking over our lives.

Charlie had started leading discussions on our *findings* increasingly often, and it had become clear that, whatever was happening, it was not one of his passing interests. Looking back, I find it hard to remember exactly how it all happened. The idea of sharing dreams was impossible, but they did—or at least, they claimed to. It resembled a kind of arms race. Charlie might read from his dream diary first, say, and then Billy would describe *his* dream, and there'd be a connection there. Charlie would be pleased, which of course would spur James on to find a connection in his own. Or else James would go first, Charlie would describe a similar dream, and then Billy, not wanting to be left out, would make out that he had experienced something similar. They never showed each other their dream diaries after the first time. Perhaps they didn't want to puncture the fantasy world they were developing between them.

And increasingly it did feel like the three of them. My reluctance to join in began to open up a division in the group. I kept hoping that my indifference might sway the others, but it didn't. James, especially, seemed to be falling harder under Charlie's spell with every passing day.

Which was another thing I resented.

I had the uncomfortable sensation that we were all building toward something. There was a purpose to what Charlie was doing, and while I couldn't figure out what it was, it made me more and more uneasy.

But as stupid as the whole thing seemed to me, I remember thinking: *What harm can it do?* Like I'd told James on the day we compared dream diaries for the first time, none of it meant anything. Dreams were just dreams. And so I figured that eventually the whole thing would burn itself out and life would get back to normal.

*It doesn't matter.*

That's what I kept telling myself.

*Incubation.*

Despite its sinister undertones, the word describes a straightforward fact: the dreams we have are influenced by the real world. Our subconscious takes everyday experiences and shatters them on the floor like a vase, then picks up a handful of pieces to form something random and new to show us while we sleep. We might recognize a few fragments, but they're joined together oddly and separated by strange cracks. Dreams are a patchwork, stitched together from the things that happen to us in our waking lives.

But sometimes the opposite can be true.

One lunchtime, James and I were in the playground, heading to Room C5b. I wasn't relishing more of the usual activity, and the feeling grew stronger as we walked, but I couldn't think of an excuse not to go.

Then I glanced behind me.

Jenny was at the far edge of the playground, walking off in the direction of the construction site. She looked as confident and self-contained as always—alone, but never lonely—and the way she moved, it was as though she'd somehow plotted a route between the other kids that allowed her to walk in a straight line without having to stop.

I watched as she continued down the small road alongside the building site. Where was she going? There was little that way apart from the tennis courts, a few outside teaching huts, and the staff parking lot, and yet she was walking with quiet assurance, some destination clearly in mind.

"What?" James said.

I didn't reply for a second. Seeing Jenny reminded me of that first lucid dream I'd had. And just as our dreams are shaped by our reality, there are times like these when our lives can be changed by the dreams we've had.

"I'll catch up with you," I said.

"Why?"

"I just need to talk to someone."

"Okay."

He shrugged slightly and then headed off.

I hesitated, but then set off back the way we'd come. Up close, the tarps were transparent enough to see the mud spattered on the far side. The raised arm of a digger hung in the air above, its thick metal teeth misshapen and rusted, and I could smell the faint scent of tar in the air. Presumably something was happening in there, but the site was so quiet that it was easy to imagine it was all an illusion: that eventually the tarps would be pulled aside like a handkerchief in a magic trick to reveal that nothing had changed.

There was nobody else around, and the world grew quieter as I walked. The tennis courts on the left were locked away behind wire mesh, while the teaching cabins on the right looked like corrugated caravans abandoned in a rough line. Up ahead, a little way past them, there was a lone wooden bench. Jenny was sitting there. She had been a minute ahead of me at most, but she was already scribbling furiously in a notebook on her lap.

I stopped a short distance away, unsure of myself now, and feeling a little stupid. This was clearly *her* place, and she was so absorbed in what she was doing that it seemed wrong to intrude. And while I'd spoken to her a handful of times since she loaned me the book, it had always been accidental: conversations after the creative writing club, or fleeting exchanges when we bumped into each other in the corridor. I'd never sought her out like this before. I had no idea what I was going to say. A dream might have brought me here, but reality found me speechless. So I was about to turn around when she looked up and saw me.

She stopped writing immediately, her face blank for a moment.

Then she called out.

"Hey."

I shifted my bag on my shoulder. "Hey."

Another beat of silence.

"Well," she said. "Are you coming or going?"

Again, I felt stupid. At the same time, turning around and leaving would make me look even more ridiculous. I walked up to the bench.

"I'm sorry," I said. "You looked busy."

"Busy?" She glanced down at the notebook. "Oh. No. Just messing around with ideas."

"Story ideas?"

She closed the book.

"Kind of. Do you want to sit down, or are you planning to stand?"

Another question that, now I was here, had only one possible answer. I sat down at one end of the bench, leaving a careful gap between us. She looked at me expectantly.

*Yes,* I realized. *I probably need a reason to be here, don't I?*

Inspiration struck.

"I saw you and realized I'd been meaning to apologize," I said. "I've kept that book you gave me for so long."

"Oh. Don't worry about it."

"I just had the impression it was important to you."

"Yeah, but I've had it for ages. Have you read all the stories yet?"

"Not quite."

"Then you should keep it a bit longer, then. Get your homework done. Because they're all good. There are some real classics in there—ones you should definitely read."

I smiled.

"To educate myself?"

"Yeah. If you're going to be a writer, you've got to know the field, haven't you? Have a bit of respect for history. As awesome as he is, I can't leave you just reading Stephen King for the rest of your life."

"I guess."

I felt even more awkward now. *If you're going to be a writer.* I wanted to be, but with recent distractions I'd barely managed to write a thing for weeks. I'd jotted down a few ideas, but they seemed flat and lifeless. It felt like I had nothing to write about. No stories to tell.

"What are you working on?" I said.

"A horror story, of course." Her face lit up with an appealing kind of glee. "Sort of, anyway. A ghost story, so it's more sad than anything else."

"Why sad?"

"Because ghost stories should be sad. Don't you think?"

Ghost stories generally made me imagine white sheets and clanking chains, and dark corridors with figures jumping out at you. But, thinking about it, I could see what Jenny meant.

"Yeah, I guess so. It must be sad to be a ghost."

"*Exactly.* If there's a ghost it means that someone's died. A person's been left behind and isn't at peace. Other people are grieving. And so on."

"No gory bits in this one, then?"

"No." She sniffed. "Well—not many."

I smiled as I remembered "Good Boy," the gruesome story she'd read out about the dog that had eaten its owner after he died. It made me think of Goodbold, strutting through the streets with his own pet, and a part of me hoped the same thing would happen to him one day. Except that, for all his faults when it came to us, he seemed to treat the animal well.

"The dog story was ace," I said.

"Thanks."

"You said it was based on a real thing. How did you even hear about that?"

"Marie told me."

"Who's Marie?" I said.

"A friend of mine." Jenny put the notebook on the bench between us. "Which reminds me, actually—I've got something for you. I don't know if you'll be interested, but Marie gave it to me, and it made me think of you. Hang on."

She bent over and rummaged around in the bag at her feet, eventually retrieving a tattered magazine. She passed it to me.

"*The Writing Life,*" I said.

"Check out the back cover."

I turned it over, scanning the details.

"It's a short story competition," Jenny said. "Open to

anybody under the age of eighteen. If you get selected, there's going to be an anthology of the winners—an actual book. The deadline's not far off."

"Okay."

I looked at the advertisement, not understanding.

Finally, it clicked.

"What—you think I should enter it?"

"Yeah! *Definitely.* I thought your story was really good. You should absolutely send it in."

"Are you going to send yours?"

"Of course. I mean, what's to lose?"

I stared down at the magazine for a few seconds, reading through the details again, more carefully this time. Crucially, there was no fee to enter. So what harm would it do? I was worried about getting rejected, of course, but Jenny thought my story was good enough.

"I've not got a pen."

She rolled her eyes. "You don't need to send it off *now.*"

"I know *that.* I mean to write down the address."

"It's fine—take the magazine. I've already got the details."

"You sure?"

"Yeah, totally." She shook her head at me, bemused. "That's why I brought it in."

*That's why I brought it in.*

I remember being excited by that. It meant that, despite the small number of times we'd interacted, Jenny had been thinking about me, and that knowledge delivered a thrill that was difficult to describe. A warmth in my stomach. I hadn't experienced anything like it before, but it was as though I'd just learned the world contained possibilities I hadn't known about.

I put the magazine into my bag. "Thank you."

"That's okay," Jenny said. "No big deal."

The next morning, I was yawning as I walked through the town, meandering to James's house almost on autopilot. The cold helped wake me up a little, at least—even though spring had officially come, Gritten seemed to hang on to its winters as hard as it did to its people. But in the town the grass was growing again, at least, and while the sun was little more than a shimmery coin occluded by clouds right then, I could feel it gathering strength. There was birdsong for what felt like the first time in months. A cautious sound that seemed not to want to tempt fate, but there.

My heart sank as I arrived at James's house.

It was normally Carl who got him ready for school and saw him off on a morning, but that day Eileen was outside on the doorstep. She was wearing a faded dressing gown, and she was wiping at the door with an old blue rag bunched up in her fist, a look of angry concentration on her face.

The gate hung on one old hinge. The wood scratched along the ground as I opened it. Eileen looked over at me sharply, and I kept my head down as I made my way up the path.

"Good morning, Mrs. Dawson."

"Is it?"

She resumed her activity, holding the door with one hand and pressing the cloth against it with the other, wiping with such ferocity that I half expected the flimsy wood to give. She shouted into the house.

"Get out here, boy. It's schooltime."

There was no immediate response. I stood there awkwardly for a few moments, watching her work. There was a bottle of disinfectant at her feet.

"Anything happen at yours last night?" she said.

The question threw me; I had no idea what she meant. After a second, perhaps taking my silence for some kind of guilt, she looked at me suspiciously.

"Were *you* out last night?"

"Mrs. Dawson?"

"Don't gape at me like that, boy. Were you out last night?"

"No."

She stared at me, evaluating me. After what felt like an eternity, she shook her head and then turned her attention back to the door.

"Someone was. One of you lot out playing silly fuckers."

Before I could say anything else, James appeared in the doorway, edging past his mother carefully, as though the woman were electric and might give him a shock if they touched.

"See you later, Dad," he called back into the house. "Love you."

Carl's voice came from somewhere far away inside the house. "Love you too."

I waited until James and I had walked out of earshot.

"Everything all right?"

"Yeah."

Which was obviously a lie, but I didn't want to press the matter. When the bus arrived, he got on first. I always led the two of us up to the back—because that felt like the place you were *meant* to sit at our age—but today James took us to a spare seat in the middle. When the doors shut and the bus started off, we sat there in silence for a time. But while I didn't want to ask James outright what had happened, I was still curious about what Eileen had said.

*Anything happen at yours last night?*

"What was your mother doing?" I said.

"Cleaning the door."

"Yeah, I saw that. What I mean is, why?"

James hesitated.

"Did you hear anything?" he said. "In the night?"

I thought about it again. As far as I could recall I'd slept through undisturbed.

"Not that I remember."

"Are you sure?"

James looked as tired as I was. But scared too.

"I don't know," I said. "What am I supposed to have heard?"

But after a moment, James turned away and looked out of the window at the bleak landscape flashing past.

"Nothing."

"Yeah. It really *sounds* like nothing."

"Someone knocking at the door. Did you hear that?"

"Knocking? No."

"Right."

"You mean, you did?"

"No, it's just what my mother said. Someone was

hammering at our door in the middle of the night. She was pissed off about it because it woke her up." James shrugged, a small, timid gesture that was barely even completed. "So she woke me and Dad up too. There was nobody there, though. I thought maybe she imagined it, except there was something on the door this morning. That was what she was doing—cleaning it off."

"Cleaning what off?"

Again, James didn't reply. I wondered if he actually knew—or if there had even been anything there at all. Eileen drank a lot, and she wasn't the type of person to admit she'd gotten something wrong. It was easy to believe she'd imagined a noise in the night, overreacted, and had just been cleaning the door this morning as a way of stubbornly pretending she was right.

The bus turned off the main road and began making its way past the abandoned factories, run-down shops, and boarded-up houses.

James said something under his breath that I didn't quite catch.

"What?" I said.

"Blood."

He was still watching the dull scenery, his voice so quiet I could barely hear him.

"She said there was blood on our door."

# FIFTEEN

-----------

## NOW

Officer Owen Holder squinted at my mother's front door.

"What do you think it is?" he said.

"I don't know. It looks like blood."

"Yeah, I guess." He tilted his head. "Maybe."

I said that word too much, and it annoyed me to hear it now. There were three crimson smears on the door, each about the size of the side of a balled-up fist, and they stood out starkly against the white wood, glinting dully in the morning light. If it had been unnerving to see them by flashlight, alone in the darkness, the sight of them now made me feel sick. They were starting to congeal, and a couple of flies had already been drawn to them.

"I think it's definitely blood," I said.

"They weren't there before?"

"You can't really miss them, can you?"

"No," Holder said. "I suppose not."

Then he leaned back, stuffing his hands in his pockets, and he frowned, as though unsure exactly what he was supposed to do about this. I wasn't sure either. I'd hesitated before calling the police, and had eventually decided it could at least wait until morning. But now, whatever the outcome, I was glad that I had. The marks on the door were clearly a message of some kind, and even if I didn't quite understand the meaning yet, it frightened me more than I wanted to admit.

I hadn't attempted to get back to sleep after being woken by the knocks. Instead, I'd checked the locks on every door and window in the house, and then sat in the darkness on my mother's bed, with the curtains parted a sliver to give me a view of the street. I had waited and watched until the silence in the air began to sing. And while there had been nobody out there, no sign of movement in the town at all, I had still had the crawling sensation of being watched.

The feeling remained now.

Holder took a long, slow breath and then glanced down the front path toward the street. He looked doubtful.

"I'm not really sure what to say, Mr. Adams. It's vandalism of a kind, I suppose. And I appreciate it must be annoying. But there's no actual *damage* been done. It's probably just a prank."

*One of you lot out playing silly fuckers.*

Despite the warmth of the morning, the memory sent a chill through me. But Holder looked to be in his late twenties at most, and I assumed he was way too young to know what had happened here all those years ago. I could have attempted to explain, but it felt like there was too much to say to bring him up to speed. And even if I did that, to understand the real significance you would need to have lived through it in the first place.

"I'd like a record made of it, at least," I said.

He sighed, then took out his phone. "Of course, sir."

He took photos of the front door from a couple of different angles, and I stood back with my arms folded, scanning the street and the nearby houses. Again, there was nothing to see. But if someone was watching me, at least they'd know I was taking the situation seriously. That—at least on the surface—I wasn't going to be intimidated.

After Holder was done and gone, I went back inside. The whole situation felt both strange and anticlimactic; something serious had happened, but the house itself looked perfectly normal, and life appeared to be going on in the same way it had over the past few days. I wasn't sure what to do.

*Clean the door, for a start.*

Yes—that was the proactive thing to do, wasn't it? So I took cloths, a bucket of water, and a bottle of disinfectant out onto the doorstep and set to work. But the whole time, I kept checking the street behind me. And even though there was nobody there, I was glad when I was finished and I could get back inside and lock the front door against the world.

The house was silent.

Who could have left those marks? It was an impossible

question to answer. When I had been reading online yesterday, I had seen numerous references to the knocks on the door at James's house. It was just one of many infamous details in the case: a piece of the puzzle known to thousands of internet obsessives. If somebody wanted to play a prank on me, there was a wealth of material for them to draw inspiration from.

And perhaps that was all it was.

But as I thought about those posts I'd read online, I also remembered the users who believed Charlie was still alive out there somewhere, and the ones who imagined he really had achieved the impossible. The sense of foreboding that had been gathering for days was stronger now. The feeling that the past was not gone, and that something awful was coming.

But if so, what?

I walked slowly up the stairs, then stood by the window, looking up at the attic. The hatch was closed, but I could almost feel the red handprints and the boxes of newspapers sealed away above me.

*It's in the house, Paul.*

*It's in the fucking house!*

The urgency of my mother's words came back to me now, along with the panic and fear straining her voice. I had found boxes full of reports on three different murders, separated by years but with a common thread that led back to me. As painful as it had been to learn what my mother had kept hidden from me all this time, I'd imagined that was all I had found. But now I wondered if there was something there I had missed. A detail that was important enough for someone to send me a message or a warning.

A threat.

The idea of that scared me.

But I needed to take another look. And I was about to reach up to open the hatch when I saw something out of the corner of my eye. I stood very still, forcing myself to keep looking upward. The window to the side of me faced out over the backyard and the woods, and I was sure there had been a flicker of movement in the tree line there.

I glanced out, watching the woods for a few seconds and trying to catch another sight of whatever it had been.

There was nothing there.

And then there was.

I couldn't be certain, but I had the impression of a figure crouching down in the undergrowth on the far side of the fence.

*Act naturally,* I told myself.

And then tried to keep myself calm. After a moment, I turned my back on the window and stood there a little longer, looking here and there, as though I hadn't seen anything. As though I wasn't sure what to do next.

In a way, that was true. Did I want to confront whoever was out there? My heart was beating with a steady message of, *No, no, no.* It was the last thing I wanted to do. But then I thought about what Jenny had told me, and I remembered running through the boy on the rugby field that day long ago, and I decided that what you wanted to do wasn't always the same as what you had to.

I headed downstairs.

The backyard was long. There was about a hundred fifty feet of undergrowth between the door and the woods, and if I went out that way, whoever was there would see me and disappear into the trees before I could reach them. But there were other routes into the Shadows.

Outside the front door, I locked it and then headed quickly off down the street. A little way along, an overgrown footpath led away from the road and toward the woods. I set off down it. Muffled by the hedges on either side, the world became so quiet that all I could hear was the bees buzzing softly in the brambles around me, and even that sound fell away as I reached the end of the path and stepped carefully between the trees.

The unease intensified. I hadn't been in these woods for twenty-five years, but I remembered them all too well. You only needed to go a few feet for civilization to disappear behind you and a profound and unnerving silence to settle. To feel trapped and lost even on the bare threads of path where the undergrowth had been trampled down.

And to feel watched.

But I wasn't a teenager anymore.

A little ways in, I turned to the left, making my way between the trees at an angle toward the back of my mother's house. If I was careful, I would be able to sneak up on whoever I'd seen at the fence.

A minute later, I judged I was nearly there. It was

punishingly hot, and I stopped to wipe sweat from my face before crouching a little and beginning to move more slowly. The distant backs of the houses began to appear gradually between the branches of the trees.

A stick *clicked* beneath my foot.

I held still for a moment. Nothing by way of response.

I continued forward, reaching the fence a few seconds later, the trees thinning out and the untidy spread of my mother's backyard suddenly visible ahead. There was nobody here. But when I looked down, the undergrowth at my feet was clearly flattened, and I could smell something in the air.

A sickly trace of dirt and sweat.

The skin on the back of my neck started itching. I turned slowly to face the woods behind me. There had always been something wrong with this place—a soft thrum of energy to the land, the same as when you got too close to an electricity generator—but the sensation right now was worse.

Somebody was out there.

Someone hidden between the trees.

"Hello?" I called out. "Anyone there?"

There was no reply. But the quiet had an edge to it, like breath being held.

"Charlie?"

I had no idea why it was his name I called, but it got a result. After a couple of seconds of silence, I heard foliage snap gently ahead of me on the left. I stood very still, my heart pounding. The woods were so dense in that direction that I couldn't see more than a few feet, but the sound hadn't come from far away. Whoever was out there was still close by.

I steeled myself, then moved tentatively, edging between the rough trunks of the trees, stepping over the coils of grass, and lifting thin spreads of branches out of the way.

And then, as I emerged into a clearing, I froze in place.

A man was at the far side.

He was about thirty feet away from me, standing with his back to me and his head bowed, his body entirely still.

"Hello?" I said.

The man did not reply. I looked closer, and saw he was wearing what appeared to be an old army jacket, worn away at the back of the shoulders so that the fabric stuck out in feathery tufts. And as I listened, I could hear him breathing.

*No,* I thought.

*No, no, no.*

Although a part of me wanted to move closer, my body wouldn't respond. I felt as rooted in place as the trees to either side of me. I reached up and pinched my nose.

I wasn't dreaming.

And then, just like that, the man moved away between the trees. I stared after him in horror, but he was out of sight almost immediately, foliage snapping as he disappeared deeper into the woods.

Then the world fell silent.

I stood there, my heart hammering.

And just as Charlie's name seemed to have come

from nowhere a moment ago, a thought came to me now that was similarly unbidden. That what I had just seen hadn't been a man at all. That it was something that had dragged itself out of the depths of the Shadows to visit me, and was now returning to its home among the trees.

# SIXTEEN

*Jesus,* Amanda thought as she arrived in Gritten.

The world around her seemed to have completely changed in the space of twenty minutes. Not long ago, she had been driving along tranquil country lanes, surrounded by sunny idyllic fields, thinking: *This isn't such a bad place.* Whereas now there were just empty industrial estates and shabby houses and shops on all sides, and what she was thinking was: *This is a fucking shithole.*

Which was admittedly harsh. In her experience, places were just places. What mattered most were the people who lived in them, and an upmarket zip code was no guarantee of anything; you found good and bad everywhere. And yet there was something especially beaten-down about Gritten. Despite the sunlight, the air seemed drab and gray, like an old wet cloth half wrung out. As she looked at the dilapidated neighborhoods she drove through, it was difficult to shake the sensation that the place was cursed in some way—that there was something poisonous in the ground here, rooted in the history of the place, that kept the land barren and the people dead inside.

Her phone was in a dock on the dashboard, the navigation showing her the route. About half a mile to go.

She slowed the car slightly as a tight bend approached, then passed a series of newly built houses on the left. The folly of hope over experience right there, she thought. It was hard to imagine someone moving to Gritten who had the option of being anywhere else instead.

Of course, some people had no choice.

A few minutes later, she parked up a little way past the address registered to Billy Roberts. The house was small and stood off by itself between two stretches of bedraggled, overgrown grass. The brickwork was crumbling away below the old windowsills, and the paint on the front door was peeling so badly it looked like something had been clawing at it. The remains of an old garage were half attached to the left-hand side, with sheets of corrugated iron scattered on the ground and a few rusted struts still poking out of the house, like a body with an arm torn off and the ripped tendons hanging loose.

Amanda's first thought was that the place had seen better days. But then she remembered the implied details she'd read about Roberts's childhood—the neglect; the extreme poverty; the allegations of abuse—and she wondered if maybe it hadn't.

She killed the engine and sent a curt message to Lyons, informing him she'd arrived. When she'd gone to his office yesterday, he'd turned out to be more than amenable to her suggestion of traveling to Gritten to talk to Billy Roberts. In itself, that had not been much of a surprise. With the possible involvement of a third party online, the murder of Michael Price had started to sprawl at the edges, and Lyons always had his eye on the prize. If Roberts turned out to be implicated or— even better—Charlie Crabtree really was still alive and they could find something that led to him, there would be gold stars all around.

But Lyons needed the rest of the day to clear her visit with the Gritten Police Department. What she hadn't expected was that, in the course of tracing other individuals connected to the original crime, she would learn from the college he worked at that Paul Adams was also back in Gritten right now. Lyons had loved that, of course: two birds with one stone. And so what she'd initially imagined as a day trip had ended with her booking a shitty local hotel and hastily packing a suitcase that was presently stuffed in the trunk of her car.

Roberts first.

She took out her phone as she approached the house and called Roberts's number again. The street was so deathly quiet that, after the call connected, she could hear the phone ringing inside the house. No answer, though. She killed the call and the house fell quiet until she knocked on the door.

She waited.

Was there movement inside?

There was a small fish-eye lens on the door, and a few seconds later Amanda had the crawling sensation that there was someone on the other side of it staring out at her. Impatiently, she looked behind her at the run-down surroundings. The house was opposite a row of closed shops, the metal shutters daubed with simple graffiti. A little way along the road was a fenced-off yard filled with piles of old car tires, an illegible wooden sign tied to the wire mesh.

She turned back to the house and knocked again.

No answer.

She took a step back.

According to the records, Billy Roberts had been unemployed for a number of years, but obviously that didn't exclude the possibility of him being out of the house somewhere. Which was fine, of course; she could come back. But she looked at the fish-eye lens again. It had felt like someone had been there, and, given Roberts's reluctance to answer the phone, she wasn't entirely convinced his attitude toward the door would be any different. She knelt down on the doorstep and poked the mail slot open.

"Mr. Roberts?"

Nothing.

She peered in as best she could, and was rewarded by a thin view of the hallway. It led down to a door that was open onto the kitchen, the broken slat on the window at the far end hanging at an angle like a guillotine. Everything she could see looked old-fashioned: the patterned wallpaper; the dust on the picture frames hanging in the hall. It was as though Roberts had changed nothing after moving back here. The beige carpet was patchy and threadbare, and there were . . .

Footprints on it.

Amanda stared for a moment.

Red footprints.

Her heart began to beat a little faster. She allowed the mail slot to close slowly, then stood up and tried the door handle. It turned easily, the door opening slowly inward on creaking hinges.

She took a step inside.

"Mr. Roberts?"

The house was completely silent.

*Check your exits.*

She scanned her surroundings. There was a door directly to her left, secured by a rusty padlock; presumably that had once led into the garage. Stairs led up, but there was nobody in the gloomy hallway above. The old hallway directly ahead of her was empty, and narrow enough for only one person at a time. Nobody was visible in what she could see of the kitchen—although she guessed there was probably a back door out of sight there.

She looked to her right. The open doorway there led into what appeared to be a front room. She couldn't see any furniture, and the bases of the walls were lined with empty cans and bottles. Nobody visible there. But that was her immediate flash point. The place she wouldn't see anyone coming from.

She stepped away from it for a moment.

Now that she was inside, the footprints leading away down the hall looked even more like blood than before. From what she could discern from the pattern, it looked like someone had walked out of the front room to the door, and then headed off down the hallway into the kitchen.

Amanda listened.

Silence.

She slipped her phone out of her pocket and keyed in the number for the police, her thumb poised over the CALL icon as she steadied herself. Then she stepped sideways into the front room.

Immediately she pressed CALL.

It was out of instinct more than anything else, because it took a second for her mind to process what she was seeing. Her attention was drawn to the dark red couch to her left, its back against the wall to the hallway. And then the still figure sitting on it. She didn't immediately recognize it as a person, only as something that was close to human but also horrifically *wrong*. The head had no discernible features and was far too large, and it was only after staring at it that she realized the man's face had been rendered unrecognizable, the skin swollen to almost impossible proportions by the bruises and cuts that had been inflicted upon it.

Amanda held the ringing phone to her ear.

*Answer, answer, answer.*

"Gritten Police Department, how—"

"Officer requesting assistance. Eighteen Gable Street. I need police and ambulance on scene as a matter of urgency. A man appears to be dead. Suspicious circumstances. Whereabouts of perpetrator unknown."

She stepped carefully toward the body as she was speaking, taking in the details. The man's hands were in his lap, every finger broken into a twisted nest. Another step, and her foot squelched slightly. She looked down. The couch wasn't red at all, she realized. It was just drenched with blood that had soaked into the carpet below it.

She looked up.

A little way past the couch, a door hung open. From the length of the room, it could only lead into the kitchen.

*Whereabouts of perpetrator unknown.*

"Ma'am, can I take your name, please?"

"Detective Amanda Beck," she said. "Just *get here now.*"

The man on the other end of the phone said something else, but Amanda lowered her phone, her heart thudding in her ears and her attention entirely focused on the open door a little way in front of her. She was thinking about the footprints in the hall. They disappeared into the kitchen, but the most obvious route there from here was this door at the far end of the room. And yet whoever had made them had gone out into the hall to the front door instead.

She remembered the sensation she'd had after knocking. The feeling that someone had been staring out at her.

*Keep calm.*

With her gaze locked on the door into the kitchen, Amanda slipped her phone into her jacket pocket and took out her keys, bunching them between her knuckles. Then she moved carefully across to the far side of the room, giving her more distance, more time, a better angle. Not that, armed as poorly as this, she would stand a chance against anyone capable of the ferocious violence that sat motionless across the room from her.

The kitchen revealed itself by increments. She could see the end of the counter, loaded with dirty plates, and then the edge of the sink. The window.

She hesitated, caught between the fear of what she might encounter in the kitchen and of the ruined, crimson thing sitting behind her now.

Panic was setting in.

*I can't do this.*

And for a few seconds, she was eight years old again. Terrified, and yet too frightened to call out because she knew there was nobody in the house who would come.

Then:

*You* can *do this,* she imagined her father saying. *I raised you better.*

She took another step sideways.

The kitchen was empty. She could see the length of it now, all the way to the alcove at the far end, where the black eye of an old washing machine was staring back at her, and she saw the pebbled glass of the back door that was hanging open against the boiler on the wall, desultory sunlight streaming in beside it.

*You're okay.*

Relief flooded through her, and she moved more quickly now, treading around the bloodstained footprints leading in from the hall. Despite the heat of the day, when she reached the door and breathed in the air, it was somehow cooler and fresher than the tortured atmosphere throbbing behind her. Out back, there was a disheveled paved area, grass springing up in the cracks between the dirty slabs, and then an expanse of trees at the far end.

Nobody in sight.

She looked down.

The bloody footprints headed across the paving stones toward the trees at the end of the yard. But they faded as they went, as though the person who had left them were disappearing as they ran. And by the time they reached the tree line, they had vanished entirely.

# SEVENTEEN

### BEFORE

I remember the last time I went into the Shadows with the others.

It was the weekend after the knocks at James's door in the night, and as usual, the four of us met in the town playground and then walked up to his house. There were numerous routes we could take, but for some reason Charlie always liked to go in from there. As we wandered down James's backyard that day, I found myself lagging a little way behind the others. The trees in front of me seemed darker and more inhospitable than usual, gradually filling the sky as we approached the fence, and my skin felt chilly in the shade of them.

I glanced behind me. There was a figure in the upstairs window of the house. Carl was standing there watching us, a reflection of the clouds slightly occluding the expression on his face. I raised my hand to acknowledge him, and for a moment he didn't respond. Then his own hand moved tentatively to the glass.

Turning back, I spread the thin wires of the back

fence and ducked underneath, stepping through into the woods, and then followed the others into the tree line. The volume dropped a notch, the quiet rush of the real world fading away behind us. The silence in the woods was eerie, and not for the first time I found myself glancing around as I trailed behind, my heart humming with that strange sensation you have when it feels like you're being watched.

Which was stupid, of course. There was nobody out here apart from us. But the woods always made me nervous. My mother had warned me it wasn't safe out here. There was little in the way of pathways, which made it easy to lose your bearings, and even if you didn't, the land itself was treacherous and unsafe. There were abandoned mines out here, and places where the ground had collapsed, leaving the trees leaning at angles, forming shattered crosses above crumbling pits. These were not friendly woods. Not a welcoming place for children to play.

And, of course, there were all Charlie's stories about the woods being haunted. The idea of that had wormed its way into my head. It was always Charlie who insisted we come out here, and always him leading the way, taking us along different routes through the trees. I had the sensation he was searching for something here, and frequently found myself peering off to the side or checking behind. It got so dark and quiet among the trees that it was easy to imagine something stalking us out here.

We walked for about half an hour that day. Then

Charlie hitched his bag off his shoulder and dropped it in the dirt.

"Here," he said. "It's not right, but it'll do."

"Where would be *right*?" I said.

I didn't expect a reply, and I didn't get one. I'd become more openly belligerent toward Charlie over the previous weeks, and in return he had begun to act as though I weren't there or hadn't spoken.

I looked around at where he'd brought us.

Much of the woods were impenetrable, but Charlie had taken us off-path today and still managed to find what amounted to a clearing. The ground was black and scorched, as though there had been a fire and the land had never quite recovered. The charred trees pointed arrow-straight from the dark soil, the branches high above spreading out like splayed fingers. There was an odd crackle of energy to the place too. I turned in a circle, breathing in the atmosphere, thinking of fairies and monsters. If anything like that had lived in the woods, this felt like a place where they would congregate. There was a sense of expectation to the air, as though the place were waiting for something to appear.

Billy had brought his own bag: an old, stained drawstring sack. He pulled a knife and a Black Widow slingshot out of it, then handed the slingshot to Charlie, but kept the knife for himself, turning it around in his hand and examining the blade. I'd seen the slingshot before, but the knife made me nervous. It was about six inches long, with a serrated edge and a wicked curve at the tip, and the little light that caught the metal revealed numerous scratches on the blade. I pictured Billy in his father's workshop, following instructions from one of his magazines to sharpen the blade.

The ground *chuffed* as Charlie kicked at it, searching for a suitable rock to fit the slingshot. When he found one, he hooked the brace of the Black Widow over his forearm, squeezed the stone into the pouch, and pulled the tubing back to its fullest extent.

I heard the creak of the rubber stretching.

He closed one eye for accuracy, and then turned and aimed at my face.

"*Fuck.*"

I reacted out of instinct, closing my eyes and throwing up a hand. He'd moved so quickly that my mind filled in the rest of the action, and I imagined the explosion of pain in my eye. It didn't come. When I lowered my hand and looked again, Charlie was smiling at me, aiming down at the ground now.

"Got you," he said.

"Jesus, man." My heart was beating so quickly that it was hard to speak. "What the fuck are you doing?"

"Just messing around."

But the nonchalance in his voice didn't reach his eyes. He turned and took aim at one of the trees. I swallowed, trying to calm myself down.

If his hand had slipped then, he'd probably have killed me.

*So do something.*

The urge was there. But he still had the slingshot. And Billy had moved closer to me now. He was prodding the point of the knife into one of the trees. Not stabbing it, exactly, more like torturing it out of idle curiosity, a blank look on his face.

The realization came to me suddenly.

*I don't know these people anymore.*

"Goodbold," Charlie said.

He fired. The trajectory of the shot was too quick for me to follow, but there was an awful crack to one side, and when I looked across I actually *saw* Goodbold standing there for a moment, one eye punched red, splinters of his skull dusting the air beside his ear. Then it was just a tree again. Charlie's shot had shattered away a chunk of bark at head height.

"Dead center," he said.

I shook my head, whether in disagreement or just to clear the vision he'd prompted.

"Not dead center," I said. "More like an eye."

"An eye, then. Still straight into his brain—or what passes for it. Your turn, James."

Charlie held the slingshot out, and James took it hesitantly, scanning the ground for a stone to use. When he found one, he loaded it into the pouch and stood with his feet apart, aiming awkwardly at the same tree Charlie had shot.

"A little to the left," Charlie said.

Handling a weapon didn't come naturally to James. I could tell he was already setting himself up for failure, the exact same way he did on the sports field. As he adjusted his aim, Charlie touched his upper arm, gently guiding him.

"A little more."

Just about whispering now.

"And a little higher as well. That's it. Now—can you see Goodbold there?"

James had one eye closed, concentrating. "Yes."

"So do it."

James released the shot, but pulled it slightly at the last second. The stone skittered off through the under-growth, and he lowered the weapon, a dejected look on his face.

"It just takes practice," Charlie said. "Have another go."

James loaded the slingshot again. "I wish we could do this to him in real life."

"We're going to," Charlie said.

For a moment, the clearing was silent other than the steady *chit* as Billy continued whittling at the tree. I looked at Charlie. The certainty that had been in his voice was mirrored in his face. He looked calm. And entirely serious.

"What do you mean?" I said. With anyone else, I might have taken it for bravado, but Charlie rarely suggested anything he didn't mean.

He looked at me.

"We're going to kill him," he said.

"I don't . . . I don't think we should do that."

"Why not? The man's a bully. And a pedophile."

"I'm pretty sure he's not *actually* a pedophile."

"Really?" Charlie frowned at me. "So what would *you* call a man that forces boys to undress in front of him?"

What I thought was that Goodbold was just a grown-up version of Hague. A frustrated man, taking out the problems of his own miserable life on the rest of us.

"He's a bully," I said.

"No, he's worse than that."

"Maybe. But, Jesus. Even if that's true, it doesn't mean we can kill him." I shook my head; this whole conversation was ridiculous. "Apart from anything else, I don't think any of us wants to go to prison."

"We won't have to," Charlie said.

"Oh yeah—of course not."

"Because we'll get *Red Hands* to do it."

And again, I could tell from his voice and his expression that he was entirely serious. I glanced around the woods, more uneasy than ever. *Who's Mister Red Hands?* Charlie had never answered my question, but deep down none of us had needed him to. It was obviously the ghost he claimed haunted these woods that he was also conjuring up in the dream world. And in a strange way, it seemed that *not* saying it out loud had made the whole thing more believable. When people think they've worked something out for themselves, they become more invested in holding on to it as truth. What I didn't know right then was why.

I looked at James and Billy now. Neither of them seemed remotely disoriented by what Charlie had said.

And the thought came again.

*I don't know these people anymore.*

"But he's not real," I said carefully. "They're just dreams."

"You're only saying that because you've not seen him."

"No, I'm saying it because it's impossible."

"James?"

We both turned to James, who stared down at the blackened ground, looking awkward.

"What is it?" I said.

James hesitated.

"I saw him," he said. "I saw him with Charlie."

"No, you didn't."

"I did—earlier this week. I had a dream I was out here in the woods, and they were both there too. Red Hands was just like Charlie described. He had on this old army coat, all frayed at the shoulders, so it looked like he'd had wings that had been ripped off him."

"And I dreamed the same thing," Charlie said. "Didn't I?"

James nodded. Then he looked at me hopefully.

"His hair was wild, Paul. And his hands were bright red. But I couldn't see his face. It was all dark. It was just a hole."

The certainty on his face frightened me. I looked away. The spaces between the trees around us felt ominous now, as though something were listening, drawn closer by the quiet madness that was unfolding in the clearing.

"Tell him the rest," Charlie said.

"You remember the other morning, right?" James took a step toward me. "The knocking in the night?"

*Oh God.*

He looked so eager. It was obvious he already believed whatever he was about to explain, and was desperate for me to believe it too. That he wanted to share it with me—to take me along on this journey he had found himself on.

"Yes," I said. "I remember."

"And the marks on the door in the morning?"

*Blood.*

"Yes."

"Charlie showed me his dream diary. His entry for the night before. That was *him*. He did it in his dream."

"No." Charlie held out his hand. "Not me."

Without being asked, James passed him the slingshot.

"It was *him* who knocked on the door," Charlie said. "Loud and heavy. I remember the dream felt even more real than usual, like the two of us were really standing there. I looked up and saw a light come on upstairs."

"*Which is exactly what happened.*" James was practically imploring me now. "My mother went downstairs, but there was nobody there. You remember, right?"

Before I could answer, Charlie shook his head.

"It was too much for me," he said. "Too real. Just before the door opened, I woke up. It was like the dream threw me out of it."

I closed my eyes, remembering Eileen wiping furiously at the door that morning—cleaning away the *blood*, if that was what it had really been. And it was obvious to me what had happened, even if the rational explanation was almost as unbelievable as what James seemed prepared to accept. Charlie had snuck out in the night and done that. Then he'd written the entry in his diary to convince James.

It was deliberate and calculated.

And it was so obvious.

But when I opened my eyes again, I saw that James believed, at least enough that he was willing to go along with it. The look on his face made me feel sick. But what could I say? I had a sudden realization of how alone I was out here, and how far the four of us were from another living soul. Charlie, standing there with the loaded slingshot. Billy, who had turned away from the tree and was watching me, the knife in his hand. And James, an innocent pawn in some game I still didn't understand.

*You need to be very careful right now,* I told myself. *Very, very careful.*

"Okay," I said slowly. "So Red Hands is going to come to life and kill Goodbold for us. How does that work?"

"It will take all four of us," Charlie said. "Between us, with his help, we can be strong enough to affect reality."

"Please, Paul," James said.

*You're insane,* I thought. *You're all insane.*

Except I wasn't sure that was true. Charlie seemed far more in control of the situation than that. The real question was what he was hoping to achieve. Because even if he'd convinced James up until now, there was no way the experiment could go much further. Sneaking into our town at night and banging on James's door was one thing, but I doubted even Charlie was capable of murdering Goodbold.

*What matters is getting out of here, Paul.*

The realization brought a shiver.

"Okay," I said. "How do we do that?"

Charlie nudged the bag on the ground with his foot and smiled at me.

"*Incubation*," he said.

# EIGHTEEN

----------

That night, I sat at the desk in my room, the house dark
and silent behind me, holding the thing Charlie had
given me in the woods that afternoon.

A doll.

It was handmade and about six inches long. The base
was an old wooden clothespin, but Charlie had wrapped
it in a patchwork of material. Scraps of old clothes; curls
of string; clumps of dried paint and dabs of glue. The
hair on what passed for its head was dark and wild,
and the face it surrounded had been painted completely
black. The body was draped in some kind of camou-
flage fabric, with pipe cleaner arms emerging from the
sleeves. Five long tendrils of red string had been attached to the end of each one—fingers, I assumed, but
they were so long that when I held the doll upright they
hung all the way down to its feet.

I turned the doll around in my hand. It was physically disgusting. There was something dirty and *itchy*

about it, like a toy that had been left under a couch or in the corner of a room that was never cleaned.

*Incubation.*

Why had I kept it? Back in the woods, I'd had no choice. Charlie had made four of these dolls, and the other three were just as intricate and carefully constructed as mine. As revolting as they were, it was obvious he'd put a great deal of work into them, and Billy and James had accepted theirs gratefully. For me to refuse my own had felt like it would be dangerous. Instead, I'd listened to what Charlie had told us, and I had pretended to agree, the whole time telling myself I would get rid of the hideous fucking thing as soon as I was safe.

And yet here it still was, in my hands now.

I stared into the black absence of its face.

After giving us the dolls, Charlie had explained what we needed to do. The idea was that if we kept this doll close to us, and focused on it before we went to sleep, it would help the figure to find us in the night. When we were dreaming lucidly, we were to transport ourselves to Room C5b and find each other there, and then Charlie would show us what to do.

It was impossible, of course. I no more believed it could happen now than I had back in the woods, and I realized that the only reason I was entertaining the whole thing was because of James. Turning my back on Charlie would mean losing my best friend. And I was afraid that abandoning James would be placing him in danger.

So I needed to play along.

And how much further could Charlie realistically take this? There *was* no shared dream world. There was no way our dreams could have a tangible effect on the real world. And there was no Red Hands.

Which meant that nothing would happen.

And tomorrow would be the end of it.

Even so, there was a limit to how far I was prepared to go. Charlie had instructed us to sleep with the doll under our pillow, but that was too horrible an idea to contemplate. I put it in the desk drawer instead. In bed, I turned off the light and lay there for a time, and when I imagined the others in their own beds, I was unnerved by how easy I found it to visualize them. The day had spooked me badly. I rolled onto my side in the darkness, and then repeated the mantras that had become familiar to me now.

*I will remember my dreams.*

*I will wake up in my dreams.*

Nothing would happen to Goodbold. James would begin to see through Charlie soon, wake up from the spell he was under, and in a few weeks all this would be forgotten.

What else *could* happen?

I still had no idea what Charlie was capable of.

*I'm dreaming.*

I remember the familiar thrill that came from becoming lucid within a dream.

And I remember the unease that came next.

Because I was standing at the bottom of the stairs in

the basement of the school, looking at Room C5b. The door across from me was closed, the meshed window to one side misty and gray. The alarm I felt made the dream blur at the edges and almost woke me up, so I knelt down and used the environment technique, placing my hand against the cold stone floor, rubbing my palm in a circle against the rough stone. The sensation anchored me.

I stood up again.

*There's nothing to be afraid of.*

This was a dream, which meant I was in control of it now and there was no need to be scared. I'd been thinking about the events of the day while falling asleep, and so it was perfectly natural that my subconscious had conjured up this place.

But there was no reason for me to stay here. With my back to the stairs, I told myself that when I turned around there would be a door at the top, and when I opened that door it would lead me out onto a beach. It was easier than trying to teleport. In a lucid dream your brain could still cling to the familiar rules of what was possible, and this was a technique I'd used before that had always worked.

I visualized it clearly, and then turned around.

The area above was gray and dead, and—

*Clank.*

I heard a distant noise. It was like a pipe being struck with a hammer. The sound reverberated and faded. I couldn't tell where it had come from, and I felt even more uneasy now. I was awake in my dream, but it felt out of my control in some way, as though somebody else were exerting their own influence on it, and they were better at it than I was.

*Clank.*

The noise again. Louder this time.

I turned around and walked across to the door to Room C5b. The window at the side was gray, but the air beyond looked like it was swirling, the room full of smoke. And there was something else there too, I realized now. A pale shape, close to the glass.

It was a face—or at least the nightmarish approximation of one. It was elongated into an oval, the eyes stretched and distorted into blurry smears, the nose little more than tiny vertical slits, and the mouth a thin black cut. As distorted as it was, though, I recognized James. His eyes widened at the sight of me, and his mouth began working in some alien fashion, forming odd shapes as he attempted to communicate with me across a divide neither of us could cross. He looked like he'd been drowned and left under the water, his image swimming before me on the other side of the window.

*Clank.*

And then suddenly a much louder noise from behind me. The awful, grinding sound of metal against metal. A screeching and scraping of rusted parts that hadn't moved in an age snapping free of their inertia.

I turned around slowly.

In the shadows beside the stairs, there was now a faint yellow triangle glowing above the doors to the old elevator. The sound of shrieking metal was coming from there. My heart started pounding so hard in my chest that it seemed impossible for me not to wake up. But I didn't.

The tone of the grinding noise changed.

*Wake up,* I told myself.

The metal doors began shuddering open.

I turned back to the room. James was still there, shaking his head from side to side now, his horrified features blurring into a slow-moving smear as he saw whatever it was that had risen out of the depths of the school and stepped out behind me.

*Wake up.*

I closed my eyes, picturing myself lying in my bed and willing myself to escape back there.

*Wake up.*

But when I opened my eyes again, the dream seemed even more vivid than before. The room was still right there in front of me, and now I could sense something standing right behind me. The skin of my back was crawling from its presence.

*Wake up.*

I smelled leaves and turned earth, and heard an awful rasping noise, like somebody breathing badly through a broken throat.

*Wake up, wake up, wake up.*

Then a wet red hand reached around my face, its rancid fingers closing over my nose and mouth and pinching them shut. I tried to breathe. Nothing came. And as I started to suffocate, I flailed around helplessly in panic.

Now I knew why I couldn't wake up.

Because this was not a dream.

# NINETEEN

## NOW

Back in my mother's house, I locked the doors and then leaned on the kitchen counter, staring out of the window at the Shadows, trying to control my breathing.

Apart from the flies flickering by the fence, the Shadows were completely still.

There was nobody out there now.

And yet I was shaking.

I remembered how, after I'd woken from the nightmare Charlie and his doll had given me years ago, I had done my best to explain it to myself. To rationalize it. *Of course* I had dreamed about the room in the basement, and about Red Hands. After the intensity of the day before, faced down by Charlie and his slingshot and the collective madness of my friends, it would almost have been strange if I hadn't.

I tried to do the same now.

The marks on the door could be a prank. And people had every right to go walking in those woods. Perhaps it was a vagrant I'd seen—a man who lived out there because there was nowhere else for him. It wouldn't be so strange for someone like that to be dressed that way, wrapped in a worn and tattered old coat.

I wanted to believe it.

But while I didn't like to admit it, I had been scared just now. I could tell myself there had been no point pursuing the man—that the woods were so dense and impenetrable I would likely have lost him quickly—but however true that might be, I knew it was not a calculation I had made at the time.

No, the sight of him had terrified me.

And I had stood there frozen—a teenager again.

A sudden clattering noise behind me now made me start. But the sound brought a familiar echo of memory from my childhood. It was just the mail slot. I turned around to see the day's mail had arrived.

I walked down the hall and picked up the spread of letters. More bills and flyers. I placed them on the side with the others, but then thought better of it. They were obviously trivial and irrelevant in the grand scheme of things, but they'd have to be gone through at some point, and a mundane distraction might help right now. Something to ground me in the real world again. So I gathered up the whole pile, took it through to the front room, and sat down on the couch.

My mother was resolutely old school and was still getting paper copies of everything. There were the standard utility bills, which I tore open and scanned without interest, along with a bank statement that I decided to leave alone for the moment. There were take-out menus, and flyers for local gardening and guttering firms.

And then there was a phone bill.

I stared at that for a few seconds after I opened it. It was a quarterly bill for the landline, and it was three sheets thick. My gaze moved down the itemized list of numbers—all of them calls my mother had made— and then moved to the next sheet, and then the last.

Going back close to two months, I found my cell phone number. The date seemed like such a long time ago. What had we talked about? I realized I couldn't remember. Nothing, probably—just a standard catch-up, which I'd doubtless hurried to the end of without thinking. It had always been my mother who phoned me, and time seemed to pass between those infrequent calls without me ever feeling a need to make contact myself.

A wave of sadness washed over me at that.

*I don't care if you ever think about me at all.*

*I'll think about you instead.*

Because that was what parents did, wasn't it? They wanted to protect their children. They wanted the best lives possible for them. And they expected nothing in return for that. But it was clear from the volume of numbers listed here that my mother had felt the need to talk to someone, and I felt guilty now that it had not been me. That I had not thought about her more than I had.

Who had she spoken to instead?

I turned back to the first sheet. There were several calls over the last month to what I recognized as Sally's phone, along with a few other numbers that meant nothing to me. One in particular stood out from the amount of contact. It was a cell phone number, and while my mother hadn't called it every day, it had been close enough. The conversations varied in length and had taken place at irregular times, often in the middle of the night. I had no idea who it was, but then, why would I? I knew so little about my mother's life.

Perhaps it wasn't quite too late to change that.

I took out my own cell phone and dialed the number. It rang for an age before cutting to an anonymous, robotic voice mail that invited me to leave a message. I didn't. Instead, I killed the call and then tried again a minute later. Maybe whoever the number belonged to just hadn't been able to get to the phone.

This time, it didn't ring at all. It just bleeped emptily.

I ended the call and then frowned at my phone. Whoever was on the other end of the line had decided they didn't want to answer and had turned their phone off. There didn't seem to be any other way of interpreting the situation, but I also couldn't think what to make of it.

I sat there for a moment, confused.

And then my phone rang—a sudden shock of noise and vibration in my hand. I looked down at the screen, expecting to see the same number there, but the call was from Sally.

"Hello?"

"It's your mother," she told me. "She's awake. She's asking for you."

I drove too quickly to the hospice. There had been no obvious urgency in what Sally had told me—no sense that I needed to get here before it was too late—but even so. My mother was awake and asking for me, and I was familiar enough with her sleeping patterns that I didn't want to miss this window to talk. After years of mostly silence between us, it felt like there was so much I wanted to ask.

After parking, I went inside and found Sally waiting for me at the desk. I signed in, and then we walked quickly.

"Is she still awake?" I said.

"She was a minute ago."

"What did she want to talk to me about?"

"I don't know." Sally looked at me sympathetically. "I wouldn't get your hopes up. She was asking for you, but she still seemed confused to me."

When we reached the room, Sally waited in the corridor. I pushed the door open slowly and saw my mother lying in the bed. She seemed smaller and weaker than yesterday, her body fading by the hour now, but her eyes were open. She looked at me as I gently closed the door, and then her gaze followed me across the room as I moved to the seat by the bed.

"Hi, Mom."

"Hello, Paul."

"Sally said there was something you wanted to tell me?"

She frowned. "Who's Sally?"

*The woman who's been your care worker for months,* I thought.

"It doesn't matter," I said.

"Is she your girlfriend?"

"Absolutely not."

"The one you won't let me meet yet?"

My mother smiled and looked at the ceiling. I said nothing. It was Jenny she was talking about—that was when and where she was right now.

"You'll have to ask your father."

My father, who had been dead for six years. Even in life, I wouldn't have wanted to ask him anything, and for a moment I couldn't work out what my mother meant.

She looked at me and smiled encouragingly, willing me on to understand.

"For the *envelopes,* Paul. You know he's the one who keeps things like that. You'll need two, won't you? And stamps, of course."

Then I understood where she was. It was the day I'd shown her the magazine that Jenny gave me, with the details of the short story competition on the back. It might have been free to enter, but that didn't mean I had everything I needed. Envelopes and stamps. I still remembered the sick feeling in my stomach at the prospect of asking my father for help, along with the dismissive look on his face when I had, after he'd made me explain what I wanted them for.

"*Not* that they'll be sending your story back." My mother tutted to herself. "Not if they know what's good for them, at any rate."

"I don't think it was very good, Mom."

"Rubbish. I snuck into your room, you see, and read it when you were at school. The one about the man walking around the streets where he grew up? I thought it was *brilliant.*"

Then she frowned to herself.

"I mean, I know I shouldn't have done that. But you never *show me anything*, Paul. I'm sorry."

I swallowed. At the time, it would have mortified me to know she'd done that, but it all felt so distant now that it scarcely seemed to matter.

"That's okay, Mom."

She looked back at the ceiling again and closed her eyes. I waited, unsure what to do or say. I'd sped here because she was awake and there had been something she wanted to tell me. Maybe it was foolish, but after what had happened at the house today, I'd imagined it might be connected to that: the knocks at the door; the man I'd seen in the woods.

But it was only this.

"Mom, do you remember me telling you I went in the attic?"

For a moment there was no response. Then she sighed.

"They're all the same."

"The . . . cases?"

"No." Her eyes still closed, she smiled as though quietly pleased about something. "They're all the same. That's why he won't find it."

"Who? And what is it he won't find?"

But she just shook her head. It seemed that whoever *he* was, and whatever she was hiding from him, she was determined to keep it a secret from me as well. Well, I could search through the newspapers again later. I forced down the frustration I felt and tried a different angle.

"Have you . . . seen anybody in the woods?"

Again, she didn't reply immediately. But the smile disappeared, and then, a few seconds later, her eyes suddenly opened and she looked at me in alarm.

"He's in the woods, Paul!"

"It's okay, Mom."

"He's in the woods. He's there *right now*!"

I reached out and calmly smoothed the edge of the cover down over the corner of the bed. It felt like a futile attempt to soothe her, but after a moment her body seemed to relax a little.

"Who is in the woods, Mom?"

"I don't want to say that horrible boy's name." She shook her head again and closed her eyes. "Not after what he did. Not after all the pain he's caused over the years."

I hesitated.

"You saw Charlie in the woods?"

She nodded absently. "Flickering in the trees."

The image disturbed me and I moved my hand away from the bed. My mother was seeing ghosts now. But I told myself she had likely been seeing them for months.

It didn't mean they were real.

"Oh," she said suddenly. "I remember."

"Remember what?"

"What I needed to tell you."

Her eyes remained closed, and her voice was fainter now. She was drifting off. The window was closing, and I didn't know how many more there would be.

I leaned closer again.

"What?"

"I'm so proud of you."

She smiled slightly. As she drifted back off to sleep, her mind was moving between times, and I knew where she was now. Standing on a railway platform with her son, waiting for him to leave, knowing he would not return. Throwing him out into the world without a thought for herself.

Silence in the room for a moment.

"Thank you," I said quietly.

"You're going to be a writer, I think."

Even though her voice was barely there now, she said it with such conviction that I was unable to reply. Instead, I just sat there, watching the covers rising and falling almost imperceptibly with every small breath she took. And then, eventually, I found the words.

"I love you," I said.

But my mother was asleep again by then.

I kissed her gently on the forehead and then sat with her for a time.

*I'm so proud of you.*

Walking outside again later, I thought about those words. They should have brought some comfort, but I knew it hadn't really been me she was talking to—or, at least, not me now. There was nothing about my present-day life for anybody to be proud of, and whatever there might have been back then had been squandered since. While my mother had been happy that I was escaping from Gritten and what happened here, the reality was that I never had. Not really. The shadow had always been there.

*You're going to be a writer.*

THE SHADOWS | 193

What a joke. A part of me was glad her mind had re-treated to a time and place where she could still believe I might amount to something.

I pushed open the doors to the hospice, and then squinted as I stepped out into the bright afternoon sun. I walked over to my car, the gravel crunching under my feet, and because of the light and the heat and the emotions churning inside me, it was only when I reached it that I realized another vehicle was parked beside it now, and that a woman was leaning against it with her arms folded, watching me.

She looked to be in her late thirties and had long brown hair tied back in a ponytail. She was not dressed for the weather—dark jeans and a long black coat—but from the look on her face, the temperature was the least of her worries.

She leaned away from the car. "Paul Adams?"

"Yes."

She nodded to herself, as though I were yet another disappointment in a long line of them.

"Detective Amanda Beck," she said. "Is there a bar around here, Paul? I don't know about you, but I could really do with a drink."

# TWENTY

---·--·-·---·-

Paul didn't drive far.

A few minutes after they'd left the hospice, he signaled and pulled into a parking lot. Amanda drove in and parked behind, then followed him into the pub. Given the general state of Gritten, she was worried it would be a pit, but it turned out to be nice enough: dark wood and polished brass; enough screens to suggest it would be lively later but quiet for the moment. Most importantly of all right now, of course, it had a bar.

*I need a drink.*

Amanda imagined she had said that numerous times in her life, usually after what had been, in hindsight, a comparatively mild day at work. Today it was genuinely true. The near-encounter back at Billy Roberts's house had caused her fight-or-flight mechanism to kick in, and after the police and ambulance arrived, the adrenaline had begun to settle listlessly in her system like sludge. Adrenaline was a poison; if you didn't use it up, it used you instead. She had been shivering as she talked to the lead detective, a man named Graham Dwyer, and her hands were still trembling a little even now.

The bartender fetched a beer for Paul automatically. Amanda ordered a vodka tonic along with a separate shot. She downed the latter in one as soon as it arrived. Paul started to get his wallet out, but she waved him away, her throat burning.

"On me."

"Thanks."

Once the order was settled, she looked around and then led him to a table to one side, as far away from the handful of other customers as possible. As they sat down, she resisted the urge to down the second drink too. Instead, she just took a sip, closing her eyes and rolling the liquid around her mouth.

"Is this about this morning?" Paul said.

Amanda swallowed slowly and opened her eyes. "This morning?"

"The marks on my mother's door," Paul said. "An officer came to the house. Holder, I think his name was. He took photos, but he didn't seem that interested."

Amanda certainly was. "What kind of marks?"

"Someone knocked on the door in the night and left fist prints on the wood. The officer thought it was probably just a prank."

"That's a weird kind of prank."

"Yeah, I thought so."

He stared back at her for a moment, as though he wanted to explain a little more but wasn't sure how. Then he shook his head.

"But you're not here because of that."

"No." Amanda got out her ID and showed him. "I'm not with the Gritten Police Department. I'm from a place called Featherbank."

She watched his reaction to that closely. If Paul Adams was behind the CC666 account, the place name would surely be familiar to him. But his face didn't show a flicker of recognition.

She put the ID away. "I'm here because of a crime that occurred there last weekend. A murder. Two boys killed one of their classmates."

That got a reaction. Paul closed his eyes and began rubbing his forehead with his fingertips. Again, she watched him. He would be forty or so now, she estimated, but had the kind of appealing face she imagined under normal circumstances could pass for much younger. Right now he seemed weighed down by the world, every single one of those years etched on his features. It seemed like she'd just added more.

"Another one," he said quietly.

"Another?"

"There have been two others over the years. At least."

*Shit.* Amanda took out her phone. "Do you have the names?"

She typed the details he gave her into her notes app. She would need to look into those later. Was it possible CC666 was involved there too?

"I didn't know about those," she admitted.

"I only found out about them yesterday. Until then, I had no idea. I assumed all that . . . that it had been forgotten about."

"Not online."

He raised his eyebrows. "Yeah, I saw. I don't understand it."

"Well, you know." Amanda shrugged, and dropped her next reference as casually as possible. "People are always interested in the unsolved and the unknown."

He shook his head. "But it wasn't *unsolved*."

"No, that's true." If he had ever heard of the forum before, he was a good actor. She made a calculation. "That's actually the name of a website. The Unsolved and the Unknown. You ever heard of it?"

"No."

"Me neither until a few days ago. The thing is, the boys in Featherbank were both members on there. They were obsessed with the Charlie Crabtree case. And there was another user who seemed to be encouraging them. This person knew a lot about what happened here in Gritten."

"Yeah, I noticed a lot of people do."

"This particular one was implying they were Charlie Crabtree."

That worked like a magic spell. For a moment, Paul's whole body was totally still. Then an expression of disbelief appeared on his face: a mixture of disgust and confusion and grief. *Nobody* was that good an actor, Amanda decided. Whatever else Paul Adams might be, and whatever troubles were going on in his life, she was sure he wasn't behind the CC666 account.

Which was almost disappointing.

"Why would anyone *do* that?" he said.

"I don't know." She hesitated. "I mean, do you think it's possible they were telling the truth?"

"No. Charlie's dead."

But he said it too quickly, in a way that seemed to be a magic spell of its own: an incantation that, if you repeated it often enough, would become true.

"How can you be sure?" she said. "From what I can tell, the police searched those woods extensively."

Paul thought about that for a while.

"I remember that," he said finally. "I remember hearing the dogs barking from my bedroom window. Every now and then, I'd spot an officer in the tree line. But the thing is, the way it reads online, Charlie vanished without a trace. And that's just not true."

"It's not?"

"No. He and the others had been in those woods so often that there were traces of him *everywhere*. The dogs would find a trail that would lead them back to another, and they'd end up going in circles. Literally chasing their tails. So, yeah, the search was extensive, but unless you've been in there, it's really not obvious how big those woods are. How easy it is to get lost in there."

All of which might be true, but she could still sense the doubt there. He wasn't as certain as he wanted to sound. Even in the face of the evidence and the weight of probability, there was a part of him that wasn't quite so sure. And she could tell the idea scared him.

"Did you know Billy Roberts was living in Gritten?" she said.

"No." He blinked. "Fuck. I had no idea."

"He was living in his parents' old house."

"I didn't even know he'd been released."

"Really?" Another truth, she thought, but this one surprised her. "Given what happened, I'd have thought you'd have been following the case over the years."

"The opposite. I've done my best not to think about it at all. After I left here, I just wanted to forget about it. Pretend it never happened."

*Jesus,* Amanda thought. *Everyone has a fucking box in their head to hide things in.* Apart from her, of course. She didn't need to close her eyes right now to recall the sight of Billy Roberts on his blood-soaked couch. The image kept pressing at the edge of her mind, and it was all she could do to keep it out. There were going to be nightmares later.

"*Was* living?" Paul said.

"I'm sorry?"

"You said Billy *was* living there."

That was sharp of him. Amanda picked up her drink and took another sip, wondering how much to tell him. But it wasn't like the news wouldn't spread quickly.

"He was found dead today," she said.

*I found him dead.*

"How?"

"I don't want to go into that right now. And I just want to stress this: I'm not officially involved in that investigation. The Gritten police already have several suspects they want to talk to. I was visiting him on a completely unrelated matter."

Paul considered that.

"You think he might be the person behind the online messages?"

Sharper still.

"I don't know. It's one line of inquiry. Do you think that's the kind of thing he would do?"

"Billy? I don't know anything about him."

*Present tense.* Even though Paul had just been told Roberts was dead, the information hadn't sunk in far enough yet for him to correct his speech. She had already been confident Paul wasn't behind the CC666 account. She was sure now he hadn't been involved in killing Billy Roberts.

So who had been?

*An unrelated matter,* she'd just told Paul, and that was likely true. While she wasn't involved in the murder investigation itself, she had been on the scene, given a detailed statement, and talked to Detective Graham Dwyer afterward. Dwyer already had a list of people he wanted to bring in and talk to. Billy Roberts had been a loose part of a local circle of drinkers who enjoyed an often volatile relationship: men who were borderline homeless, and who fell out and fought viciously within the space of half a bottle, all the suppressed anger and resentment exploding out of them. In advance of forensics, those connections would be the natural focus of the investigation, and Amanda figured the odds were good Dwyer would turn out to be right.

But she couldn't rid herself of the feeling she'd had outside Roberts's door earlier—the sensation that someone had been standing on the other side of that flimsy wood, staring out at her. If that was the case, it suggested a killer far more in control of themselves than the working theory supported. And Amanda didn't like to believe that whoever had done the terrible things she'd seen inside that house had been cool and collected while they did it.

Because what kind of monster was that?

Paul was staring off into space, looking helpless and almost overloaded by the information she'd given him.

"I'm sorry for dredging up bad memories," she said.

He shook his head.

"Believe me, they were all already being dredged."

"Your mother . . . isn't well?"

"She's dying."

"Well, I was trying to be circumspect about things."

"There's really no need."

She nodded, remembering what it had been like when her father was dying. The endless visits; the smell of the hospital; the way he seemed diminished by every passing day, shrinking into a figure that didn't fit with the size of the man who filled her memories. It had seemed impossible. But everything is okay until it isn't. People are there, large as life and taken for granted, and then they aren't.

"Well, I'm sorry," she said. "It must be very hard for you right now."

"I think it's probably harder for her."

Paul picked up his beer and downed half of it in one gulp.

Amanda waited.

"I hadn't seen her in a long time," he said. "Not been back *here*. You know how it can feel like you put something away and forget about it, and it's like it's gone? But then you realize it's actually been there the whole time."

"Like a box that won't stay shut?" she said.

"Exactly."

"Believe me, I know that one every day. You're staying at your mother's house, right?"

He nodded.

"I'm surprised you didn't opt for a hotel," she said.

"Lecturers don't get paid that much."

"Even so."

He didn't answer, and she found herself trying to imagine how it must feel, returning to a childhood home with so much sour history in its walls and floorboards. Especially when, unlike Billy Roberts, Paul probably hadn't needed to. But looking at him now, Amanda recognized that a lot of the weight he was carrying was guilt, and she wondered if, despite not wanting to think about what had happened here, a part of him had decided that maybe, deep down, he needed to.

"I don't know," he said eventually, speaking slowly as though he were working out the same thing for himself. "As difficult as it's been, I think I owe my mother. She looked after me when I was a kid. Protected me. Raised me. Maybe it's the least I can do. Although, obviously, it's too late now."

"Not necessarily."

Her phone buzzed. She checked it and found a message from Lyons requesting an update on what the hell was going on. It was worded so politely she could tell he was furious at being kept in the dark. Well, he could wait. She scrolled back up, hoping there might be an update from Theo, but there was nothing. The mysterious user behind the CC666 account clearly hadn't taken the bait yet. And, of course, if it turned out to have been Billy Roberts, now they never would.

A flash of the scene earlier.

She pushed it away and drained her glass.

"Okay," she said. "I need to go."

"Well, thanks for the drink."

"That's okay. Now that I know that lecturers don't earn much, I'm relieved I could help out. I'll probably be in touch. It might be handy to talk about what happened here, even if it's just to give me an idea of what I'm looking for."

"I don't know how much help I can be."

"Me neither. But we'll see." She stood up. "In the meantime, is there anyone else in the area it's worth me talking to?"

At that, Paul looked past her toward the door of the pub.

Up until then, he'd come across as so unguarded that she hadn't doubted a single thing he'd said. But there was something different about his manner now. He didn't look like someone scanning his memory for a name, so much as someone who already had one in mind and was deciding whether or not to say it.

"No," he said eventually. "Nobody."

# TWENTY-ONE

············

When I drove back to Gritten Wood later, I didn't go straight to my mother's house.

As I turned off the main road, I could see the wall of the Shadows in the distance: a black and solid presence at the base of the sky. Soon it would be night, and I felt nervous about sleeping in my old room after everything that had happened today. With everything I'd learned churning in my head. With the house ticking and creaking around me, and the trees at the end of the yard full of darkness and ghosts.

Of course, there were ghosts everywhere here.

I parked in front of a different property and stared out of the car window. The yard was enormously overgrown, with brambles arching over the lawn like rolls of barbed wire. The undergrowth closest to the house rose high enough to reach the dirty black glass of the ground-floor windows. The place was little more than a shell. I had the sense that the woods behind had spread

their fingers down the backyard and were slowly clenching their fist, reclaiming the building for the wilds.

James's old house.

I had a dim memory of my mother telling me Carl
and Eileen had moved away years ago. Perhaps they
had tried to sell this place beforehand, but who was
going to buy a home in Gritten Wood? The town was
slowly dying, the houses like lights going off one by
one, the old bulbs never replaced. The building beside
me now had clearly been abandoned for years, and the
heart had gone out of it long before.

*Billy is dead,* I thought.

The words signified something clear, but still didn't
seem to map onto the world in a way that I could grasp.
It seemed like it should be important to me—that I
should be feeling something. Perhaps I should be glad.
Pleased that, after what he did, the bastard had finally
gotten what he deserved. That would be the natural reaction to have, wouldn't it? But every time I searched
inside myself for a reaction to the news, I couldn't
find it.

The truth was that, in every way that mattered, Billy
had been dead to me for twenty-five years. He was just
an old photograph I had long since stopped looking at.
Back then I would have been happy to kill him myself
for what he'd done, but the time since had tempered
that. Looking back, I could see that Billy had always
been easily manipulated. He'd had a difficult childhood, and I could only imagine his adult life had been
hard too. The only emotion his death raised in me now

was an odd kind of sadness. A sense of how many lives had been ruined by what happened here, and what a waste it had all been.

And now another boy had been killed.

*Charlie's dead.*

That was what I'd said to Amanda, but the words had come out of instinct. It was what I'd told myself over the years, because I had to. I looked past the house now, toward the woods. The most likely explanation for Charlie's disappearance remained that he was out there in the Shadows somewhere—that after what he and Billy did, he'd woken up and wandered off, and that his bones were moldering away somewhere deep between the trees, pulled apart by tangles of grass and lost in the undergrowth.

And yet my skin was crawling.

As the evening darkened around me, I thought about knocks in the night, and figures in the woods, and what my mother had said about seeing Charlie flickering in the trees.

About someone online pretending to be him.

*Do you think it's possible they were telling the truth?*

Right then, I wished I felt anything like as sure as I'd tried to sound in the pub, but the reality was that I could still feel him everywhere. As I started the engine again and drove away, I was frightened by the thought of it. If Charlie was still alive, then what was happening here?

*Billy is dead.*

The words came again as I drove. And despite what Amanda had said about it being unrelated and suspects having already been identified, the dread rose up inside me. Because red handprints were once again being pressed onto the world and I couldn't escape the feeling that something awful was going to happen again. And most of all, there were my mother's words.

*You shouldn't be here.*

When I parked outside the house, I took a few seconds to calm myself. I was almost scared to go inside, and that wouldn't do. Coming back here to Gritten had scrambled me; that was all. And while there were difficult moments still to come, the important thing was this would all be over before too much longer. When my business here was done, I could go back to my life and forget about it all again. In the meantime, it was understandable that I was seeing spirits in the shadows. It didn't mean they were really there.

*The past is the past.*

And it couldn't hurt me now.

The house was dark and gloomy as I unlocked the front door and turned the handle. The door jammed on something for a second, then opened more slowly than it should. There was something stuck beneath the bottom of the wood. I opened the door wide enough to squeeze my body inside, then closed it behind me. Whatever had been trapped beneath it came loose.

I flicked the light switch beside me.

And then froze.

*What is that?*

Except I already knew. I forced myself to crouch down by the mat, and fought back the revulsion that came as I touched the thing that had been pushed through my mother's mail slot. The fabric was dusty and old. It had come away in places, revealing gummy patches of glue beneath. And when I turned the doll around and looked into its pitch-black face, the red string fingers tickled against the back of my hand.

What was it?

The answer that came brought a shiver as I imagined the vast, dark expanse of the woods behind me right then.

*Incubation.*

# TWENTY-TWO

## BEFORE

The morning after the nightmare with Red Hands, I remember feeling scared as I walked through the town to James's house. I knew that the dream I'd had—the experience of being outside the room in the basement of the school, and what happened there with Red Hands—had only been a dream: one that might have felt lucid at the time, but which couldn't have been, really. I hadn't been able to breathe simply because it had been a nightmare and I had never been in control of what was happening at all. But no matter how hard I tried to rationalize it to myself, the awful residue of it had stayed with me. The knowledge that Charlie had somehow got so far into my head was frightening.

James looked tired and apprehensive. As we walked to the bus stop together, it was obvious that whatever he'd dreamed the night before was on his mind as well. Neither of us mentioned it until the bus left the main road.

"So . . . how did it go?" James said.

"How did what go?"

"Last night. The experiment. What did you dream?"

I forced myself to shrug as though it were nothing. At the same time, I had dutifully written a basic account of the dream in my diary that morning, and if I was going to end up reading it out at lunchtime there didn't seem much point in lying now about what had happened.

"I did dream about the room," I admitted.

"I did too. What happened in yours?"

"*Nothing* happened."

"But you just said it was about the room?"

"Yeah."

I would have been happy to leave it at that, but he was waiting for me to carry on, unwilling to let it go. He looked scared by whatever his own dream had been about. So I sighed, and told him a little bit about being outside the room and seeing him floating behind the glass. But I played down how scary the whole thing had been, and I certainly didn't mention what had happened at the end.

"And nobody *else* was there," I said. "Honestly, I'm not even sure it was you. It was just a stupid dream."

James looked away, out of the window.

"What about you?" I said.

"I don't want to talk about it."

"Why?"

"Because it was horrible." He shook his head. "I'm worried about what we've done, Paul. I think we might have done something really bad."

*Something ridiculous, more like it.*

And yet I didn't say that. There was something in his tone of voice that bothered me. The day before, I hadn't believed for one second that Charlie would dare repeat his door-knocking trick and try to do anything to Goodbold. This morning, though, I no longer felt quite so sure.

"Everything will be fine," I said. "We'll get to school, and it will just be the usual. Goodbold will be there, trust me. And he'll be the same bastard he always is."

James didn't reply.

The bus juddered and rattled.

"You'll see," I said.

But Goodbold was not in school that morning.

After we trudged to the changing rooms to get ready for soccer, a different sports teacher, Mr. Dewhurst, arrived to take us down to the field. Under normal circumstances that would have been a good sign. Dewhurst ran a far tighter ship than Goodbold, and there would be less violence on the field as a result. But it might have been the first day since starting at Gritten that I'd have been glad to see Goodbold instead, and as we set out into the streets and I saw Charlie smiling to himself, the unease I'd felt since waking up that morning intensified.

Something had happened.

*I'm worried about what we've done, Paul.*

By lunchtime, the nerves were humming inside me. James and I walked down to room C5b, our footsteps echoing in the empty stairwell, and it was clear that whatever had been weighing on James first thing that morning had become heavier over the last few hours. As he pushed open the door, I felt an urge to reassure him again. To tell him not to worry. That everything was going to be all right.

Except I couldn't find the words.

Charlie and Billy were in their usual seats, but the rest of the room seemed darker today. It took me a second to realize why. The lights closest to the door had been turned off, which left the two of them illuminated at the back, drawing you toward them from out of the shadows. Was that by design? I thought it probably was. Charlie stage-managed everything so carefully.

As James and I made our way between the seats, I decided I wasn't prepared to be manipulated by him any longer. We weren't alone in the woods right now, miles from anyone; there was no danger here. So I allowed a little of the anger I'd suppressed yesterday to surface now. Wherever this experiment was heading, I decided it had to stop.

"So," I said. "What the fuck is going on?"

"Sit down."

I ignored Charlie—but of course James did as he was told. His hands were trembling as he took his dream diary out of his bag.

"What did we all dream?" Charlie said.

"I asked you what's going on."

He smiled patiently.

"James?"

James looked up at me nervously. "I want Paul to go first."

Charlie shook his head. "No."

"I don't want to say what I dreamed."

"I'll do it, then."

Charlie held out his hand for James's dream diary, the gesture delivered with total confidence that his command would be obeyed.

"You don't have to," I told James.

But Charlie's hand remained out, and I watched as James did exactly as he'd been instructed. He didn't want his entry to be read out, but such was the hold Charlie had over him that he was incapable of refusing.

Charlie opened James's diary.

"'I dreamed I was in Room C5b,'" he read. "'Charlie and Billy were there too. Paul wasn't. The air was strange and liquid, so it was like swimming through water. When I went to the door, I looked through the window at the side and Paul was standing there.'"

James glanced at me, and then quickly away.

"'I couldn't see him properly,'" Charlie continued. "'His face was distorted and it was like he wasn't properly in the dream. He seemed frightened. I started trying to talk to him, but I don't think he could hear what I was saying. And then he wasn't there anymore.'"

James was staring down at the floor now, completely unable to meet my eye. I couldn't believe what I was hearing. His dream matched mine almost exactly, and even taking *incubation* into account, there was no way they could have ended up so similar. There was only one explanation I could think of for what I was hearing.

He'd written his diary entry after talking to me on the bus.

*I want Paul to go first.*

Because I would have read my account of my dream, and then he would have read his, and they would have been the same. And in that moment, he would have impressed Charlie and proved him right, even though he knew deep down it was all a fantasy and a lie.

*Jesus,* I thought.

After everything we'd been through over the years—all those times I'd stuck up for him and protected him—he was so far gone that he was prepared to use me to help confirm Charlie's delusions.

"Bullshit," I said.

Charlie broke off from reading.

"What?"

"I said this is bullshit."

"Why?" Charlie looked from me to the book and back again, playing confused. "This is what James has written down. What are you saying?"

For a moment, I was too angry—too *hurt*—to answer. I looked from one of them to the other. Charlie waiting for my reply. Billy indifferent to it. And James, still looking down, so obviously ashamed of himself that I couldn't get the words out.

*I'm saying my best friend is a liar.*

"Paul?" Charlie said.

"Finish reading what James dreamed."

But instead, Charlie put James's diary on the desk.

"You've always doubted this, haven't you?" he said. "Why don't you tell us what *you* dreamed? I can finish James's account afterward."

I looked down at my bag, on the floor at my feet with my dream diary inside. But I couldn't read from that now, could I? Not without either confirming what James had written or challenging him outright about it, and both seemed unbearable to me right then.

"Just finish reading what James wrote," I said.

"In a minute," Charlie said. "But actually, I think I'll read from mine first—or rather, Billy will. That way we can avoid any doubts or suspicion. You go first, Billy."

They swapped dream diaries and Billy started reading.

"'Billy and James and I were here in the room,'" he said. "'At first, I wasn't sure if the two of them were lucid in the same way I was, but I thought they were. Paul wasn't there. I could sense that he was somewhere close by, but he didn't want to join us for some reason. I was disappointed, because I knew it might take all four of us at first to accomplish what we wanted to do. It would be much harder with just three, especially if there was someone nearby who didn't believe. Paul didn't want to join us—'"

Charlie held up a hand. "Stop there, Billy. I'll read the beginning of yours now."

I shook my head. "This is fucking crazy."

"'Me and Charlie were in the room,'" Charlie read. "'James was there too, but he was flickery, like he hadn't managed to be as there as me and Charlie were—like he wasn't as connected. I could see Charlie clearly, though. Paul wasn't anywhere around. He wasn't there at all.'"

Charlie stopped and looked up at me. "What did *you* dream, Paul?"

I didn't answer, and the silence in the air began ringing. After a moment, James looked up at me, with an imploring expression on his face that only intensified the sick feeling inside me. In his own sad way, he was doing this in an attempt to bring me back into the fold. To give me an opportunity to invest in Charlie's fantasy the same way he had.

I stared back at him, my face hardening.

"I didn't dream anything like that," I said flatly. "I wasn't there. I didn't see any of you."

"That you remember," Charlie corrected me. "James wrote down that *he* saw you."

"I think I'm done with this whole thing."

"Yes." Charlie leaned back. "I think that might be for the best. You being involved is hampering the three of us. That's why we couldn't connect properly—because you weren't properly committed."

"James?" I said.

And then I stood there, waiting to see if James was going to say anything. Come to his senses and confess, perhaps; put an end to this whole charade. It was obvious from Charlie's words that he was attempting to banish me from the group right then, and this was my supposed best friend's chance to speak up and stop all this.

To leave here with me.

But he said nothing.

"You're right." I came back to life and picked up my bag. "I guess I'll see you guys around."

I walked over to the door. When I reached it, I paused and looked back. Because even though I knew that nothing could possibly have happened, the fact remained that Goodbold was not in school today.

"How did it all end?" I called over.

"The dream broke apart," Charlie said. "Because of you. I remember James and Billy drifting away from me, and the dream beginning to fade. Red Hands and I got as far as Goodbold's house by ourselves, but I knew the two of us wouldn't be strong enough to get inside by ourselves. All because of you."

I shook my head and gave a half laugh.

"So *nothing* happened."

Charlie smiled.

"We managed to kill his dog," he said.

# TWENTY-THREE

Goodbold was back at school the next day.

For obvious reasons, I found myself watching him out of the corner of my eye. On a superficial level, nothing about him had changed: he still lumbered about the same as always, rolling his shoulders, that whistle on a cord around his neck. But if you knew to look for it, it seemed to me that he was walking a little more slowly than usual, the way someone might while recovering from an operation. And every now and then I caught him looking around suspiciously, as though searching for someone.

There was no way I could know for certain if Charlie really had killed his dog. It wasn't the kind of incident that would have been reported in the news or made its way into the school's grapevine of gossip. But Goodbold did seem hurt to me. When I saw his face in unguarded moments, it was as though some cruel damage had been done to him and he couldn't understand why.

And so, while there was no way I could know for sure, I did.

Because I saw Charlie and the others watching Goodbold too. That first day he was back, I remember seeing the three of them sitting on a bench together at break time. While I'd done my best to avoid them since yesterday, I was near enough to see Goodbold walking past on playground duty, and then what happened as he reached their bench.

James was staring down at the ground. Billy was looking off to one side. But Charlie was staring straight at Goodbold the whole time, watching him as he approached.

I saw Goodbold glance indifferently at them.

Then back again more intently.

And then he came to a halt.

Because Charlie was smiling at him. It was a *knowing* smile—one that was easily deniable, but which communicated just enough of a message for Goodbold to understand what lay behind it. To let him know it was Charlie who had done this terrible thing to him, and that there was nothing he could do about it.

The moment seemed to last for an age. It felt like my heart stopped in my chest as I wondered what was going to happen. Whether Goodbold might approach Charlie and challenge him. Or perhaps even lose control and attack him.

And yet Goodbold did none of those things.

He just stood there. But the expression on his face changed. It was as though he couldn't quite comprehend what he was seeing—as though even if, right then, he understood the *what* of it, he couldn't make sense of the *why*. And in those few seconds I saw the man in a different light. I remembered the occasions when I'd seen him walking his dog in Gritten, and I found myself picturing a lonely home life, and the frustrations and disappointments of his everyday existence. I imagined him waking up the previous morning and coming downstairs, stepping out into his yard, and seeing what had been taken from him. And despite all the indignities he'd forced on us over the months, I felt sorry for him.

Then he turned from Charlie and walked away.

And life carried on for all of us.

Over the weeks that followed, it was easy enough to avoid James. The town was small, but there were routes through it that avoided his house on a morning. I found it easy to ignore him during the wait at the bus stop. On the journey itself, he sat in the front and so was always ahead of me by the time I disembarked. On the way home, I'd often see him stalking across the bridge over the main road, his head bowed and his hands stuffed in his pockets, slumped and walking too quickly, as if he were trying to escape from something.

At school, I imagine the three of them spent most of their time in Room C5b, and I had no reason to go there anymore. Likewise the woods. On weekends I kept well away from the Shadows. I had no desire to encounter the three of them out there in the wilds, making their stupid plans, buying into each other's fantasies, and communing with the monster from their dreams.

I couldn't get away from them entirely, of course. I saw them in classes, and occasionally in the playground. While I did my best to ignore them, it was always uncomfortable, because I had the impression they weren't ignoring me—or at least that Charlie wasn't. Every now and then my skin would crawl and I'd look up to see the three of them nearby, Charlie with a smirk on his face, a sly and victorious expression.

*You might have removed yourself from the game,* he seemed to be saying. *But the game isn't finished with you yet.*

And each time, I would look away and wonder why I had ever been friends with him at all. It had been because of James, of course. But I never saw James looking at me. He would always be staring at the ground instead, embarrassed and awkward, and I remember thinking he seemed increasingly out of sorts with the other two. There had been shifting power divisions between the four of us as a group, but my presence had balanced things out a little; it seemed like, without me around, Charlie and Billy had grown closer again, and that James was being dominated.

There was one lunchtime when I was at the edge of the playground and I saw the three of them in the distance. James was walking between the other two, and he looked so broken down that he reminded me of a prisoner being led somewhere against his will.

But he had made his choice, hadn't he?

I stared after them for a moment, telling myself I didn't care, and that I didn't need him.

*Fuck him.*

Then I hitched my bag up on my shoulder and walked past the construction site toward the tennis courts and the bench.

Because I had someone else to spend my time with.

# TWENTY-FOUR

--------

## NOW

*I'm surprised you didn't opt for a hotel.*

That was what Amanda had said to me yesterday. The comment had thrown me at the time. It had never occurred to me to do that, and I wondered why I hadn't. It wasn't a matter of money, so perhaps a part of me had wanted to punish myself. Or possibly, thinking about the way my life had faltered and failed over the years in the shadow of what had happened, maybe on some subconscious level I'd decided it needed to be done—almost like a dare to myself.

*See? Everything is okay.*

If so, the delivery of Charlie's doll changed that. There was no way I was going to stay in the house that night. I packed my things, including the boxes my mother had kept, then got into my car and drove back to Gritten. I found the cheapest hotel I could and checked in, deciding that I would figure out what to do in the morning.

But I'd never been able to sleep well in hotels. And even there, away from the house, I still had the same sense of threat and foreboding. The knocks on the door might have been a prank, and the figure I'd seen in the woods a stranger, but there was no way of rationalizing away the delivery of the doll.

Someone was out there. Someone was targeting me.

And however much I told myself it was impossible, I couldn't escape the feeling that Charlie was behind it. I tossed and turned as morning approached, remembering the way he'd looked at me in the weeks after I left the group. The sense I'd had back then that things were not over.

*The game isn't finished with you yet.*

The early hours found me outside, walking the streets of Gritten.

At this hour, the world was quiet and peaceful. There was no breeze, just the push of cool air against me, an almost welcome sensation in advance of the heat I knew would come later. Ribbons and threads of clouds hung low in the dawn sky. They were so close that they seemed like spirits that had descended to peer at me, and so still that it was hard to imagine them ever moving on.

I wandered down roads I remembered well. There were endless rows of anonymous red-brick terraces squashed uncomfortably against each other. Back then, there had been clotheslines strung across the streets above, with laundry hanging down from them like tattered flags. The streets had changed a little, but they remained familiar. And while I told myself I was walking aimlessly—just drifting—I knew that wasn't true, and eventually I found myself at the top of a hill I knew better than most.

Jenny's old house was just ahead of me.

I stopped a little way up the street. The house looked almost the same as it had twenty-five years ago. My gaze moved to one of the upstairs windows, the one that had been her bedroom, and I pictured her single bed with its plain covers, the desk with a small television on it, the acoustic guitar on a stand in one corner. The walls had been filled with shelves. They stretched all the way from the ceiling to the floor—clearly homemade—and always looked too flimsy to support the sheer number of books loaded onto them. It was only the foundations of more books below that had prevented the whole edifice from collapsing.

God, I could still see it all so clearly.

I remembered the first time I'd come here, and how it had been a surprise to see Jenny out of school uniform. When she opened the door, she was dressed in jeans, a faded Iron Maiden T-shirt that looked a couple of sizes too big for her, and an open, black-and-white-checked flannel.

The two of us had gone upstairs.

*I'm sorry about the mess,* she told me.

There had been no need for her to apologize. The contrast with my own bedroom had struck me immediately, and I'd felt ashamed thinking of the bare floorboards and plain mattress, the piles of clothes and books, the damp walls. Even the idea of having my own wardrobe or bookcase was alien to me, never mind a television.

*You should see my room,* I'd said.

That got me a raised eyebrow.

*That's very forward of you.*

I smiled at the memory now. It had made me blush back then, but at the same time, the squirming sensation in my stomach had been nice. And both feelings had returned shortly afterward, when Jenny had finished bagging up the books she wanted to take to her beloved secondhand shop.

*We should head downstairs,* she said. *We don't want my mom getting suspicious, do we?*

A little way down the street now, the front door opened.

I felt an urge to hide, but there was nowhere to go. Maybe it wouldn't be Jenny emerging from the house—but then it was, of course. I watched as she stepped out onto the path, called something back into the house, then made her way to the street, hitching a bag over her shoulder. Not a plastic bag full of books this time, but something much more grown-up: designer and expensive. She was going to turn and see me at any moment, standing in the middle of the sidewalk like an idiot.

*You're not a teenager anymore.*

No. And so instead of hesitating any longer, I started walking. She turned her head and did a double-take as she saw me. Then she smiled.

"Hey, stranger."

"I'm like a bad penny," I said. "Keep turning up."

"That's harsh; you're worth more than that. What brings you to these parts at this time?"

"My feet. I'm not stalking you, honestly. I was just walking."

"Yeah, yeah. I believe you. Thousands wouldn't."

She gestured back at the house. "Hey, you want to come in for a bit? See my mom?"

I couldn't really imagine doing that right now.

"Thanks. But I might not be the best company. And I really *was* just out walking."

"Sounds serious." She patted her bag. "I was just heading out to get some breakfast first thing. Do some reading. Make some notes. Walk with me?"

"Sure."

I fell into step beside her. As we walked, I remembered how the two of us had done this so often that summer: meandering through the streets side by side, talking shit and sharing our aspirations for the future.

As the weeks had passed, it had felt like our lives were becoming slowly intertwined, and there had been a gentle tension between the two of us: a shared knowledge that something was building. A lot of time had passed since then, of course, and everything had changed, but the ease that came from age and experience right now was just as pleasant in its own way.

"Why *did* we lose touch?" Jenny said.

"I don't know."

I put my hands in my pockets, thinking back on the times she'd come to see me at college, and then the handful of occasions we'd seen each other afterward, and all I knew was that it had become increasingly awkward. Jenny had been my first love, and when you're young you cling to that long past the point when you know it should be over. You know you need to let each other go, but it's so sad and difficult, and so you don't until you have to. Until the hurt of keeping someone out-weighs the hurt of losing them.

"I don't know," I said again. "It was a long time ago. All I know is that it's good to see you again now."

"It is, isn't it?" She smiled at me. "So: Any develop-ments?"

I faltered slightly.

"I don't want to talk about that right now."

"Yeah, I can tell. All the more reason for you to, I reckon."

And so, after a moment's hesitation, I did. I told her about the knocks on the door and the figure I'd seen in the woods. The fact that Billy was dead.

"Well," she said of the latter, "I'm glad about that."

"I thought you would be. I know I should be too."

"Yeah, but you were always more sensitive." She frowned. "So what do you think is happening?"

"I don't know. But do you remember the dolls Char-lie made?"

"I remember you telling me about them."

"Someone put one through my mother's mail slot yesterday."

"*What?*"

Jenny came to a stop beside me, looking horrified.

"Why would anyone do that?" she said.

That was one of the questions that was bothering me. So far, the attention I'd received had been threaten-ing but not harmful. Perhaps that meant whoever was behind it just wanted to frighten me away, for some rea-son. But the behavior also seemed to be escalating—

building toward something—and I couldn't shake the sensation that I was in danger here.

But there was a question that scared me more. *Who*?

"I don't know," I said.

"You need to go to the police," Jenny told me.

I looked at her.

"I don't," I said. "I can always just leave."

And as I said it, I realized I meant it—that the thought had arrived along with the doll yesterday, even if I hadn't admitted it to myself until now. I could leave. No law compelled me to stay here in Gritten. If I would be letting my mother down by doing so, I had lived with worse guilt over the years, and hadn't she told me herself that I shouldn't be here?

There was no need for me to stay.

Jenny smiled sadly.

"I don't think you're going to do that this time, Paul."

And then she reached out and touched my arm.

It was the first physical contact we'd had in over twenty years. The sensation sent a jolt through me, and when she left her hand there I felt warmth spreading through my skin.

*I don't think you're going to do that this time.*

"I owe it to my mother, right?" I said.

"No, you owe it to *yourself*. And you know what? I think a part of you wants to. After all, you didn't have to come back here at all, did you? You didn't have to stay in the house or look in the attic. But you did."

"Yes."

"Because deep down, you know you need to."

I didn't reply. After a moment, she moved her hand.

"This is me, by the way."

I looked to the side and realized we were standing outside a café on one of the main roads. I'd been so engrossed in talking to her that I hadn't paid attention to the world around us.

"I'll leave you to it, then," I said. "But thank you."

"Hey—anytime."

And then she walked inside, leaving me alone on the sidewalk, my arm still tingling from the contact. Her words stayed with me too, and I knew she was right. Yes, I could pack my things into the car and be gone from here. It would be the easiest thing in the world to do. But not what I needed to do.

And I realized there was another question that needed to be asked about the doll. Not just why and who, but *how*? I didn't know what had happened to the other three dolls, but I couldn't remember getting rid of mine. I supposed it should have been in the box along with everything else from back then. But it hadn't been. And if the doll that had been delivered to me was my own, then how had someone else gotten hold of it?

There was only one answer I could think of.

They had to have been in the house at some point.

# TWENTY-FIVE

---

It was midmorning when the autopsy results for Billy Roberts finally came through, and Amanda already felt dead on her feet. Hotels did not agree with her. Or was it the other way around? The thought momentarily baffled her. Then she shook her head, took a sip of cheap coffee, and tried to concentrate on the screen in front of her.

It wasn't easy. One of the many things she had learned from this case was that dreams occurred in the shallowest part of sleep. Last night, the uncomfortable mattress had done its best to keep her there and had helped to supply a wealth of them.

The nightmare, of course.

Given some of the horrors Amanda had witnessed in her career, she might have expected any bad dreams to be grim and visceral, but the most common one she had was superficially benign. Everything around her was pitch-black, and there was a feeling of vast space on every side, as though the whole world had been swept empty and clean. There was no sound. There was no real sensation at all, in fact, beyond the tight knot of awareness in her mind that somewhere out there in the darkness a child was lost. That he was going to die if she didn't find him. And that she was not going to do so in time.

She always woke from the dream in a state of profound distress, with an ache in her chest. It was not a pain so much as an absence: a feeling of hopelessness and despair. This morning, that feeling had been compounded by panic. The bedroom around her was almost as dark as the world in the nightmare, and what little she could see in the gloom was unfamiliar and threatening.

She had sat up quickly.

Where was she? For a few seconds, she hadn't been able to think. In that time, she had felt like a child again herself, the despair heightened by the dim knowledge that her father was dead, and if she cried out nobody would come.

At least she knew where she was right now. The Gritten Police Department cafeteria. It was a classic of its kind: a small room with beige chairs and old folding tables with the Formica chipped at the edges. The catering arrangements amounted to a vending machine in one corner. She took another sip of the shit coffee she'd gotten from it and thought, *Focus, woman*. Then she opened the autopsy report on her laptop.

There were photos attached, but she avoided them for the moment. It turned out there was more than enough devil in the details themselves, and she scanned them as dispassionately as she could. Time of death was estimated to be late morning yesterday. That information made her shiver. She had been sure the killer was still in the house when she arrived, and the forensics report all but confirmed it. When she had knocked, there had been a monster on the other side of that door, staring back out at her.

Christ, if she'd tried the handle right then . . .

She did her best to shake the thought away and read on. The cause of death appeared to be a savage knife wound to Roberts's throat, but as she'd observed at the scene itself, there were numerous other injuries listed in the report: cuts to his face and arms; extensive bruising to the head and body; bones that had been methodically broken. Billy Roberts had been badly tortured prior to his actual death, and marks around his wrists suggested he'd been handcuffed for much of his ordeal.

Amanda steeled herself and opened one of the photos.

It showed a close-up of what was left of his face. She leaned back slightly, recoiling from the image. Over the course of her research she had seen photographs of Billy Roberts as a teenager, and the one that had stuck with her was from the press coverage: the surly face staring back at the camera, somewhere in that nebulous state between boy and man. The discrepancy between the teenage photograph and the sight before her now was stark in every possible way.

*Who did this to you, Billy?* she thought.

But, as always, another question pressed at her. Right now it seemed more important than ever.

*And why?*

Detective Graham Dwyer was fairly sure he had the answer to both questions.

"Walt Barnaby, Jimmy Till, and Stephen Hyde," he said. "They're fucking scumbags."

Amanda followed him down one of the Gritten department's ancient corridors, caught between the need to keep up and the desire not to. Dwyer was a large man. The back of his barely tucked-in shirt was stained with sweat, and his thin gray hair was damp with it; she could smell him even from a distance, and it was obviously he didn't care in the slightest. It was equally clear that he was tolerating her presence here rather than welcoming it—that whatever strings Lyons had pulled higher up in Gritten had become a little more tangled on the way down.

Which was understandable, she supposed; she would probably have been the same if their situations had been reversed. But then she considered that. Maybe it wasn't true anymore. She remembered the investigation into the little boy's disappearance, and how she had initially resented another officer being drafted in to assist her, whereas now all she did was miss him.

"That's three people," she said.

Dwyer didn't break stride. "Well counted."

"I only saw one set of footprints at the scene," she said.

"One set of *bloody* footprints."

"Indicating one *bloody* killer."

"Who will be one of the three men I mentioned."

Dwyer led her into his office. It was tidier than she'd been expecting, the shelves lined with carefully labeled box files, the desk clear aside from his computer and some neatly stacked brown folders. The window behind the desk—mercifully—was open.

Dwyer sat down heavily in his chair and sighed.

"You have to understand, you don't know these people. Barnaby, Till, and Hyde. Like I said—complete scumbags. If you don't believe me, the files are right there." He gestured at the pile of folders without making any effort to pass them to her. "Be my guest."

"Thank you."

She flicked through them, thinking that Dwyer's definition of *fucking scumbag* differed slightly from hers. Maybe she was mellowing as she aged, but she found herself feeling slightly sorry for the three men. They were all in their forties, but looked much older in the mug shots that had been taken. Sallow skin. Bedraggled hair. Wild eyes. She recognized the type, of course, and could read between the lines of the various arrests and charges. These were the type of men who had drifted to the edge of society, or fallen through its cracks. You found them everywhere: drinking in the daytime in cheap, rough pubs; sitting with cans in the park; passing out in each other's houses and flats, the days and nights blurring into one. A volatile network of friends where the threat of violence was always humming away below the surface. All it took was one wrong word or perceived slight. One falling-out.

Dwyer was staring at her.

"We have all three in custody," he said. "We have numerous witnesses who say they were drinking with Billy Roberts in the house on the day before his murder."

Amanda remembered the raised voices she'd heard in the brief phone call she'd made to Roberts.

"And what else?"

"They all say they left at some point." Dwyer spread his hands. "Except none of them can corroborate that. And their stories all conflict."

"Maybe they were drunk."

Dwyer laughed. "Oh, they were certainly that."

"Okay," she said. "Was anything taken from the house?"

"Who can tell? And before you ask, we're waiting on forensics. My guess is we're going to find tons of that."

"Well, you already said they were all in the house."

Dwyer ignored her.

"We're searching what passes for their properties. We're also talking to them—or trying to. Two of them are still plastered. But trust me. I know from experience that one of them will turn out to be the *bloody killer*."

Amanda put the files back down on the desk, torn between the instinct she had to disagree with Dwyer and the knowledge that he was probably right. There was no reason to believe Billy Roberts's murder was in any way connected to what had happened in Featherbank, and more often than not the most obvious solution turned out to be the correct one. Dwyer was placing his bet in exactly the same way she would probably have if she'd been in his shoes. Not everything had to have a deeper meaning; sometimes a cigar was just a cigar.

And yet.

The ferocity of what had been done to Roberts had stayed with her. Yes, the level of violence fit with a perpetrator whose mind had been ravaged by years of drink and drugs and God only knew what else. But it still felt like there had been more *control* to what had happened in his house than that, and that there was something here they were missing.

"You look worried," Dwyer said.

"I am."

"About what?"

"I'm worried this has something to do with why I'm here."

Dwyer rolled his eyes.

"Detective Beck," he said, "I know why you're here. And let me tell you, places like this one have long memories. Nobody has forgotten what happened. But the thing is, nobody likes to think about it either. It's done. It's the past. Life moves on."

"Someone left blood on Paul Adams's door."

"Apparently so. I said people don't like to think about it. But maybe they don't mind *other people* thinking about it."

She leaned on the desk. "Charlie Crabtree was never found."

There was silence in the room for a moment. Dwyer's gaze settled on her, and there was stone in it, as though she'd transgressed, crossed a boundary.

She didn't care.

"If you're wrong," she said quietly, "the killer is still out there. And what I'm *worried* about is what he might do next."

She was about to say more when her phone buzzed in her pocket. She stood back from the desk, and took it out to find a message from Theo:

*CALL ME ASAP.*

Dwyer raised an eyebrow sarcastically.

"What have you got there?" he said. "A confession?"

She looked back at him.

"Yeah," she said. "Maybe."

She went out into the corridor to phone Theo back, leaning against the wall as she waited for him to answer the call. When he did, she could hear the low thrum of activity in the hard drives he spent his working life surrounded by. Or at least imagined she could.

"It's Amanda here," she said. "What have we got?"

"We've not had an actual reply from CC666," he said. "But there was a hit on the link I sent. I could bore you with all the information it's given me about the user's computer, but I won't for now. The important thing is that the IP address turned out to be easy to pin down. I've got it to within a couple of streets. A place called Brenfield. It's about a hundred miles from Gritten."

"How long ago was this?"

"Last night. Sorry, I missed it until now."

"That's okay."

Whoever was behind the CC666 account, it obviously wasn't Billy Roberts. The place name nagged at

her though. *Brenfield*. She'd seen it in the files somewhere. But she was so tired it was difficult to trawl
through the sheer amount of information she'd absorbed
over the past few days.

The sound on the line altered slightly, and she pictured Theo moving about in his dark room, shifting
between screens.

"You recognize the place name, right?" he said.

"I've had a busy couple of days."

"Fair enough."

So he told her. And Amanda remembered. And even
as she listened, she was already heading off quickly
down the corridor.

# TWENTY-SIX

----------

Sitting on the edge of the bed in my hotel room, I picked up my cell phone and made a call. I wasn't quite sure what I was going to ask, or what I was going to do with whatever I learned afterward, but I knew I had to do something.

It took a few seconds for her to answer.

"Sally Longfellow speaking."

"Hi, Sally," I said. "It's Paul Adams here."

"Paul, hello. I'm at home right now. How is Daphne today?"

"I haven't gone in to see her yet."

"I know it's hard. Well, I imagine she's sleeping." She lowered her voice slightly. "As sad as it is, that's really the best you can hope for at this stage, isn't it?"

I wasn't in the mood and decided to cut to the chase.

"I suppose so," I said. "What I actually wanted to do was ask a little more about the circumstances of my mother's accident."

"Of course. What would you like to know?"

"She fell, right?"

"Yes."

I waited, staring out of the window at the street below, but it seemed that Sally was unwilling to add more without being prompted. If it was possible to hear defensiveness in silence, then the call seemed full of it. Maybe she thought I was planning to blame her for what had happened—for being negligent in some way.

"Was she going up- or downstairs when she fell?"

"I really don't know. Does that matter?"

"I'm not sure." I shook my head. The question had come from nowhere, and yet it suddenly felt important, for some reason. "Did she say anything afterward about what happened?"

"No. She was quite badly hurt. And you know what your mother is like, Mr. Adams. I'm not sure she understood anything had happened at all."

"How long was she lying there?"

"Again, I don't know. All I can tell you is that I got there as quickly as possible."

I paused. I'd assumed it had been a scheduled visit.

"Hang on. So . . . you *knew* she'd fallen?"

"Not that she'd fallen, but Daphne had an alert. We call them a bat signal—meant *in a nice way,* of course. It's basically a pager that patients carry with them that sends a signal through to our phones. I got an alert from Daphne, so I tried to call the house. When there was no answer, I drove straight over."

I thought about that.

"She was conscious after the fall?"

"She wasn't when I arrived, but obviously, she must have been. All I can tell you, Mr. Adams, is that I was on the premises within half an hour. It would have been sooner, but it was late in the evening."

*She must have been.*

Unless for some reason she had pressed it *before* the fall. Maybe because something or someone in the house had frightened her.

"Mr. Adams? Is there anything else?"

"Yes, sorry." I shook my head. "There is just one more thing, actually. Was the door unlocked when you arrived?"

Silence for a moment.

"I have a set of keys. Well—you have them now."

"Yes. But did you use them that night?"

More silence as she tried to remember.

"Now that you say it, I'm not entirely sure. I don't *think* I did. I knocked, and when there was no response I went straight inside. But I don't think I had to use the key."

"Okay. Thank you."

"But what—"

I ended the call. Which was intolerably rude, of course, but given the circumstances I figured the universe would forgive me even if Sally didn't.

I stared out of the window at the street and the shops opposite the hotel, the people going about their business, and tried to balance what I knew already with what I'd just learned.

On the night of my mother's fall, she had sent an

alert signaling she needed help, and the door had been unlocked when Sally arrived. There was an obvious, innocent narrative you could construct from that, which was clearly what people had done.

Except that my mother was disoriented and scared of something. She claimed to have seen Charlie in the woods. And if it had been my doll that was mailed to me, then someone else must have been in the house at some point. I wondered now if there might have been more to my mother's fall than everyone thought. That maybe she hadn't been alone that night.

That perhaps she hadn't fallen at all.

And as I sat there in the hotel room, feeling lost and frightened, the thought kept returning to me.

*The game isn't finished with you yet.*

And so I made a decision.

That did not, however, mean that my determination would survive an encounter with reality, and I began to feel foolish before I'd even arrived at the police station. The sensation was compounded when I walked inside. The reception had barely changed over the years, and for a moment I remembered walking in here beside my mother, lost and numb, and with her arm around me, guiding me behind the two officers who had led us there.

But I wasn't a teenager anymore.

At the desk, I asked for Amanda first, but after some initial confusion it turned out she wasn't on the premises. So then I asked for Officer Owen Holder, the man who had seen the blood left on my mother's door, and then I waited in the reception for a while.

"Mr. Adams?" When he arrived, Holder looked distinctly nonplussed to see me but did his best to hide it. "Follow me."

He led me through to a small room on one side of reception. It was more of a storeroom than an office, but it had a computer, and he sat down on the far side of the desk and tapped at the keyboard. I sat across from him and waited. From the changing expressions on his face, I thought he was worried he hadn't logged the door-pounding incident as I'd asked him to, and then he seemed suddenly relieved to discover he had.

"Has there been more . . . damage to your property?"

"It's not my property," I said. "It's my mother's house."

"Yes, of course."

"My mother had an accident—a fall down the stairs. Except I'm not sure that's what really happened."

"Oh?"

"I think that someone else might have been in the house."

Holder had been peering at the computer, but he looked up at me now. On the way here, I'd been imagining that might sound ridiculous spoken out loud, and perhaps it did, but it also felt right. Holder leaned back from the screen and stared at me thoughtfully.

"Go on."

I told him everything that had happened. To begin with he simply nodded along, but then he leaned forward again, searched out a pen and paper on the desk, and began making notes. He seemed skeptical about the man I'd seen in the woods.

But then I put the doll of Red Hands on the desk.

Holder looked up from his writing and froze.

"What in God's name is that?" he said.

"It's a doll," I said. "Someone put it through my mother's mail slot. Charlie Crabtree made it a long time ago. Charlie was—"

"I know who Charlie Crabtree was."

Holder picked up the doll tentatively and examined it. He was too young to recall the case itself, but perhaps I'd underestimated the memory that places can have: the way stories are retold over the years. And Gritten, in particular, had always been like that. It held close to its people and tales, even if nobody wanted to talk about them outright.

"It's . . . disgusting," Holder said finally.

"Yes. It is."

He put it down, then moved his hands below the desk. I wondered if, without even realizing it, he was rubbing his fingers against his trousers, trying to remove the invisible stain he felt the doll carried with it.

"And you say someone pushed this through your mail slot?"

"My mother's door," I said. "But yes."

Holder's gaze remained fixed on the doll. It was as though he were seeing something in real life that before now he'd only ever read about in history books. I could tell he was troubled by what I'd told him, but that he was also struggling to work out what to do about it.

But at least he was listening to me.

"You know who Charlie Crabtree was," I said.

"Of course. Everybody around here does."

"So you know what happened. You know *what* this is."

"Yes. And I know who you are. I'll be honest with you, Mr. Adams. That's the only reason I took the marks on your door—your mother's door, I mean—as seriously as I did. And . . ."

He looked off to one side, suddenly awkward.

"And?" I prompted.

"And so I also understand that coming back here must be very difficult for you, especially after all this time."

I waited.

"What I *mean*," he said, "is that grief can do strange things to a person. And I'm genuinely not meaning that rudely. But what I'm wondering is if maybe you've built all this up in your head a bit. Enough for it to seem like more than it is. To *make* more of it, even."

Again, I said nothing.

I'd been prepared to feel foolish coming here, or to be told there wasn't enough evidence for the police to do anything, but I hadn't expected to be accused of lying—even indirectly—about what had happened. For a moment, I felt embarrassed, but then Jenny's words came back to me.

*You used to be more decisive.*

"I'm not making this up," I said.

"I'm *really* not saying that."

"Yes, you are."

My voice sounded cold. Holder was right in at least

one way: all the emotions of the past few days were bubbling up, and I was in danger of saying something I shouldn't. Losing control of myself wasn't going to help.

"Where is Detective Amanda Beck?" I said.

"Who?" He shook his head. "That's the officer from Featherbank, right? I don't know where she is. I think she might have gone."

"What about Billy Roberts? You know that he's dead?"

"Of course I do." Holder looked at me, his face almost plaintive now. He gestured at the doll. "But that has nothing to do with *this*. We already have individuals in custody, and—"

"Who? Who do you have?"

Holder took a second to gather himself.

"I'm really not at liberty to divulge that information right now, Mr. Adams."

"You think I'm lying." I stood up and picked up the doll. "Or that I've lost my mind."

"No, I'm just—"

"Thank you for absolutely fucking nothing."

"Mr. Adams—"

But I wasn't prepared to listen to whatever else he had to say. And by the time I got back to the car, I was even more furious. I felt exactly as powerless and frustrated as I had as a teenager. I opened the trunk and threw the doll in so hard it almost bounced out, then slammed the lid down loudly enough to attract glances from passersby.

Which I ignored.

Then I stood on the sidewalk, unsure what to do next. The police station was on a busy main road, lined mostly by shops, and there were dozens of people wandering along in the sunshine, bags in hand. I found myself searching their faces, looking for anyone familiar, or who seemed to be watching me.

*Are you here somewhere?*

Was it really Charlie I was looking out for?

As I stood there in the sun, surrounded by the mundane activity of ordinary life, it seemed absurd to be thinking such a thing. And yet I realized I really was doing just that. Scanning the people around me for the face of a boy I hadn't seen in twenty-five years. Dyed black hair swept to one side. Empty eyes. Grown up now, but not so far removed from what he had been that I wouldn't recognize him.

A boy who nobody knew for sure was really gone.

The world carried on around me, apparently oblivious. Nobody appeared to be paying me even the slightest attention.

I started walking.

Partly it was because I didn't know what else to do, but there was also the thought in the back of my mind that if someone really *was* following me, this might be the best way of spotting them. So I wandered along, doing my best to pretend to appear careless while keeping an eye on the people around me.

Nothing.

And then twenty minutes later, I realized what street I had found myself on. I looked around in wonder, hardly recognizing the bright new shops, the sidewalks that had been swept clear of trash. When I'd been a teenager, most of these units had been boarded up, and the ones that weren't had been run-down. Now everything was taken and thriving. There were even trees planted neatly in little fenced-off plots along the road.

*It can't still be here.*

I started walking a little more quickly now.

That first time I'd ever visited Jenny's house, this was the street she'd brought me to, her carrying a bag full of books. She had taken me to a shop that—like so many here back then—had appeared derelict at first glance. The door had been old and flimsy, the windows had wire mesh across the outside, and the glass behind had been so misty with dust that it was difficult to see through.

*It can't still be here. . . .*

And yet it was.

I stopped on the corner. The door was new, the wire mesh was gone, and the glass was clean. But in so many ways it felt like the place hadn't changed at all. I looked up. The green sign had been repainted, but it still stretched the length of the shop, the name written in an elaborate cursive script, like something from another age.

*Johnson & Ross.*

I stood there for a moment, staring at the place. It was so familiar, and the world around me was suddenly so quiet, it was difficult to escape the sensation that I'd somehow traveled back in time.

I reached out and turned the handle slowly.

Pushed.

A bell tinkled within.

And then, feeling as nervous as I had twenty-five years ago on that first visit with Jenny, I stepped into the shop, out of the present and into the past.

# TWENTY-SEVEN

## BEFORE

I fell in love with Johnson & Ross the second I followed Jenny inside that first day.

The door led into a cramped main room. I was immediately assailed by a cacophony of sensation; the whole store was alive with texture. Books were packed in shelves along every wall, filling cabinets and covering the surface of tables, and there was a comforting, musty aroma to the air, as though all the leather and paper surrounding me had saturated it over the years. I remember exactly what it was like. Not only was I seeing the books, I was feeling them on my skin and breathing them deep inside me as well.

Jenny led me down one of the overcrowded aisles. But in that moment I was distracted—looking around in wonder, almost shocked by my visceral reaction to the shop. Walking in here was like receiving an embrace from someone who had cared for me when I was too young to remember them properly. I had never been here before, and yet it felt like coming home.

The counter turned out to be little more than a cave among the shelves and cabinets. At first glance, I couldn't work out how anyone got behind it, but a woman was sitting there with a newspaper open on the counter before her. She was in her forties, her long hair dyed so blond that it was practically white, and she was wearing small glasses. She peered curiously at me over the top of the frames as we approached.

Then she looked at Jenny and smiled warmly, clearly delighted to see her.

"Jenny! And what have you brought me today?"

Jenny held up the bag of books. "A few from last month."

"I was *not* talking about the books, young lady."

Jenny glanced back at me, and for the first time that I could remember she looked slightly nervous herself.

"I'm her . . . trainee," I said.

"Ah!" The woman seemed even more pleased now. She closed the newspaper and gave Jenny a conspiratorial wink. "The one you told me *all* about, right?"

"This is Paul," Jenny said. "Yes."

From the look on her face, it was like she was no longer sure this was such a good idea. But then she turned to me.

"And this is my friend Marie."

It turned out that Marie was the *Johnson* of the bookshop's name. *Ross* had been the name of the man who'd owned it before, and whom she'd worked for until he retired several years earlier.

"But I kept his name on there as well," Marie told

me. "Tradition is important, isn't it? You've got to have *lineage*. Places are like people. They have to know where they came from—and where they are now—or else they'll never know where they're going."

I agreed that was true, but it was honestly difficult to do anything else. Marie was a force of nature. She spent the next twenty minutes bustling around, dragging me off to see different parts of the shop and bombarding me with questions the whole time. The latter were often accompanied by amused glances in Jenny's direction, as though they were designed to tease her as much as probe me.

"So how did you two meet?"

"We go to the same school," I said.

"That's no answer at all. Jenny goes to school with lots of boys, and I don't recall her ever bringing any of *them* to meet me before."

Jenny raised an eyebrow.

"And you wonder why?" she said.

But I could tell that her nerves had settled a little now, and she seemed quietly pleased, as though meeting Marie were a kind of initiation that I was so far managing to pass. It was obvious she and Marie had known each other for a long time and that the woman's opinion of me mattered. For my own part, it was nice to see Jenny relax a little. I admired how self-contained she always seemed, but it was also good to see her more relaxed, more at ease.

*Seeing someone in their sauce,* as my mother would say.

I didn't understand it at the time, but looking back

now I can see this whole encounter for what it was. Marie, older and more experienced than Jenny and me, was effectively grabbing our hands and pulling us together, forcing us closer toward the flirtation we were still both tentatively circling.

"We're in the creative writing club together," I said.

"Which I already told you," Jenny added.

"Of course, yes." Marie feigned forgetfulness. "Well, when you get to my age. The creative writing club—that reminds me. Did you send your story in to that competition?"

Jenny pulled a face. "Yeah. Not that anything will come of it."

"Hush. You're a very good writer. Have you read any of her stories, Paul?"

"Only the one in the club. Well—I mean, I listened to that. The one about the dog."

Marie laughed.

"I liked that one. A bit close to home, maybe, but some of the best stories are."

"Marie is a font of local knowledge," Jenny told me.

"There are plenty of stories around these parts, believe me."

"I know," Jenny said. "I *know*."

The idea of that pulled me up a little. For as long as I could recall, I'd thought of Gritten as a gray and dull place, and I'd dreamed of escaping from it and ending up somewhere better. It had never occurred to me before then that where I lived might be just as interesting in its own way as whatever place I imagined myself going.

"Paul sent a story in too." Jenny looked at me. "I think?"

"Yeah."

I had followed my mother's instructions. I remembered the way my father had sneered at me when I asked him for two envelopes and stamps: one to send the story; the other for a self-addressed envelope if it got rejected and returned.

*When* it got rejected.

"But nothing's going to come of mine either." I turned to Jenny and added quickly: "Not that I mean nothing will come of yours. I'm sure it will. Yours will be way better than mine."

"You haven't read mine yet."

"No. But I'd like to. I mean—if you want me to."

"Yeah, of course. But only if you want to."

Marie followed our exchange, her gaze moving back and forth between us, an incredulous expression on her face.

"*Teenagers.*"

"What was that?" Jenny said.

"Nothing, love. Anyway—let me see what you've got for me, bookwise."

Jenny began unloading the bag, and the two of them went through the contents. The books were all second-hand, and I assumed they had been bought from here. As I watched Marie checking the penciled prices on the inside covers and making a list of figures on a sheet of paper, I guessed that, for at least some of her customers, this place effectively functioned as a library as much as a bookshop.

Marie peered over her glasses at me.

"Would you be kind enough to do me a favor, Paul?"

"Of course."

"Excellent! I like him very much already, Jenny. Right, you look like a big, strong lad, and I have a box of books out back that I could do with someone bringing in. Would you be kind enough to do that for me?"

"Sure."

Marie retrieved a set of keys from below the counter and held them out for me.

"You can head through there." She nodded toward the back of the shop. "Just follow the corridor. My car's out back. Old orange Ford. You can't miss it, it's the only one there."

I took the keys.

"The box is in the trunk. Be careful, though. The metal really catches the sun and I don't want you burning your hands." She raised an eyebrow at Jenny. "I'm sure Jenny doesn't want that either."

I had time to see Jenny go horribly red before I quickly shut the comment away inside my head and hurried to the back of the shop.

The last half term of school seemed to crawl by. I found myself counting the days until the summer holiday, desperate to see the back of Gritten Park for at least a little while.

I did my best to avoid Charlie, Billy, and James, and for the most part I succeeded. Not always, of course. There would be those times when I'd see them—times that never felt entirely like accidents. James would be staring at the ground, and Charlie would be smiling beside him, as though showing off a trophy he'd won.

I always looked away quickly.

*Fuck them.*

But even when I didn't run into them directly, there were times when I could *feel* them somehow. Whenever I was near the stairs that led down to Room C5b, it was like I could sense a heartbeat pulsing steadily below me, and I found myself wondering what was going on down there. What the three of them might be dreaming up together.

But I spent as much time with Jenny as possible. We'd share her bench at break and lunchtimes, until it began to seem more like *ours* than *hers*. We'd compare notes on books we'd read and stories we'd thought of; sit and talk; sometimes stroll around the grounds together. On weekends, I'd visit her house. Her mother was always home, so our opportunities were limited, but I remember we spent a lot of time in her room, kissing and fooling around. The connection between us was blossoming. I had never felt so comfortable and relaxed with anyone—so able to be myself without worrying that being *me* was a problem—and the knowledge that she felt the same was enough to take my breath away.

And, of course, we'd go to the bookshop.

Marie provided us with coffee and cake, and the occasional filthy comment, but the latter became increasingly less embarrassing. Partly because Jenny and I were more relaxed with each other, but also because Marie was a little way behind us by then. But mostly, the three of us just talked. I liked Marie and took to helping her out during our visits: moving and unpacking boxes, organizing shelves.

One time, she was chatting to Jenny when a customer approached the counter. She called me over.

"Paul? Will you serve this gentleman for me, please?"

"Sure."

I had absolutely no idea how to work the register. I pressed a few of the more obvious buttons, fumbled with the drawer, and did the math in my head.

Marie came over to me afterward.

"The summer holidays are coming up soon, right?"

"Ten days." I feigned checking a watch I didn't have. "Sixteen hours, ten minutes, and fifteen seconds."

She laughed.

"Well, I was thinking. You're going to have a lot of time free." She glanced at Jenny. "And I figure you're going to be in the area. So I was wondering if you'd like a job?"

I blinked, then looked around the shop.

"You mean *here*?"

"Let me show you how to work the register," she said quickly.

My mother was pleased that I'd found a part-time job to occupy my time.

"In a *bookshop* too!" she said.

I might have expected my father to be happy as well, but I'd long since given up hope of impressing him, and if anything the bookshop part of the equation—and a secondhand one, at that—seemed to be worthy of even greater disdain than usual. But rather than being discouraged, I found myself quietly emboldened. It felt like working in Johnson & Ross somehow brought me closer to my dream.

When the holidays began, I helped Marie three days a week, and once I'd mastered the register I found the work rewarding. There were shelves to be organized, boxes to be packed and unloaded, and regular customers to begin to get to know. Marie was far less provocative without Jenny around to tease. She showed me some of the more expensive books in the shop, and even began to teach me how to recognize what might be a valuable edition myself. I liked her more and more. And Jenny had been right: Marie was full of stories. She was like a walking repository of the area's history, and not a day went by when she didn't regale me with some wild local tale.

Late at night, after my parents had gone to bed, I continued to attempt writing tales of my own. It was hard. While I wasn't short of ideas, the problem came when I sat down at my desk and attempted to put them into words. Marie was a natural storyteller, and I suspected that Jenny was too. But not me. Ideas that felt good in my head came out flat and lifeless on paper. I started a lot, and finished nothing.

The rest of the time, I spent with Jenny.

The strength of my feelings for her frightened me. It was strange to think that at the beginning of the school year I'd barely noticed her at all. Now I could hardly stop thinking about her. My heart beat oddly, as though my pulse had been taking secret classes and learning fresh and unfamiliar tricks. When we weren't at her house, we walked slowly around the streets of her part of Gritten. She showed me the park she'd played in as a little girl, the shops she remembered that weren't there anymore. On one level it was all inconsequential, but the intimacy rendered each detail vivid and special. The weather was hot and bright, and I suddenly found myself noticing color everywhere. Summer was coming. A world that had previously been drab and gray was growing more vibrant by the day.

And I didn't see Charlie or Billy or James at all.

All these years later, when I first saw Jenny upon returning to Gritten, she reminded me there were good memories for me here as well as bad ones. That was true. All of them were here, as I fell in love for the first time. The three weeks at the beginning of that holiday are the happiest of my whole life.

It was in the fourth that everything went wrong.

# TWENTY-EIGHT

------------

## NOW

Walking into Johnson & Ross again after all these years brought an almost overwhelming explosion of recognition.

The exterior might have been rejuvenated, but so little had changed inside. The shelves and cabinets were all filled with books, many of them so old and worn that it was easy to believe they were the same ones that had been here back then. The smell and the atmosphere were exactly as I remembered. Every sensation was so intense that I recalled my first visit here, and how it had felt like *coming home,* and for a moment I wondered if that could have been some impossible flash-forward from then to now. A buried memory emerging not from the past but the future.

I made my way a little unsteadily down the aisle.

There was nobody at the counter. As I glanced around and listened, there didn't seem to be any other customers in the shop either. It had often been like that when

I'd worked here. In less busy moments that summer, I would just sit quietly, breathing in the books. There had been times when it felt like I could hear the pages around me rustling slightly, as though the stories within were shuffling softly in their sleep.

Marie couldn't still be here, could she?

I didn't know which answer to that question made me more apprehensive. That she had moved on, or that I might be about to see her again after all this time.

How would either of those make me feel?

A noise from the back of the shop.

"Be right there," a woman's voice called. "Bear with me."

My heart began beating faster. *It's not too late,* I thought; even now, I could turn around and be out of here before she appeared. But I forced myself to wait. Finally, she emerged from between the stacks. She was visibly older—that bleached blond hair cut short, and now naturally white—and she was walking a little awkwardly, but to my eyes she was as unchanged as the shop itself.

Marie wasn't expecting to see me, of course, so there were a couple of seconds when she peered at me blankly, perhaps thrown by the intensity with which I was looking back at her. But then she recognized me, and she broke out in a smile that sent the crinkles at the corners of her eyes flaring wider.

"*Paul.*"

She walked over slowly, then hugged me.

How was it going to feel to see her after all this time?

Again, it was like coming home.

Marie turned over the sign in the door to CLOSED, then made us both coffee in the small kitchen area behind the counter.

"There's no cake, I'm afraid."

"That's okay," I said. "I'm not hungry."

"No. But it certainly looks like you could do with the coffee."

Did I? I still felt tired from this morning, but I hadn't realized how obvious it was. Maybe that was another reason the police had thought I was losing my grip on things.

"I've not been sleeping well."

"Understandably. It can't be easy."

"I'm glad you're still here," I said.

"That's not easy either. I've hung on for as long as I can. I don't think I've got much left in me, though."

"I don't believe that for one second."

She smiled, then blew on her coffee and took a sip.

"I'm sorry to hear about your mother, Paul. She's a lovely woman."

That surprised me. "You know her?"

"A little. Not well, but she used to come in here quite a lot."

I thought about that.

"It seems like she'd become quite a reader."

"After your father died. Yes."

I nodded to myself.

My father had been tough and unforgiving, a man who worked the land when the jobs were there, but always seemed more proud of the way the land worked him, as though hardness achieved through suffering were something to covet. Books had never made sense to him—and so neither had I, his quiet, bookish son, always squirreled away upstairs, lost in the stories of others or fumbling to create tales of his own.

I remembered the photograph I'd seen of my mother as a child, lying in the sunlit grass with a book open before her. And I found it easy to picture her, freed from my father's disapproval, finally pursuing a suppressed passion for reading. It might have been a comforting image, but instead I thought of a lonely woman, desperate for contact, searching for solace and connection in the only places she could find them, and a tremendous surge of guilt went through me that I had not been one of them.

*You never show me anything, Paul.*

"How was she?" I said. "Recently, I mean."

Marie hesitated.

"It's fine." I sipped my own coffee. "I want to hear. I already know she was confused a lot of the time."

"Yes. Sometimes she was."

Marie put her cup on the counter and looked down at it thoughtfully. We both knew she had told me something in the past that had led to unimaginable consequences, and I could see she was weighing the effect her words might have now.

"Go on," I said.

"She would ask after you."

"Me?"

"Yes. There were times when she thought you were still working here. And then other days when she'd be looking for books by you. She kept saying I needed to get some of your books in. She always told me they'd fly off the shelves."

I didn't reply.

"I said I'd try, of course." Marie smiled. "I told her I thought we'd had a couple in before, but they'd already sold. That kind of thing."

"That must have been . . . hard to deal with."

"It was never hard to be kind to your mother, Paul."

*No*, I thought. It wouldn't have been. Because my mother herself had always been kind, not just to me but to everyone. The knowledge brought a burst of sadness. It occurred to me now that I had wasted so many years, and that there was so much I wanted to say to her while there was still time for her to hear.

"She had lots of friends, you know," Marie said. "She wasn't unhappy. And she was very proud of you."

"She had no reason to be."

"Well, now. I'm sure that's not true."

I fell silent.

*You're going to be a writer, I think.*

Once upon a time, I had imagined that too. But I remembered a day that year, just before the end of the final term, when I had come downstairs to find an envelope waiting for me. Even from the kitchen doorway, I had recognized my own handwriting on the front, along with the stamp I'd stuck to the corner. In the weeks after sending my short story off to the competition, I'd done my best not to think about it, telling myself the story wasn't very good, that it wasn't going to be accepted, and that there was no point in getting my hopes up. But the knowledge it was out there had still created a soft fluttering in my heart, as though a bird were living there. It felt like a part of me had left this place and gone off into the world, and deep down I had allowed myself to imagine it might find a home out there.

When I opened the envelope, the short story was inside, along with a form rejection slip expressing regret that, on this occasion, my submission had not been successful.

I remembered reading it a few times, and how it had felt like whatever had been living in my chest those past few weeks had died.

"I teach a bit of creative writing now," I confessed to Marie. "That's one part of what I do. But I don't actually write anymore."

"That's a shame. Why did you stop?"

"Because I knew I would never be good enough."

But that wasn't strictly true. The reality was that I'd never worked hard enough to find out, and I should be honest about that.

"After what happened, it felt like there was only one story that would ever matter. And I don't think I've ever had the words to write about that."

"Perhaps that will change."

"I don't think so. It's not a story that has an ending."

"Not yet."

I thought about the people poring over the case online. Complete strangers who were still determined to solve the mystery of Charlie's disappearance even after all these years.

"There's been too much water under the bridge," I said. "It's ancient history now. All a long way behind me."

Marie smiled again.

"I don't think time works that way, Paul. As you get older, it all begins to blur into one. You start to think life was never any kind of straight line. It was always more of a . . . scribble."

She laughed quietly: a throwaway comment. But the description struck me. Everywhere I looked in Gritten, I could see traces of the past beneath the details the years had etched on top. Places. People. The past was all still there below the present: not a line, but a scribble. However much you tried to forget it, perhaps without realizing it you were only ever running in place.

I was about to say something else—ask more about my mother, the books she had liked, the things she had said—when my phone buzzed in my pocket.

A call from Sally.

I answered it. And then I listened, and found myself responding in the right places, quietly and formally and almost out of instinct. Marie watched me the whole time, her face full of sympathy. Because she knew.

When the call ended, all the questions I had been intending to ask a minute earlier had deserted me. There was only really a handful of words left to speak, and I did so blankly.

"My mother died," I said.

Sally wasn't at the hospice when I arrived, and a nurse showed me up to the room. She was respectful but professional. *I'm so sorry about your mother,* she told me in the foyer, and then didn't speak at all as we walked together. There were no doubt countless formalities and procedures to attend to, but it was clear from her manner that those could come later.

For now, there was simply this.

We stopped outside the door.

"Take as long as you need," she said.

*Twenty-five years,* I thought.

It was quiet and peaceful in the room. I closed the door gently, as though I'd walked in on a person waking slowly rather than someone who never would. My mother was lying on the bed, the same as always, but while her head was propped up on the pillow it already looked slightly lost in the cushion of it. I sat down beside the bed, struck by the absence in the room. My mother's skin was yellow and as thin as tracing paper over the contours of the skull beneath. Her eyes were closed and her mouth slightly open. She was impossibly, inhumanly still. Except not *she* at all, I thought. Because this was not my mother. Her body was here, but she was not.

There had been occasions during my previous visits when her breath had been so shallow and her body so motionless that I had wondered if she'd passed. Only the soft beep of the machinery by the bedside had convinced me otherwise, and even that had seemed like a trick at times. That machine was silent now, and the difference was completely profound. I've never been a religious man, but some spark of animation had so obviously departed this room that it was difficult not to wonder where it could have gone. It didn't seem possible for it to have disappeared entirely. That didn't make any sense.

I felt numb. But in a strange way, the silence in the room was so solemn that it seemed ill-suited to emotion. It would come, I knew. Because despite everything, I had loved my mother.

Which I had told her yesterday, when she was asleep.

When she wouldn't have heard.

I thought about how different things might have been between us if Charlie and Billy hadn't done what they did. What altered courses my life might have taken, and where my mother and I could have ended up in place of this moment right now.

*Damn you,* I thought.

The events of the past few days had frightened me, and that fear remained. The sense of threat was still there.

But there was anger burning beside it now.

A short time later—I wasn't sure how long—I became aware of quiet voices outside the room, and then there was a tentative knock at the door. I stood up and made my way over. The nurse was out in the corridor, and Sally had arrived too.

"I'm so sorry, Mr. Adams."

Sally rested her hand gently against my arm, then passed me a tissue. I realized at some point I must have been crying.

"Yeah, the window's open," I said. "My hay fever's hell at this time of year."

Sally smiled gently.

"Listen," I said. "Thank you. For everything you've done. I suppose I don't have much of a right to say that, after everything, but my mom would have wanted me to thank you. And I'm sorry about earlier."

"You don't need to apologize. And you're welcome."

She began to talk me through the practicalities of what would happen next, and the arrangements I would need to make. The words washed over me. I knew I should be remembering all of this, but I couldn't concentrate. All that filtered through was that it was going to take a few days to organize.

"Are you able to stay?" Sally said.

I thought about everything that had happened. How scared I had been. How all I really wanted was to get away from here and forget the past. And how—whatever was happening here—that wasn't what I was going to do.

Because, alongside the fear, that anger was still burning.

"Yes," I said. "I am."

# TWENTY-NINE

----------

Night had fallen by the time Amanda arrived back from Brenfield, the town they had traced the CC666 account to, and she drove slowly and carefully along the main road that led to Gritten Wood. The streetlights above bathed the car in intermittent waves of amber: a hypnotic effect that seemed to be pushing her into a kind of dream state. The world outside the car didn't quite feel real. She was trying to concentrate, but her mind had become slippery and her thoughts were refusing to take hold.

She took the turn off to the left when it arrived. The town ahead was dark and dead, the streets little more than dirt paths and the houses like hand-built wooden shacks half buried in the gloom on their separate patches of land. As she drove, she spotted a few lit windows here and there—small stamps of brightness in the night—but saw no real signs of life.

And, looming over it all in the distance, the black wall of the woods.

A couple of minutes later, she parked outside a house that seemed even more deserted than the rest and got out of the car. The clap of the door closing echoed around the empty streets, and she glanced around a little nervously, as though she might have disturbed someone or something. There was nobody around. But despite the lack of visible activity, she still had the sensation of eyes turning to look at her.

Of her presence being noticed.

And after the events of the last two days, that scared her.

She turned to the house. The front gate was broken and dangling from a single rusted hinge. She pushed past it and headed up the overgrown path to the front door. The cracked windows to either side were gray and misty, the inside of the glass plastered with yellowing newspaper. With a flashlight she might have been able to make out the headlines there—tales from a different age—but the sensation of being watched was so strong that she was reluctant to draw attention to herself.

She tried the door handle.

Locked, of course.

She took a step back and looked up at the blistered wood of the house's face. The windows above were as smoke-dark as busted light bulbs, and a portion of the guttering was hanging loose. Moss was growing between the beams above the door.

*Fuck it.*

She took out her phone and turned on the flashlight, then stepped carefully into the thicket of grass to one side of the path, shining the light through a window where a patch of newspaper had curled away from the pane. The beam played silently over the empty room inside, pools of light and shadow rolling over bare floorboards and damp-speckled walls.

Amanda turned off the light.

There was nobody here; the house was derelict and long since abandoned. But this was where Eileen and Carl Dawson had lived, and where James Dawson had grown up twenty-five years ago. This was where Charlie Crabtree had always insisted on setting out from when he led the boys on their treks into the woods that lay behind.

Eileen and Carl Dawson had continued living here until around ten years ago, at which point Carl had inherited a small amount of money and the couple had decided to finally move away from Gritten Wood. They hadn't been able to sell the house, though, because who would want to buy a property in a place like this? But even so. They had packed up their things and gotten away from here, leaving the house and all the bad memories it held sealed up behind them.

And they had moved a hundred miles away to Brenfield.

Back in the car, Amanda drove a few streets on and parked outside the address registered to Daphne Adams. This was supposed to be where Paul was staying. And yet, while the property had been marginally better maintained than the one she'd just seen, there was the same sense of emptiness to it as she walked up the front path. The house itself was dark and quiet, and her heart sank as she approached. She glanced back at the street. Paul's car wasn't here. He wasn't going to be either.

She knocked and waited.

Not expecting a response, and not getting one.

The frustration rose; she needed to speak to him. Where the fuck was he? She knew he had gone to the Gritten Police Department earlier and reported a doll being pushed through his mail slot, but the officer he'd spoken to—Holder—hadn't taken the matter seriously. It was one of a litany of errors that had been made, and she supposed some of them were hers. She didn't even have a contact number for Paul. She'd discovered he was here in Gritten by talking to the college he worked at, but there was nobody there to answer her calls at this time of night. She had a sneaking suspicion that Theo would have been able to help her out there, but she'd already tried the number she had for him, and he'd left work for the day.

She stepped back.

The yard wasn't as overgrown here as at the Dawsons' old house, and after a moment's hesitation Amanda flicked on her phone's flashlight again, then made her way across to the side of the house, and down the tangled path that led toward the back. She listened carefully the whole time, hearing nothing but the slight rush of the night's breeze. When she reached the backyard, she shone the beam across it. The light didn't penetrate far, but she could make out the dim line of the wire fence at the bottom, and sense the vast, impenetrable blackness of the woods beyond it.

The woods where Charlie Crabtree had vanished.

She shivered.

*Charlie's dead.*

Amanda was no longer sure that was true. And as she stared at the dark expanse of those endless trees, she wondered who or what might be moving around out there right now.

Despite heading out to Brenfield earlier, she had never gotten as far as Carl and Eileen Dawson's house there. She had called ahead to the Brenfield department as a courtesy while en route, and had been told that the police were already at the property. Because that morning a man and a woman had been found butchered there.

*I'm worried this has something to do with why I'm here.*

She remembered Dwyer rolling his eyes at that, and what she'd then told him. That if he was wrong, it meant the killer was still out there, and she was worried about what he might do next.

*Where are you, Paul?*

Amanda stared at the pitch-black woods before her now. The Shadows, they called them here. She heard nothing beyond the heavy silence there, but she could sense the weight of the history that lay within them. History that seemed to have returned now.

History that was taking life after life.

# PART THREE

# THIRTY

The fourth week of the summer vacation.

I was at Jenny's house, up in her bedroom. We were kissing and fooling around. Her mother didn't seem to mind Jenny spending time alone with a boy in her room, but the door was open and she was constantly up and down the stairs, working tirelessly. At one point, we heard her out in the upstairs hallway and quickly broke apart, Jenny standing up and moving away from the bed, where we'd been half lying. I remember her mother was singing absently to herself as she made her way along the hall, constantly moving from one task to another.

Jenny and I listened for a moment. When we heard her footsteps on the stairs again, Jenny smiled at me and sat back down on the bed.

"As nice as this is," she whispered, "it would be better to have a bit more privacy, wouldn't it?"

My heart did one of those surprising new tricks.

"Yes," I said. "It really would."

It wasn't like I hadn't thought about it. And, of course, with my parents both out all day, it had also occurred to me that my own house would offer exactly that. I just hadn't had the courage to mention it before. And also, after spending time at Jenny's, I was painfully aware of how threadbare and run-down my house was in comparison. But it was stupid to be ashamed.

"You could come to mine one day instead."

"Yeah?"

"My parents aren't home much."

She smiled. "That sounds like a good idea, then."

"I'm at work tomorrow. Maybe Friday?"

"Yeah. That would be great."

We stared at each other for a moment, and I realized she was just as nervous and excited as I was.

"Oh." She stood up suddenly. "I've got something to show you."

She walked over to a chest of drawers. There was a spread of papers and books beside the television there.

"Actually, I got it a few days ago, but I wasn't sure if you'd want to see it or not."

"What is it?"

She picked up a slim hardback book.

"It's the anthology. From the competition? They sent me a copy."

"Oh wow." I was embarrassed but also touched that she had been worried about showing it to me. "It's fine, honestly. I'd love to see it. It looks amazing."

She smiled and brought the book over to the bed. It had no sleeve, but was beautifully produced. The cover was pale blue, with the title and the list of contributors—

twelve in all. I found her name and ran my fingers over the texture of it.

"It looks so professional," I said.

"*I know.*"

"Your first publication."

"Actually, I had a story published when I was seven. In *Kicks* magazine."

"Okay—*second publication,* then. First with your name on the cover, though. First of many, I reckon."

"Thank you." She smiled. "I am really pleased."

"It's awesome."

It really was. The disappointment from my own rejection had faded a little now, but it would never have occurred to me to resent Jenny's success. I looked at the cover and imagined seeing my own name on a book like this, and was determined to redouble my efforts. Maybe one day I'd have something of my own to show her in return.

The spine gave a quiet but satisfying *click* as I opened it, and then, holding the book carefully, I flicked through the first couple of pages until I found the contents.

"You're meant to read it," Jenny said. "Not preserve it."

"I just want to be careful."

"It's not *that* big a deal."

"It so totally is."

I moved my gaze down the list of contributors. It was non-alphabetical, and I found her close to the bottom.

"Red Hands," by Jenny Chambers.

I stared at that title for a few seconds, a chill running down my back. I almost felt the urge to pinch my nose shut, but there was no need—I could tell I wasn't dreaming right then. The one thing I didn't know how to do was make sense of what I was seeing.

"Paul?"

I was aware of Jenny frowning. And yet I just kept staring at those two impossible words. "Red Hands." The rest of the text on the page began to crawl before my eyes. For over three weeks, I'd done my best to forget about Charlie and his stupid stories, and this seemed like an ambush he'd somehow managed to plan in advance. Like a trick was being played on me.

"Paul?"

"Sorry." I shook my head, then quickly searched through the book, looking for the start of the story. "Just give me a minute."

I found the page, and started to read.

Red Hands
    By Jenny Chambers
    It was nearly midnight when the man in the woods called for the boy to go to him. . . .

I flinched as Jenny touched my arm. She pulled her hand away as though shocked.

"Jesus—what's the matter? You look like you've seen a ghost." She attempted a smile. "And you've not even read it yet."

I looked at her, feeling sick.

"Is that what this is? A ghost story?"

"Sort of. It's the one I told you about."

"The sad one."

"Yeah." She rubbed my arm. This time neither of us recoiled. "What's wrong, Paul?"

"I don't know. Can I read it first?"

"Yes." She moved away from me slightly. "Of course."

The story was about a young boy who was drawn out of his house in the dead of night by a man calling to him from the woods. The boy snuck quietly down the upstairs hallway so as not to wake his mother, whom it was clear he resented in some way. Downstairs, he unlocked the back door as silently as he could, then stepped out into the cold and the dark. His backyard was overgrown, full of wavering black grass.

The man was standing on the edge of the tree line at the bottom. The boy couldn't see the man's face, only that he was a large, hulking figure.

When the man turned and headed off into the woods, the boy followed him.

There were eloquent paragraphs describing the boy making his way into a forest that became increasingly frightening and fairy-tale-like as he went. But while the boy was scared, he kept going anyway, even when the man was sometimes only a vague presence between the trees ahead. The boy brushed the foliage aside in the darkness. Vines caught his ankles. Sticks and twigs cracked beneath his feet.

And eventually he found the man.

Just as it seemed he was too tired to continue, the boy caught sight of a campfire up ahead, the flames dancing and flickering between the trees.

He heard something snap and saw sparks of fire rising in the smoke. Stepping forward, he found himself in a clearing where wood gathered from the forest was burning in a pit of soft gray ash, the sticks there like bones glowing in the heat.

The man was sitting cross-legged, his face somehow in shadow, but the boy could see his hands, resting on the stained knees of his jeans, and they were bright red in the light. They were red from the blood that was still seeping out of the jagged incisions he had made across his wrists. It hurt the boy to see that. The man was still bleeding, even though those wounds were so many years old now.

The boy sat down in the undergrowth, on the far side of the fire. The man's expression was unknowable, but the blood was still visible, the cuts there vicious and terrible. The fire was cracking and spitting between them.

And finally, the boy's father began to speak.

When I finished reading, I sat there in silence for a few seconds. I still had no idea what to say, so I found myself reading sentences over and over again, pretending I hadn't finished while I tried to gather my thoughts.

"Do you like it?"

Jenny sounded anxious. Given my reaction so far, I could hardly blame her.

"I think it's brilliant," I said.

"Really?"

"Yeah, really."

And I did. In terms of quality, it was miles ahead of anything I'd ever managed to write. Despite my unease with the subject matter, I'd found myself there with the boy while I read it—scared for him, but also intrigued by the man he was following. Jenny had added enough subtle detail throughout for the ending to seem inevitable when it arrived, and for understanding to flow backward from it. The boy lived alone with his mother, and the man calling for him was the ghost of his father, lost to suicide years earlier. The boy needed to talk to him, to understand what had happened and why. It was a metaphor for grief and loss, and for the damage done to those left behind in the wake of tragedy.

So, yes, I thought the story was brilliant.

Did I like it, though?

Not one bit.

It was far too close to the dream Charlie had shared with us, and the fantasies he'd spun, to be a coincidence. The four of us searching the woods for something we never found. The stories of a ghost among the trees. A man with bright red hands and a face that could not be seen.

But how was it possible for Jenny to know about any of that? As far as I knew, she had never spoken to Charlie at all, or to Billy or James. And yet this couldn't possibly have happened by chance.

So there had to be some explanation for it.

"I think it's amazing," I told her again. "Where did you get the idea for it?"

But as I asked the question, I realized I already knew.

The next day, I arrived early for work.

Marie had given me a set of keys, so I opened up and set about my usual tasks. There were only a handful of customers to serve, and a single delivery to sort. I worked methodically but blankly, questions whirling in my head. In my own way, I felt as desperate as the boy in Jenny's story, but there was also a part of me that didn't want to know. A part of me that was frightened of what I might learn.

Marie turned up just after ten, at which point the shop was empty aside from me. I stood up, surrounded by piles of books in the sorting area behind the counter. My heart was beating fast. If I didn't do this immediately, I might not do it at all.

"I need to talk to you about something."

Marie stared at me curiously for a second.

"Well," she said. "Good morning to you, as well."

"Sorry."

And then I just stood there. Marie sighed and put her bag down on the counter, then spoke more softly.

"What's the matter, Paul?"

"Jenny's story," I said.

"What about it?"

"The one she wrote for the competition. 'Red Hands.'"

Marie shook her head. "I don't know, I haven't read that one. Slow down a bit here. Talk me through what's bothering you."

"The story is called 'Red Hands,'" I said. "It's about

a boy going into the woods. His father's there—that's who the boy is looking for—but his father is dead. He's a ghost. He killed himself years earlier, and his hands are covered in blood."

The description came out in a blurt, but I saw Marie's expression go from curious to alarmed as I spoke. She might not have read the story itself, but she knew exactly what I was talking about.

"It's based on something you told her, isn't it?" I said.

"Oh dear." She closed her eyes and rubbed the skin between them. "Yes, I think so. I had no idea she would write about that one, though. You need to be careful when you do that. Not all stories belong to you, after all. People can get upset."

"I need to know what happened," I said. "The real story."

Marie opened her eyes and stared at me for a few seconds. She looked suddenly tired, and as though she were weighing me up in some way.

"Please," I said.

"Your parents, Paul."

"What about them?"

"Your mom and dad. They're both still alive?"

"Yeah." A flash of my father's face. "Unfortunately."

"You'll miss them when they're gone." But then she smiled sadly and corrected herself. "Of course, that's not necessarily true. But all right. What do you want to know?"

"Everything."

I already knew some of it, because Jenny had told me what she could remember. Several years ago, a man had come out to Gritten Wood, walked away into the trees, and committed suicide there. The rumor was that he had left a child behind. That had been the jumping-off point for Jenny's story. From there, she'd imagined how that boy might feel years later.

Marie was silent for a moment.

"The strange thing is, I only told her any of it because of you," she said. "This was a while ago. She was talking about you—she said there was a boy in her writing class that she liked. A new boy, from Gritten Wood. Don't look so embarrassed."

"I'm not."

What I actually felt was a trickle of horror inside me. *I only told her any of it because of you.* The idea that any of this—whatever *this* was—might somehow be my fault was hard to accept.

"I just said to be careful," Marie told me. "It was a joke, really. I said that the woods out there were supposed to be haunted because of what happened."

"I never heard anything about it."

"Yes, but *you* grew up there," Marie said. "When something awful happens in a place, people there have a way of closing up. They decide the best thing to do is not to talk about it and hope it all goes away. Maybe sometimes it even does."

"Someone really killed themselves in the Shadows?"

"Yes."

"Who?"

"I honestly can't remember his name, Paul. This was a long time ago."

"How long?"

But then I realized why she'd asked if my parents were both still alive.

"About sixteen years?"

"Yes. Sometime in the seventies. It was in the local paper, but I can't recall the details. It was mostly just people talking. Gossip."

"*Why* did he kill himself?"

"All kinds of reasons, I imagine." Marie looked at me sadly. "People's lives can be very complicated, Paul. From what I understand, the man was in the army for a while and was affected by that."

*In the army for a while.*

Another resonance. I remembered the description Charlie had given of Red Hands, and how that had become the way the rest of us pictured him too. Living off the land; as much a part of the woods as in them; a battered old fatigue coat, the shoulders worn away like feathers.

"What about the child he left behind?"

"It was a little more complicated than that." Marie shook her head. "Are you sure you want to hear all this? Because think about it. Maybe there are *reasons* you've never heard this before now. Perhaps it's better for everyone to forget."

"I need to know," I said.

"All right. I don't know if any of this is true, but it's what I heard back then. The man was married to someone in Gritten Wood—your town—at the time, and his wife was pregnant. But he was also involved with a second woman as well. From another part of Gritten—I don't know where. And this other woman had ended up pregnant too."

"So the man had *two* children?"

"Yes. The second woman—she knew he was married, of course, and she wanted him to leave his wife. But he didn't do that. He chose his wife instead. But when he confessed to her, she rejected him—threw him out. And because of that, he went off into the woods and did what he did."

Marie spread her hands, looking slightly helpless.

"But I don't know any of this for a *fact,* Paul. It's just rumors I heard at the time. Some of it second-, even thirdhand. I'm not sure if any of it's true."

I nodded to myself.

Marie might not have been certain, but I was. I thought about James. How his mother always seemed to resent him. How his biological father had disappeared before he was born. I'd always assumed James's father had abandoned his family, and that James had been a constant reminder to Eileen of that hurt. But nobody had ever told me that was what had happened.

And then I thought about Charlie. How similar he and James sometimes looked. The way that when we'd first arrived at the school, Charlie had seemed to seek James out, keen to bend him to his will and bring him under his control. To isolate him from me. The way he always seemed to have some plan in mind, with the rest of us in the dark, trailing a few steps behind him.

When something awful happens, like Marie had just told me, people try to forget about it. Normal people, at least. But I thought about Jenny's story now—about the little boy desperate to find his father; to talk to him; to be accepted by him—and I wondered if damaged people did something else instead.

If perhaps they went out searching.

# THIRTY-ONE

---------------

*You have to do something about Charlie.*

On the morning of the final day, I remember waking just after dawn. The sun was streaming in through the thin curtains over the window by my desk, the room already warmed by it. But despite the heat, I was shivering. For the first time in months, I couldn't remember the precise details of the dream I'd just woken from, only that it had involved Charlie. The dread from it was still there, seeping slowly across my thoughts like black ink spreading through tissue paper.

I lay still for a moment, calming myself down.

Trying to think of anything else.

My parents had both left for work early and the house was silent. Downstairs, I knew there would be the usual list of chores waiting for me to complete. They would occupy me for a few hours this morning. And then, this afternoon, Jenny was coming around.

*It would be nice to have a bit more privacy, wouldn't it?*

My heart leaped for a different reason at that.

And yet the dream lingered. After a time, I went and sat down at my desk, drawing the curtains and looking out at the tangle of our backyard and the woods at the far end. The world was sunlit and rich with life: walled and carpeted in a thousand shades of yellow and green, dew still glinting on the grass. But I knew now that, sixteen years ago, a man had walked into those woods and slit his wrists, his life spilling out into the foliage.

On a different day, I would have taken out my dream diary and written in it. Today, I decided not to. All I really remembered from last night was Charlie, and I didn't want to put his name in my book.

*You have to do something about him.*

That same thought arriving again, this time with more force and urgency to it. After what I'd learned yesterday, I couldn't escape the feeling that something bad was going to happen—that Charlie was dangerous in some way. But at the same time, I had no idea *what* I was supposed to do. Find an adult, I supposed, and talk to them. Tell them what I knew, and some of what I suspected. Start with the dreams, and then try to explain how everything had gradually become so dark. I could tell them about Goodbold's dog, and about Red Hands, and how I no longer knew if Charlie was deluded and needed help, or if he was planning . . .

Something.

Nobody was going to listen to me.

But still. I had to try. So I would make a plan, I decided. I would work out exactly what story I needed to tell, and who I was going to tell it to. Marie was probably the best choice. Out of all the adults I could think of, she would be the most open to listening, and she already knew some of the background.

She could help me work out what to do.

Making that decision gave me the freedom to put it out of my head for a while. I showered and dressed, made scrambled eggs for breakfast, and then turned to the list of tasks that had been left for me on the kitchen table. There was tidying and cleaning to be done, and my mother had written a shopping list and left me some money. I did the house stuff first, and then finally, late morning, I set out to the shop.

The day was hot and bright, but I remember there was also an odd feel to the town. The streets were quiet, which wasn't unusual for this time on a working day, but they seemed even more deserted than usual. On my way to the grocery store, I didn't see another soul; it was as though everybody had been removed from the world and I had been left completely alone. There was a hush to the air and a strange sepia quality to the light. The roads, the houses, the trees—they all looked like they had been soaked in an amber liquid that had yet to fully drain from the air.

I was almost relieved when I reached the store and found actual people inside. Normality resumed. I collected together the items on my mother's shopping list and the assistant bagged them carefully at the register. By the time I was outside again, back in that heavy silence, the plastic bag handles were already tight and digging into the creases of my fingers.

For some reason, I didn't want to head home right away. There was still an hour or so before Jenny was due to come around, and I knew the only thing I'd do with that time was pace and worry. Although the atmosphere that day was unusual, it was also beautiful in its own strange way, so I decided to walk for a time, and I took a more circuitous route back to the house than normal, enjoying the warmth and the peace.

And as I did so, I felt buoyed. I'd been avoiding a lot of the town's streets and lanes over the past months, careful to avoid Charlie, Billy, and James, and now I wondered why. This was *my* town, after all. My home. This afternoon Jenny was coming to my house, and what were the other three in the light of that? A few sad boys, lost in a fantasy, while my own world was blossoming, its petals opening, the future ahead of me full of possibility. Right then, I felt more than strong enough to face them down if I had to.

The walk took me around the edge of the town, and then up past the old playground at its heart. If I was going to see them anywhere, it would be here, and sure enough, as I approached along the dusty lane, I saw there was someone there.

James.

He was alone for the moment, sitting on the bottom rung of the ancient jungle gym. When I had been younger, that thing had seemed huge, the ground perilously far away when you were at the top, but in reality it was hardly taller than I was now. Even so, James looked small in comparison to it, sitting hunched over. When I'd seen him in the last weeks of classes, he'd seemed diminished and drained, as though the life were slowly being sucked from him, but now he appeared almost skeletal, the shadow of his body all but indistinguishable from the ones cast by the thin metal frame around him.

My resolve faltered a little. But I made myself continue.

He looked up as I got nearer, his face hollow, and when he saw me he looked quickly away.

I walked past deliberately slowly.

I wasn't sure why. Perhaps it was a show of dominance—some attempt to make him realize I didn't care—but if so, that was stupid. Because I did care. In those few moments, in fact, the events of the past couple of months fell away. My life had moved far enough on from his betrayal that, even if I didn't entirely forgive him for what he'd done, I at least understood the reasons why, and pitied him slightly because of them.

After I'd passed, I looked back and noticed again how fragile he seemed. How *scared*. And that's the memory of James I have from that day: a lost little boy who didn't know how to escape from the situation he'd found himself in. Sitting there waiting, a condemned prisoner anticipating punishment.

*You have to do something about Charlie.*

That thought again. It wasn't rational, but there are moments in life like that, I think—moments you understand on some level are pivotal. Where everything will change, and you'll regret it forever if you don't do something you know you should.

Perhaps it was the strangeness of the day that made

me believe this was such a moment. That whatever Charlie had been planning was coming to a head, and that if I turned around and walked away now I would never shake the guilt from it.

*You have to do something about Charlie.*

*Before it's too late.*

And so I walked slowly back to the playground. I stepped over the shin-high wooden fence that separated it from the road, and approached the jungle gym. James's back was to me. I don't know if he heard me, but he didn't seem startled as I put the shopping bags down on the ground. He just turned and looked at me with those sad, haunted eyes.

"Hey," I said. "There's something I need to tell you."

I remember the sense of relief I had when I got back home afterward. I packed the groceries away with a swing in my step. Perhaps I was even feeling slightly triumphant.

*You have to do something about Charlie.*

And I had.

I'd told James everything I'd learned from Marie, which meant that any duty of mine had been fulfilled, and it was now his responsibility to act on what I'd said. I had no idea if the information I'd given him would help or change anything, but right then it didn't feel like that mattered. The important thing was that it was now in James's hands to deal with, not mine.

I'd also managed to do it without giving away any ground. When I'd started talking, I'd seen a flash of something on his face. Hope, perhaps. But my own expression had quickly killed that dead. I'd made sure he understood I wasn't there to rescue him, or to rebuild bridges. It was just that I had to warn him, and so I did. He'd shaken his head, confused, but I could tell that what I was saying chimed with him in some way, as though I'd given him a piece of a puzzle he knew fitted somewhere, even if he didn't quite know yet where to place it.

*Be careful.*

Those were the last words I ever said to him, and I said them coldly, making sure the message behind them was clear. We weren't friends again now, and we wouldn't be in the future.

Then I'd picked up the plastic bags and come home.

I remember I finished putting the shopping away and then pushed the encounter from my mind. By that point, it wasn't too long until Jenny would be here, and I decided to let myself feel excited about that instead. There was an odd mixture of excitement and fear in my chest, my heart beating a little faster with every passing minute.

One o'clock.

The time came and went.

For a while afterward I paced around the living room, frequently checking out the front window, expecting to see her here at any moment, bright and beautiful in the afternoon sun, opening the gate and walking up to the house.

But the street and front path remained empty.

And then I spent the next few hours wondering what had gone wrong. Perhaps she had come to her senses about me and changed her mind. Or maybe something had come up and she hadn't been able to make it and right then she was stuck at home, feeling awful about letting me down. Her mother might have found out where she was going and told her no. I oscillated between all the likely explanations for her not showing up. The possibilities circled me.

A knock at the door locked them into place.

I was up in my room at that point, looking out at the woods. I ran quickly down the stairs. By then I'd given up on Jenny coming around, and my parents would be back home soon anyway, but I still thought it must be her. That would be fine too. Everything else could wait, I told myself. Maybe I could even introduce her to my mother.

But when I opened the door, there were two police officers standing there. Their car was parked out front of the house, its lights rotating pointlessly in the late afternoon sun.

"Paul Adams?" one of the officers said.

"Yes."

He rested his forearm on the side of the door and peered inside past me, as though searching for something. Then he looked me up and down, his face set hard, devoid of emotion.

"Am I right in thinking you knew a girl called Jenny Chambers?"

"Yes." I paused. "Why?"

He looked at me as though I already knew.

"Oh, she's dead."

# THIRTY-TWO

## NOW

*I am dreaming right now.*

Even after so many years, I had never lost the sense of wonder that accompanied that realization, and it arrived again now as I found myself staring at Gritten Park School, amazed as always that my sleeping mind was capable of conjuring up something so realistic. I've perfected it over all these years, and much of what Charlie originally said was true.

I crouched down and employed the environment technique: rubbing my palm over the ground and feeling the rough texture of the road. A tapping sound was coming from nearby. I looked to my right and saw the tarp stretched tight around the construction area. That was long gone in real life, of course. But this was the school as it had been then, not as it was now.

I stood up and drifted past the building site, and then the tennis courts and the corrugated huts. The dream had added layers of rust to the latter, and positioned them at odd angles in the grass, as though they had been dropped carelessly from the sky.

The bench was a little way along.

Jenny was waiting there for me. She appeared exactly as my mind had created her a few nights earlier: still recognizable as the girl I remembered, but aged to match the years that had passed. Even just sitting down, there was a confidence and poise to her. But her old school bag was at her feet, and there was a notebook open on her lap. The past and the present, superimposed.

*Not a line,* I thought. *A scribble.*

And my heart ached to see her.

She closed the notebook and smiled at me. "Hey there, you."

But both the smile and the greeting seemed slightly more forced than the previous times I'd dreamed her. I remembered walking down here for the first time as a teenager, and how I'd been worried I might be disturbing her. That hadn't been true then, but I had the strange sensation it was now. That even though this was my dream, and she was only a figment of my imagination, she would rather I wasn't bothering her.

"Hey there," I said. "Do you mind?"

"Not if you don't."

I sat down beside her on the bench, allowing a little distance between us.

"Are you okay?" I said.

"Honestly?" She looked away. "I'm tired, Paul. I want to go back to sleep."

The way she phrased it, it was as though she were dreaming me rather than the other way around, and I felt a stab of guilt at conjuring her: an old sensation. *Why did we lose touch?* Jenny asked me last night. Thinking back on the times I'd dreamed of her after her death, here in Gritten and then at college, the answer was clear: because it had begun to feel like this. Whatever else he had done, Charlie had given me a tool to use, and I had. In a lucid dream, you could do anything, and so I had brought Jenny back to life in an attempt to assuage the pain and the grief I felt. But my subconscious had known, and it had become clear it was time to stop.

I had thought it would be harmless to see her again now. That it would make being back in Gritten, and everything I had to do and face here, easier to bear. And I supposed that, for a time, it did. But I knew it couldn't last, and that it was time to let her go again now.

"I'm sorry," I said.

"You don't need to be. I know you miss me."

"Always."

"But I should leave. Before I do, though, I wanted to give you two things."

"What?"

"Do you remember when the police arrived?"

I thought back to that day. The two officers couldn't question me without one of my parents present, but they asked if they could come in, and of course I said yes. They wouldn't tell me what had happened to Jenny.

*Oh, she's dead.*

The words had echoed in my head, but that had been all they were, and they didn't seem to relate to anything that could possibly be real. If they were true, then the world should have ended.

And yet the world was carrying on.

"They thought it was me that killed you," I said.

Jenny smiled. "Of course they did. I *was* coming to see you, after all. And it's often the boyfriend, right?"

"Right."

It had been about half an hour before my mother got home, at which point she insisted on driving me to the police station so I could be interviewed under supervision. I remembered how numb I had felt, and how the officers had forced us to stop at the playground so I could see what I had supposedly done. The way my mother had protected me so fiercely. She knew me. Even without me saying anything, she knew I hadn't done that.

The whole time, there had been other officers searching our house for evidence that would incriminate me. A weapon, perhaps. Bloodstained clothing. There was nothing for them to find, of course, and it wasn't long before Billy wandered into the town, his own clothes saturated with blood, carrying his dream diary and the knife he and Charlie had used to murder Jenny.

Jenny smiled at me sadly now.

"You never showed me your town before," she said. "I was so excited to see you that day that I arrived about half an hour early. And I figured I'd walk around a bit."

"Why?"

"I wanted to see you in your sauce."

I closed my eyes at that—at my mother's phrasing coming from the image of Jenny my sleeping mind was generating—but it was a mistake to close your eyes in a lucid dream. You needed sensation to make the world around you solid. So I opened them again, gripped the rough edge of the bench, and listened to the distant tapping of the drill, trying to anchor myself.

"When I got to the playground," Jenny continued, "James was gone. He obviously took your warning seriously. But Charlie and Billy were there. They were waiting and they had their plan. They were angry."

"I don't need to hear this," I said.

"Yes, you do. They beckoned to me. I'm not sure why I went over. I guess I was curious what they wanted, after everything you'd told me about them. By the time I saw the knife, it was too late."

Again, I wanted to close my eyes.

"They held me down and took turns stabbing me," Jenny said. "It almost didn't hurt at first, because I couldn't believe what was happening. I think I was in shock. But then it did. Whichever one wasn't stabbing me was putting handprints of my blood on the ground. I fought so hard, because I remember realizing I was going to die, and how much I didn't want to. I wanted to live so very much." She looked at me sadly. "But I didn't."

*A total of fifty-seven wounds were recorded on the body,* I remembered.

*The victim's head all but severed.*

"They stuffed my body under one of the bushes when they were done," she said. "And then they went off to the woods and took sleeping pills, imagining they were going to escape this world forever. Which is ridiculous, of course."

"Except that Charlie really disappeared."

"*Nobody* disappears, Paul. Nobody is ever really gone."

I thought about it and nodded.

"The police were right though," I said. "It really *was* me who killed you."

Jenny shook her head.

"Paul, you didn't know what would happen. That's the first thing I want to give you. You did your best, which is all any of us can do. You were helping a friend. And you were just a kid. It wasn't your fault. None of this is."

She sounded so earnest that a part of me almost believed her.

"I've spent so long wishing," I said.

"Wishing what?"

"That I'd kept walking that day. That I'd said nothing. Because it's not fair. It should have been James they killed, not you. And it would have been if it hadn't been for me."

The underlying sadness of what I'd just said hit me. For years I had blamed myself for what I did. I had wished I hadn't spoken to James that day, and that things had been different.

What a waste that seemed now. Why had I never

wished that Charlie and Billy hadn't killed anybody that day? Perhaps simply because they had, and so the act had taken on an inevitability: the murder becoming something that couldn't be avoided, the effects only mitigated and shifted in favor of different people, different lives. But the truth was that there would have been a death on my conscience whatever I'd done.

"*It's not your fault,*" Jenny said. "And now the second thing."

She reached down and rummaged in her bag, then took out the magazine and passed it to me.

*The Writing Life.*

I remembered how touched I'd been that she'd brought this for me. How it meant she'd been thinking of me. But then the text on the cover swam out of focus, and I realized the dream was slipping out of my control.

"They're all the same," Jenny said. "That's why he won't find it."

My mother's words. I rubbed the pages of the magazine between my finger and thumb, desperate to stay.

"What does that mean?"

But despite my efforts, everything around me was beginning to fade. The awareness of lying in bed in the hotel room was becoming more real than my presence on the bench, and I was going to wake up. But even though Jenny couldn't possibly know the answer to my question, it seemed urgent to hear her reply.

"*What's the same?*" I said. "What won't he find?"

As I stared at what was left of her, a sudden flash of revelation went through me, and I thought I might understand. And even though the dream was all but gone now, and the room in the real world was solidifying around me, I saw her smile one last time before I woke completely, her face mouthing words I felt as much as heard.

*Goodbye, Paul.*

# THIRTY-THREE

------------

I felt spaced out as I drove to my mother's house—so intent on getting there that I barely registered the journey.

That wasn't entirely due to the inevitable drowsiness that came with lucid dreaming. Now that the idea had occurred to me, it felt important to get there quickly and see if it could possibly be true. On the face of it, what I was thinking was madness, and yet something had clicked into place, and I needed to check in order to be certain. And as I drove, it was as though my mind were already ahead of me, waiting there at the house, urging me onward to join it.

*They're all the same.*

*That's why he won't find it.*

When I parked and got out, the street was empty. But, while it might have been my imagination, the air right then seemed to have the same off-kilter feel as it had on the day of the murder.

Once inside the house, I paused in the hall. At the

top of the stairs, dust was turning slowly in the air, casually disturbed by the front door opening. The place was as silent as ever, but the heaviness in the air had taken on a different texture today. It was quieter and emptier, and it felt like there was a sadness to the house, as though somehow it knew the person who had lived here for so many years was gone now, and the building itself was grieving for the loss.

I was still nervous about whoever had delivered the doll, but the need to know had overtaken that. I went upstairs to my old room and spread the contents of the box out onto the table.

The magazine.

The book with Jenny's name on the cover.

The notebooks.

I looked at those now. There were eight in total, and I'd paid little attention to them until now. My dream diary had been on top of the pile, the first one I'd opened, and I hadn't been interested in looking through the others and reading all my miserable teenage attempts at writing. All the desultory attempts at storytelling I'd long since abandoned.

But now I picked one up and opened it.

Nothing.

Another.

Nothing.

Then I opened the third. And before me, I saw not my own handwriting, but Charlie's tight, black, spidery crawl.

I closed it instinctively, my heart beating harder.

My mind returned to the first time the four of us had

compared results, the lunchtime Charlie had performed the seemingly impossible trick of appearing to share James's dream. How that day I'd noticed he and I had exactly the same brand of notebook.

*It's in the house now, Paul.*

*They're all the same.*

*That's why he won't find it.*

But Charlie's diary was supposed to have disappeared with him. He and Billy both had theirs with them on the day of the murder—presumably as part of the ritual Charlie had devised. Which meant that I was holding something that vanished from the world at the same time he did. There was an impossible piece of magic in my hands.

*Magic.*

I scanned through some of the entries toward the end of the notebook. They were all variations on the same theme: Red Hands; the woods; Billy and James. Most of them were vague, but two entries stood out as being more specific than the others. There was a lengthy passage describing the dream in which he'd killed Goodbold's dog, and further back, a similarly detailed entry about knocking on James's door in the night. In both cases, of course, Charlie had known what he'd done in real life and had been able to be more precise.

I flicked back further, until I found the entry I was most interested in.

*I am sitting with him in the woods.*

*It is very dark here, but I can tell he is wearing that old army jacket, the one with the weathered*

*fabric on the shoulders that looks like feathers,*
*like an angel that's had his wings clipped down*
*to stumps.*

It was exactly as I remembered from reading it that
lunchtime. Charlie had told James to pass me his dream
diary so that I could see the truth for myself. Back then,
I'd looked down at the same tight, black handwriting,
with that day's date recorded at the top, and the dream
had been so close to what James had already described
that it had seemed impossible for it to be a coincidence.
And yet I hadn't been able to explain how it had been
accomplished.

Charlie's trick.

I turned back a page and started reading.

*I am sitting with him in the woods.*

And then another.

*I am sitting with him in the woods.*

I kept flicking back. The entries for that whole week
were all but identical. While Charlie had changed some
of the words, the subject matter was exactly the same. In
each one, a boy and a monster emerged from the woods
and saw James in his backyard, looking back at them.

And after all these years, I finally understood.

*Incubation.*

Charlie had spent weeks seeding us with stories about
the woods being haunted. Every weekend, he'd taken

us in there, always insisting on entering them through James's backyard. So it had been almost inevitable that all of us, including James, would dream about them eventually.

I thought about Jenny giving me the magazine. At the time, I'd imagined it had been a coincidence that she had brought it in on the same day I decided to seek her out and talk to her. But she hadn't, of course; I'd gotten it backward. That was the day she'd given it to me simply because that was the day I'd spoken to her. She had brought it in every day, and whichever day I'd spoken to her, it would have seemed like a coincidence then too.

And Charlie had done something similar. He had prepared entry after entry, so that he had one ready for whenever James finally described something that was a close enough match.

*It happened much sooner than I was expecting.*

Frustration rolled through me. How easily I could have stopped everything back then, if only I'd realized. That lunchtime, the three of them had been watching me, waiting for my response to the diary entry, and I remembered how powerless I'd felt. The whole time, all I'd needed to do was turn back one single page.

And if I had, none of the rest of it would have happened.

I closed the diary.

"How did you get this, Mom?" I said quietly.

The house, of course, remained silent.

I walked through to my mother's bedroom. I drew the curtains and stared out at the street. The sun was beating down so hard now that the air above my car was shimmering in the heat. There was still nobody in sight; the town was dead and silent.

At my side, the diary felt heavy in my hand.

*How did you get this?*

The question made me feel sick. Because, while there were numerous possible explanations for its presence in the house, they all ultimately came down to the same thing.

My mother had known more about Charlie's disappearance than she had told me.

I looked up at the ceiling, picturing the red hands in the attic and the boxes of newspapers my mother had collected. When I'd first discovered them, I'd imagined she had hoarded them over the years, taking it upon herself to protect me from the knowledge and the guilt.

But now I wondered if that guilt had really been her own. If she knew what had happened to Charlie, then at least some of the blame for the copycat killings rested with her. She could have done something to stop them.

And yet, for some reason, she had not.

I looked down, out of the window again.

And the street was no longer empty.

A figure was standing at the far side of my car. They were slightly silhouetted by the sun behind, their features occluded by the haze above the vehicle, but I could tell they were staring back at me. I recognized them immediately, and twenty-five years fell away in the space of a single heartbeat.

The figure raised a hand.

After a moment of hesitation, I did the same.

I left the dream diary on the bed and then went downstairs. Outside the door, the warmth and brightness hit me. The figure was walking away now, heading slowly off up the street. But there was no need for me to chase them. I knew where they were going.

I turned around and locked the door.

And then, moving slowly myself now, I began to follow.

# THIRTY-FOUR

For the second morning in a row, Amanda found herself sitting in the Gritten Police Department cafeteria, hunched over her laptop. Depressingly, it seemed to have become her office for the time being. She took a sip of the coffee. It hadn't improved.

Nor had the overall situation.

They had three murders so far, with each of the victims connected to the original Red Hands killing. While Amanda didn't understand what was happening yet, she didn't believe that was likely to be the end of it.

They needed to find Paul Adams.

Officers first thing had found a booking for him at a hotel in Gritten. There was an irony there, she supposed. She hadn't been able to find him last night because he'd taken her advice to get out of the house. But according to the hotel, he wasn't in his room and his vehicle wasn't in the parking lot. She figured that meant he was most likely at his mother's house, and after discussing matters with a still-reluctant Detective

Graham Dwyer, Holder had been sent out to Gritten Wood to see if Paul was there.

She glanced at her phone now, resting on the table beside the laptop.

Nothing.

Attempting to distract herself, she turned her attention to her laptop. The scene in Brenfield was still being processed, but the family's history was on file.

Carl and Eileen Dawson had moved to Brenfield just over ten years ago. The reason for the relocation seemed to be so they could be closer to their son, James. Reading between the lines, it appeared that James Dawson had struggled badly in the aftermath of the murder in Gritten. He had left for college, but then dropped out after two terms, and most of his life since had been itinerant. There were minor drug convictions on his record, as well as a few for low-level antisocial behavior. There was also a long list of addresses on file, with gaps between them suggesting he had been homeless at times.

All in all, it reminded Amanda of how Billy Roberts had lived following his release from prison. Except that James Dawson had people who cared about him. Ten years ago, Carl Dawson inherited money after the death of his mother. He and Eileen had bought the house in Brenfield, which was where their son was loosely based at the time, and James had lived with them from then on.

The sacrifices parents make for their children.

And yet, from the details on-screen, there was evidence this particular garden had not been entirely rosy.

Police had been called to the address on several occasions by concerned neighbors, and one time Eileen Dawson had actually been arrested and removed from the property. No charges were pressed, and the woman eventually returned. Amanda was more used to the scenario being the opposite way around gender-wise, but that did nothing to make it any less depressing. Not least because it was one reason why those same concerned neighbors had not immediately called the police in the early hours of yesterday, when they had heard shouts and screams from inside the Dawson house.

Curtains had still twitched, of course. Shortly before dawn, one of the neighbors heard the Dawsons' front door open, and they had seen a man dressed in black emerge from the property. The neighbor assumed it had been Carl Dawson, but it was dark and they had no real description to go on. At any rate, there had been something disturbing enough about the whole scenario for her to pick up the phone. Attending officers found two bodies in the front room. While the scene was still being processed, it appeared that Eileen Dawson had been dispatched quickly. And then the killer had taken more time with James.

Amanda's heart broke a little at that.

From everything she'd read online about the history of the case, she found it hard to picture James Dawson as anything other than a small, vulnerable child, and learning what had become of his life in the years since only increased that impression. He was a boy who had never fully recovered from what had happened. The supposed friends he had embraced had groomed him, intending to kill him, and as an adult he had clearly struggled to find a niche for himself in the world. It was as though he had been stuck in a nascent state, never growing or flourishing, just remaining frozen forever, his existence defined by a moment of trauma.

If you tried, Amanda thought, perhaps you could make an argument that what had happened to Billy Roberts amounted to some kind of justice. But there could be no attempt to do so here. Whatever the damaged furniture of his life, James Dawson had not deserved an ending like this.

Was he the person behind the CC666 account?

It seemed likely; a computer had been recovered from the house and was being analyzed. But if so, she didn't understand *why*.

Regardless, the most important question right now was where Carl Dawson was.

The door to the cafeteria opened. Amanda looked around to see Dwyer walk in, bringing the smell of cooked food wafting in along with him. He moved over to her table and sat down opposite, landing so heavily that she wasn't sure the furniture would stand the impact, then put a greasy wrapper down on the table and began extracting a sandwich from it.

"Holder just checked in," he said. "He told me there's no sign of Adams at his mother's house. His car's there, though."

"That's sort of a sign."

"Holder's not very bright."

"Has he checked inside?"

"House is locked. He did look through a few of the

windows and nothing was obviously out of place. No probable cause to break in. Maybe Adams just went to the shops."

"We need to find him."

"So you say."

There were a few seconds of silence, as Dwyer swallowed and wiped his lips delicately with a napkin she hadn't noticed. Then his manner shifted a little.

"I was there, you know," he said.

"What do you mean?"

"Just what I said. I was the attending officer that day. I was at the playground when the girl's body was found. And then there were two of us that went to Adams's house afterward. I got to have a look around while we were waiting for his mother to get back. At that point, me and my partner, we both thought he did it."

"Obvious, right?" Amanda said.

"Exactly."

Dwyer took another bite of his sandwich. She waited for him to chew and swallow it.

"In hindsight, that was unfair of me." He shrugged. "You play the odds, right? There was something weird about Adams—about all of them—but my hunch that day was wrong. Maybe what I've been thinking now is too. You think this guy—Carl Dawson—is involved?"

Amanda leaned back.

"In some capacity?" she said. "Sure. I mean, his family are dead and he's gone missing. In a situation like this, it's a natural assumption to make."

"Like I said, you play the odds."

"You do. But whether he's *responsible,* I have no

idea. And we can't place him at the scene for Billy Roberts yet."

"We can't be sure that's even the same perp."

But if Dwyer was still half clinging to his original theory, he no longer seemed as convinced by it as he had been yesterday. It was just too much of a coincidence. Billy Roberts and James Dawson—two boys who had been involved in the killing here twenty-five years ago—had been tortured and murdered. And however much he might not have wanted to rake up the past, she could tell he was just as concerned as she was.

"Dawson knew all three victims," he said. "I like him for it."

She was about to answer when her cell phone started ringing. The screen told her it was Theo.

"Hang on."

She answered the call and pressed the phone to her ear. As always, the soft sound of his computers and their ghosts was humming the background.

"Hey, Theo," she said. "Amanda here."

"Hello there. You wanted the phone number for Paul Adams, right?"

"Right."

"He's actually on a pay-as-you-go, but I got it from his card details. Don't ask me how, but here you go."

She made a note of the number he gave her.

"Thanks, Theo."

"There's something else. I'm going to have to pass this on to the relevant authorities but I figured I'd tell you first. I've got a number for Carl Dawson too."

Her heart leaped. And as she noted it down, something else occurred to her.

"Can you tell me where Dawson is?" she said.

"You want the moon on a stick, Amanda. But yes, probably. Just give me a second. The more towers it pings, the easier it is." She heard him typing in the background. "Ah—bingo."

"You've got him? Where is he?"

"About two miles away from you," Theo said. "In Gritten Wood."

# THIRTY-FIVE

- - - - • - - - •- - - -

After the murder, the old playground had been de-
molished and paved over. When I left Gritten, nothing
had been added to the empty stretch of stone there, as
though nobody had known what to do with it and it
had been enough just to cover it up for the moment.
But now there were benches there, circling a tree in
the center.

And yet, as I approached, I could still picture it just
as it had been back then. And the figure waiting for me
on one of the benches reminded me so much of James
that day, so fragile and scared, that it was easy to imagine I'd slipped backward in time.

I stopped in front of him.

"Mr. Dawson."

James's stepfather was staring down at his hands.
I took in the mottled skin of his bald skull, and the
gnarled, ancient roughness of his hands. When he finally raised his head, his face was thin and drawn, his

eyes sunken into the sockets. He looked impossibly sad. I could sense waves of grief beating off him, and it felt like something more profound than loss, as though now that he was facing down the final days of his life, he was grieving for all the things he'd done with it, and all the things he hadn't.

*How old everyone has got,* I thought.

And how strange that a generation I remembered as being strong and sturdy and reliable was now vanishing away into old age.

"Paul." He gestured to the bench. "Sit down, please."

I sat at the far end, leaving a comfortable space between us. There was no sense of physical threat from him; if anything, age had only enhanced the gentle, harmless feeling he'd always exuded. But I suspected that he had been behind the events of the last few days, and now that he had finally decided to show himself to me I wanted to maintain a degree of distance between us until I understood why.

"I'm sorry," he said. "I'm so sorry about Daphne."

"Thank you."

He sounded utterly broken. But then I remembered that the man sitting next to me now had been friends with my mother since childhood—that he had known her far longer than I had. And I remembered the photograph I'd seen of the two of them, both looking so young, Carl whispering something to my mother that had made her laugh wildly.

"I'm sorry for your loss too," I said.

He nodded once.

"Did you manage to see her?" I said.

"Not after the accident."

There was the slightest of breezes. I turned my face to the sun and closed my eyes for a moment.

"I'm guessing I have you to thank for the doll?"

"Yes," he said. "I'm sorry."

"How did you get it?"

"It was James's."

I opened my eyes. So not mine at all. I wondered what had happened to it. Perhaps I would never know. The box of belongings in the house contained many things from that year, but not everything deserved to be kept.

"James held on to it all this time?"

"He hasn't lived the most stable life," Carl said. "But yes. He always kept that, for some reason."

"We all carry so much with us, don't we?"

"Yes," he said. "We do."

I hadn't given much thought to what James's life had been like after we left Gritten, but I supposed I'd always imagined he'd been happy. It made me sad to know he hadn't. That the guilt he felt had trailed him too, and he'd been unable to put it down and leave it behind.

"The knocks at the door?" I said. "That was you?"

"Yes."

"And it was you I saw in the woods that day?"

Carl nodded.

"Why?" I said.

"I was trying to frighten you away."

Which had nearly worked. But, of course, Carl had

been there when it had all happened. He knew what buttons to push.

"I'm sorry," he said. "I didn't know what else to do. I honestly never thought you'd come back here. Daphne always told me you wouldn't. But then you arrived at the house, and I knew it was only a matter of time before you found it."

*It's in the house, Paul.*

"Charlie's dream diary," I said.

"You found it, then?"

"Yes. Why did my mother have it?"

There was a long silence then. I stared across the old playground, watching the bushes at the far side wavering ever so slightly in the breeze.

Waiting.

"Are you sure you want to know?" he said.

After everything that had happened, the anger flared.

"Do you know," I said, "people keep asking me that. And for a long time, maybe the answer was no. I *didn't* want to know about any of it. But I'm here now, despite everybody's predictions about me. And so, yes. I would fucking well like to know."

Carl looked up at the sky.

"I just wanted to keep everybody safe," he said. "But now that Daphne's gone, perhaps it doesn't matter anymore. Maybe nothing does. And, God, I'm so fucking tired. So I'll tell you, if that's what you want. Then you can carry it all too. And you can decide what to do about it."

*"Tell me how my mother got the diary."*

He continued staring at the sky for a moment, lost in

memory, and then looked down and rubbed his hands together.

"First I need to tell you what happened that day."

Carl and Eileen had both been home on the day Charlie and Billy murdered Jenny. Carl had been working upstairs, and, as always, he'd listened to James leaving the house with a heavy heart. There had been many days that year when he'd felt like that: watching Charlie lead us all down the backyard and into the woods, feeling powerless to intervene. He knew who Charlie was—the illegitimate son of Eileen's former husband—and he didn't trust his involvement in James's life. But it had never felt like his place to say anything.

As he told me this, I recalled the last day I'd gone into the woods with them. The way I'd seen Carl reluctantly raise his hand to the glass when I'd waved at him.

"And, of course, by that point you weren't with them," Carl said. "But that day, you spoke to him here. You told him the truth. And instead of meeting Charlie and Billy, he came home."

He had heard the argument begin, walking out of his makeshift office and standing quietly at the top of the stairs for a time, listening to the furious words being exchanged between James and his mother. The fallout from what I'd done had been ugly. Eileen had been sobbing and shouting. For his part, James had seemed resolute. Determined to discover the truth about his father.

"I always thought we should have told him sooner,"

he said. "But Eileen was adamant. She didn't want to think about what had happened; she just wanted to forget. At that point, I didn't know how James had found out, but a part of me was glad he had. But it was a matter for them to sort out between them, so I went back to work."

The argument downstairs continued for a time, and then settled into a kind of silence. Carl carried on working, imagining he'd be able to help with the situation later. That was his role in the house: to calm things down; to look after everybody and keep things working. He had always been the peacemaker.

He took a deep breath.

"But then I heard screaming."

He could never be sure exactly what had happened, but it seemed that at some point Charlie had come in through the back door.

"That boy was crazy. You know that, right?"

I nodded, remembering. "Yeah. I know."

"He really did believe in that dream world he'd made up. He thought he would find his father by doing what he did. But, of course, the whole thing was ridiculous. I think when he woke up in the woods, he was so upset and frustrated and angry that he came to our house to take it out on Eileen."

Carl hadn't seen it happen, but from what he could gather afterward, Charlie had begun screaming abuse at Eileen, and then attacked her, pushing her to the floor and starting to beat her. James had stood there for a moment, watching the boy he imagined had been his friend trying to kill his mother. Knowing that he had been betrayed. Understanding that the foundations of his existence had been undermined in a single afternoon.

And as Charlie continued his attack on Eileen, James picked up a knife.

When Carl had finished, I sat there in silence for a moment.

"James killed Charlie?"

Carl nodded.

"You could make an argument that he was acting in self-defense—or at least, protecting his mother. But it went way beyond that. He lost control of himself. I think that everything that had happened—everything he'd learned that day—it all came pouring out in that moment. He was still stabbing Charlie when I came downstairs. I had to wrestle the knife off him."

He blinked the memory away.

"Why didn't you call the police?" I said.

"I thought about it. But then . . . well. I made a decision. Standing there right then, I knew our lives had changed forever, and I wanted to limit the damage." He looked at me suddenly. "I love James, you know."

I nodded, remembering.

Like his own son.

"And I knew that he was going to be in real trouble. I had no idea what I was doing, but someone needed to take charge. James was sobbing; Eileen was hysterical. *Someone* needed to look after them both. So it came down to me. Like it always did."

He shook his head and fell silent. I waited.

After a while, he took another deep breath.

"We wrapped Charlie's body in plastic sheeting, packed up tightly, and stuck it up in the attic, surrounded by boxes and carpets. We cleaned up. And then we waited. We didn't know what he'd done at that point, and by the time Billy was arrested that evening, it was too late to change anything. We'd hidden the body; we'd tidied the scene. We were all guilty. The police came to talk to us the next day, but they had no reason to suspect us of anything. They never searched the house or anything like that. I kept waiting for it all to go wrong, but it didn't. What was left of Charlie was sealed away above us, but in the end it was easy to pretend it had all just . . . gone away."

He spread his hands as though he couldn't quite believe it. He was wrong, though. The three of them might have gotten away with the crime, but the repercussions of Charlie's disappearance were still being felt even now. People were dying because of this secret. What happened that day had stretched its fingers out in the twenty-five years since, and it still had a grip on the world.

"James never really recovered," Carl said. "He's had a difficult life. The drinking. Drugs. Eileen and I came into some money, and we moved to be closer to him. He's always needed someone to look after him."

"Yes," I said.

"And I did my best to help. I tried to convince him that what happened had only ever been a bad dream." Carl laughed flatly at the irony. "Over time, I think he's come to accept that's true. He believes that Charlie really did disappear that day. He talks about it all the time. Reinforcing it to himself. He needs that to be what happened so he doesn't have to remember."

I thought about what Amanda had told me.

"Does he talk about it online?"

"What do you mean?"

"I don't know."

Amanda had believed the user on the forum she mentioned had been encouraging the killers in her hometown. I wondered now if perhaps she'd misinterpreted the messages she'd seen. If it was possible they had been designed not to incite so much as to bolster a belief the user needed to cling to. That Charlie wasn't dead. That what Carl had just described to me had never really happened.

None of which answered my original question.

"How was my mother involved?"

"She wasn't." He looked at me. "Paul, you *have* to believe me on that. She had nothing to do with what happened."

"But?"

He looked away.

"But it was hard. The guilt. The pressure. And Daphne was my best friend. We really . . . well. We cared about each other."

I thought again of the photograph of the two of them, and then also the conversation I'd overheard as a child.

*You can do so much better, you know?*

The silence that had followed before his reply.

*I really don't think I can.*

By then, of course, my mother and father had been

married for years, and Carl had already taken on the responsibility of raising James. At the time, the exchange had not seemed loaded to me, but I was old enough now to imagine a weight to the words and the spaces between them. The rules that had to be followed. The chances not taken. The things left unspoken and the lives unexplored.

"You told her what you'd done?"

"A few years afterward."

"What did she say?"

"That I'd done the right thing. That nothing good could come from telling the truth. Because she understood I was doing the best for James, and that it was better for it all to be forgotten. And so all these years, she kept it a secret."

Yes. That was exactly what my mother must have done. Out of duty, and friendship, and perhaps even lost love. But it had been a burden she had found hard to shoulder. I thought about the red hands in the attic and the newspaper reports she had collected. She had understood the consequences of her silence, and it had tormented her. But she had carried it anyway.

One generation sacrificing so much to protect the next.

"But the last year or so," Carl said, "she started calling me. It was obvious from what she was saying that she was . . . losing her grip on everything a little. She kept talking to me about what happened. I was worried what she might say to other people, and so a couple of weeks ago, I came back to Gritten."

"You went to see her?"

"I tried to talk to her, but she wasn't herself."

"So you pushed her down the stairs?"

"No!"

The sudden shock in his voice and the expression on his face were genuine.

"Tell me what happened, then."

"I decided the best thing was to get the body out of our old house. That way, if Daphne *did* say something, there would be no evidence there for anyone to find. So that night, I took the remains out into the woods and scattered them. Covered them up a bit. I tried my best to make it look like they could have been there a long time."

*He's in the woods, Paul!*

*Flickering in the trees.*

"Maybe Daphne saw the flashlight. But whatever, she knew what I was doing. The problem was Charlie's dream diary, you see? James had taken that, and I brought it back with me. But I realized I couldn't leave that in the woods with him. His remains were just bones, but the diary hadn't been exposed to the elements—it might as well have been brand-new. So my plan was to burn it. I left it on the kitchen counter when I went out into the woods. And when I got back . . . it wasn't there anymore."

"My mother came in and took it?"

"She must have. But by then it was too late for me to do anything about it. I went to your house, and the emergency services were outside."

*They're all the same.*

I understood what had happened now. My mother

had taken the diary and hidden it among the other identical notebooks. She had gotten that far, but her body was no longer strong enough.

"So she was coming down the stairs," I said quietly.

"What?"

"It doesn't matter."

Silence settled between us.

Then Carl sighed.

"I'm tired, Paul. Now you know everything. And like I said, it's up to you what you do with what I've told you." He gestured behind us. "Charlie is out there in the woods now, and sooner or later he'll be found. It'll be over. In the meantime, you need to decide what to do. You can ruin what's left of three people's lives. You can damage your mother's memory. Or you can—"

"Forget?"

"Yes. I suppose so."

I looked away, considering everything he'd said. Thinking through the chain of events, the network of cause and effect. If what he'd told me was true, did I blame anybody for the way they'd behaved? I wasn't sure I did. Everybody had been trying to do their best. To protect the people they loved. To shield them from harm. To carry the separate burdens that had been handed to them. Perhaps it was time for me to shoulder my share of that.

It was my mother's words that came back to me then.

"You could have done so much better, you know," I said.

There was a whole lifetime of regret etched on Carl's face. I thought that what I'd said was probably true of everyone, and maybe it was only as you approached the end of your life that you appreciated the force of it.

"Yes," he said. "I know."

*Then you can carry it all too.*

*And you can decide what to do about it.*

And I was about to say something else, but then I looked up and saw the police cars that were arriving.

# THIRTY-SIX

---------

Dwyer drove way too quickly, and the car skidded to a halt beside what had once been the playground in Gritten Wood. A second car pulled up behind, almost running into the back of them.

Amanda looked out of the passenger window and saw two people sitting on one of the benches. She recognized Paul, and she assumed from the cell phone trace that Theo was still feeding to her that the other man was Carl Dawson.

Dwyer clearly had no doubts: he was already out of the car, moving much more quickly than she'd ever have pegged him for. She was still unclipping her seat belt as he was stepping over the small fence with his badge held out in front of him.

"Mr. Dawson?" she heard him call. "Mr. Carl Dawson?"

She raced to catch up with him. Behind her, she heard doors slamming. Both cars had parked on the same side of the area: not great procedure, but there was a dense horseshoe of bushes around the far side of the playground, and Carl Dawson looked too surprised to put up much of a chase. He had stood up, though, and moved away from the bench toward the center of the area. Paul was still sitting down, obviously confused by what was happening, but Carl had a look of panic on his face, as though he weren't remotely surprised to see the police here.

As though he would have tried to run if he could.

But that was out of the question as Dwyer reached him. The badge went away with one hand and the other was resting against the top of Dawson's arm before she'd even seen him move.

"Carl Dawson, right? Calm down, mate. We just want to have a word, okay?"

Dawson was frozen in place now. Amanda stepped past the pair of them and walked across to where Paul was still sitting on the bench. He stood up as she reached him.

"What's going on?"

"Nothing." She held out her palms, evaluating him. He looked shaken but unharmed. "Are you okay?"

But he just stared past her. She could hear more officers joining them in the playground behind, along with bursts of radio static.

"Calm down, Paul," she said.

"What's happening?"

"We just need to talk to Mr. Dawson."

"About what?"

"I can't tell you that right now."

His gaze turned to her for a moment, and she saw

the look of desperation on his face. His hands were by his side, fists clenching and unclenching. She turned around. Dwyer was leading Dawson over to the car, one arm practically looped over the older man's shoulders. From behind, it looked as if they might have been friends, one of them helping the other home after a night out.

And then she saw Dawson slump a little, as though the air had been taken out of him, and she knew Dwyer had just told him what they were arresting him for. The suspected murder of his wife and stepson, and of Billy Roberts.

For a brief moment, Carl Dawson glanced back to where she and Paul were standing. She had never seen such loss on a man's face before. It seemed as though everything he'd struggled and worked for over the years had been taken away from him. As if, in that single moment, he was looking back on his whole life and realizing every second of it was pointless and wasted.

And then Dwyer was leading him off toward the car again.

"What's he done?" Paul said.

Amanda turned back.

"He hasn't necessarily done anything. We just need to talk to him." She put a hand on his shoulder and spoke quietly. "Are you sure you're okay?"

"I'm fine."

"Why were you here with him?"

"We were just talking."

She heard a car door slam behind her.

"*What* were you talking about?" she said.

Paul had been staring over her shoulder, and when he looked at her now, she found it impossible to read the expression on his face. It reminded her of when she'd asked him in the pub if there was anyone else here in Gritten she should talk to. As though he was wrestling with something inside himself, unsure of how much to tell her.

"My mother," he said.

"What about her?"

"She died."

"I know," she said. "I'm sorry."

"And Carl was her friend."

She looked behind her at the car, where Dwyer was waiting, Carl Dawson in the backseat. They had three brutal murders, and the man was connected to all the victims. *I like him for it,* Dwyer had told her back at the department, and surely he was right. That was playing the odds, after all. If not him, then who? But, looking back at Paul again now, she thought there was something she was missing—that there was more going on here than they realized.

"Paul?" she said.

*Goddamn it. Help me out here.*

But his face had gone blank. Whatever decision he'd been agonizing over, he'd clearly made his choice. And when he spoke, it seemed more like he was talking to himself.

"Carl was her friend," he said again.

Then he looked down and turned away.

"That's all."

# THIRTY-SEVEN

My father used to burn things.

It was one of the few memories I had of him from my early childhood. I seemed to have gotten through my entire adult life without the need to make a fire of any kind, and yet they had been regular occurrences back then. When I was still young enough for my father not to hate me, I would stand with him in the backyard and watch as he snapped kindling, leaving thin strips of wood hanging from the ends like claws, and help him sweep rustling piles of leaves into the firepit we had there. Newspapers; rubbish; clusters of branches and sharp ropes of brambles. Everything he wanted to dispose of was burned, and then the ashes would be raked over the following day, ready for the fires to come. I supposed that was just the way my father was. When something was no longer useful to him, he took it upon himself to obliterate it from the world.

Perhaps he'd had the right idea.

I stood on the back step now, holding the first of the boxes.

It was evening, and everywhere I looked, the shadows were thickening. Night fell quickly in Gritten, and it would be dark soon. Even now, the face of the woods at the end of the yard had faded into a patchwork of black and gray, occluded further by the mist rising from the tangle of undergrowth below. The air was cooling, and there was a slight breeze that brought the smell of earth and leaves to me.

I'd been in a daze all afternoon, shocked and confused by what had happened: first by everything Carl had told me, and then by the arrival of the police. Amanda had refused to explain what they wanted to talk to Carl about, and I hadn't heard from her since. Of course, the same held true in reverse. I hadn't told her what Carl had said, nor had I called and volunteered the information afterward. Back in the playground, it had simply been too soon. It had felt like the decision Carl left me with had been forced upon me and what I really needed was a chance to think and work out the best thing to do.

If I told the truth, three people's lives would be destroyed and my mother's involvement would become common knowledge. And to what end? I had gone back and forth, the whole time attempting to distract myself with practicalities. I'd collected my mother's things from the hospice. I'd obtained a death certificate. I'd looked into funeral arrangements.

But a decision had to be made.

I thought I'd made it now.

I carried the box across the yard. The firepit was a little overgrown, but the bricks at the edges had held, and it was more or less as I remembered: a pale ulcer on the green skin of the lawn. I inverted the box and emptied the newspapers into the pit, then kicked them into a heap in the center, each contact raising puffs of old ash and the sour, dirty aroma of fires long past.

Then I went back inside.

This felt like work that should be done in the dark, so I'd left the lights off in the house for now. There was still enough daylight left to make my way down to the front door where I'd gathered everything together.

I picked up the second box and carried it out to the firepit.

Emptied it.

Was I doing the right thing?

I looked up. The sky above was dark blue and speckled with a faint prickling of stars. No answers to be found there.

I went back inside again and collected the third box, then emptied it into the pit, the pile of newspapers there as dull gray as old bone.

One more to go.

The final box, then. It was already much darker inside than when I'd started, and there was a heaviness to the air, as though my actions were somehow adding to the house rather than subtracting from it. As I carried the box out to the pit, the breeze picked up and the grass around me shivered. I emptied out the contents. My old notebooks. My dream diary. The creative writing magazine. The doll Charlie had given to James.

The slim hardback book with Jenny's story about Red Hands.

But not Charlie's dream diary.

I frowned.

Where was that?

It took me a moment to realize it must still be upstairs in my mother's room. When I had seen Carl outside earlier, I had put it down on the bed before following him to the playground. I went back inside again and climbed the stairs slowly. The upstairs hallway was almost pitch-black, as though the house were gathering the night inside itself, and when I walked into my mother's room, it was full of shapes and shadows. But the diary was obvious: a stark black rectangle on the stripped mattress.

I picked it up.

*Am I doing the right thing, Mom?*

What my mother would have wanted me to do had been foremost on my mind all afternoon. She had decided to steal the diary from Carl for a reason. After so many years of hoarding guilt, perhaps a part of her had wanted the truth to come out. But equally, at that point her mind had been slipping. She *had* kept Carl's secret all this time. Because they had been friends, if not more.

*Am I doing the right thing?*

I wasn't sure what she would say if she were here now, and the dark house offered no more answers than the night sky outside. Maybe there weren't any, I thought. Perhaps life was just a matter of doing what you thought was best at the time and then living with the consequences as best you could afterward. What would my mother have said if she were here now? Probably that I was a grown man. That she'd raised me and protected me as best she could. And that she was gone now, which meant I had to decide what to do for myself.

A noise downstairs.

I stood still for a moment.

Listening.

Nothing more. It was just the house stretching out after the heat of the day, preparing to sleep. Maybe on some level it even knew what I was about to do, and was readying itself to be locked up and forgotten for a time.

I took the diary out into the upstairs hallway.

Then hesitated, looking down the stairs.

It was very dark down there now, and the house felt even more full than it had before. My spine started tingling. Since returning to Gritten, I had never felt entirely alone in here, but that had been because every corner and surface contained memories. Right now I was feeling a different kind of presence.

*Someone is downstairs.*

The thought came from nowhere.

There was no reason to believe it was true. Everything that had happened here had been down to Carl trying to frighten me away. And yet the silence was ringing in my ears, and some primal part of me was on edge.

I stared down at the front door. I'd put the chain on when I arrived. The back door was unlocked, though.

Could the sound I'd heard have been that door clicking open?

*You need to get outside.*

Once the thought came, it was suddenly urgent.

I went down the stairs, moving quickly but trying to stay as quiet as I could, wincing at every quiet creak. At the bottom, I glanced behind me along the dark corridor. The kitchen was dark and the back door was closed. There was nobody there.

But as I turned back and reached for the chain to unlock the front door, the ghost of a man stepped out from the shadows in the living room beside me. He moved so fast I hardly had time to register him before pain exploded in my lungs, the world spun about me, and the darkness in the hallway filled with stars.

# THIRTY-EIGHT

"He's lying about something," Dwyer said.

Amanda stared down at the monitor on the desk and nodded. The screen was showing footage from the camera in the interview room. Carl Dawson was sitting at the desk there, his elbows on the surface and his face obscured by his hands. What was left of his hair was pushed up, splayed by his fingers. It had been ten minutes since they'd left him alone for a break, and as far as she could tell from watching the monitor he hadn't moved at all.

*He's lying about something.*

He was lying about a lot of things, she thought.

For one, Dawson claimed to have been back in Gritten for several days. To a certain degree, that fit with activity they'd found on his credit card, but it didn't make sense in other ways. *Why* was he here? He'd come to see Daphne Adams, apparently, but that didn't add up. He'd returned to Gritten on the day *before* her accident, and yet when they checked with the hospice, there was no record of him ever visiting her afterward. So what the hell had he been doing?

"He had no answer when it came to Daphne," she said.

"Yeah, he clammed up. Because he's lying."

"Is he, though?"

"Of course he is," Dwyer said. "If he came to see her, he failed pretty miserably. Let's be honest, it's not like she was doing a lot of running around."

"No."

Dwyer was right, and yet a flicker of doubt remained in her mind. For some reason, Dawson wasn't telling them everything, but she thought there was a grain of truth in what he *had* said. It was like they had one picture and he had another, and some parts matched while others didn't. Perhaps he really had come to see Daphne Adams, but there was more to it than that, and despite the hours of pressure they had put him under, he wouldn't explain what it was.

There was something they were missing.

Dwyer said, "Don't you like him for the killings?"

"I'm not sure." She looked at him. "You still do, I can tell."

He shrugged. "We can link him to all three victims. We know he was here in Gritten at the time Billy Roberts was murdered. And it's not that long a drive back home. So, yeah, I like him quite a lot."

"Motive, though?"

"Years of domestic abuse on file. Perhaps he finally snapped."

Amanda looked at the screen.

Dawson still hadn't moved.

"Maybe," she said.

"Here's what I think," Dwyer said. "Dawson comes back here for some reason—let's say it's possible it really *was* to see Daphne Adams. She's dying, he's upset. He's had a miserable fucking life, and he's full of resentment. And there are all these bad memories in Gritten. So he stews for a while, then ends up tracking down Billy Roberts and it all explodes. Afterward, he goes home and loses his shit with his family."

"Then comes back to have a chat with Paul Adams?"

Dwyer shrugged again. "If you believe that's what they were really doing."

Amanda had no answer to that. Paul had clearly been wrestling with something back at the playground. When she had first met him, she had been confident he was telling her the truth, which made it that much easier to notice the difference when he wasn't. But she also had a feeling that whatever he wasn't prepared to tell her, it was something separate from the murders. If he had known anything about the killings, she was sure he would have told her. Appearances could be deceptive, of course, but he struck her as too decent for that.

"I can't see them being in it together," she said.

"They're in *something* together."

"Paul had no motive to hurt Eileen and James."

"He did for Billy Roberts, though."

"Sure. But when I spoke to him, I really don't think he even knew Billy was out of prison. Honestly, I think Paul has done his best to forget what happened here in Gritten. I read people well, and he was genuinely shocked when I told him." She gestured at the monitor. "And, of course, that's the other thing."

"What is?"

"Carl Dawson's face when you told him."

That moment back at the playground was still etched in her mind. And ever since they had started the interviews, Dawson had seemed like a broken man to her. There had been no bursting into tears, shouted denials, or collapsing with shock. There was an emptiness to him, but also a strange kind of resolve. As though he had carried heavier weights than this before, and whatever it took, he was going to do so again now.

Dwyer looked at the screen.

"I still like him for it," he said.

Amanda sighed to herself. Whatever her reservations, there was a good chance that Dwyer was right. And anyway, especially with Paul refusing to talk, Dawson was all they had right now.

"Round three?" she said.

"Oh, let's."

The office they had retreated to was only two doors down from the interview room. As they reached it, Amanda's phone rang. She took it out of her pocket, wondering if it might be Paul. But she'd programmed his number into her cell, and she didn't recognize the one flashing up now.

"You make a start," she told Dwyer. "I'll join you in a second."

"Fine by me."

Carl Dawson looked up as Dwyer walked in, his face still lost and empty, and then the door closed, blocking her view. She answered the call and leaned back against the wall.

"Detective Amanda Beck," she said.

"Detective Beck?"

It was a woman's voice. Amanda couldn't place it, but even with just those two words she registered the urgency and panic.

She leaned away from the wall.

"Yes. Who is this, please?"

"It's Mary."

"Mary?"

"Mary Price? You came to our home a few days ago to talk about our son's murder. I really need to speak to you. I'm so scared."

Michael Price's mother. Amanda recalled sitting in a front room still scattered with the boy's posses-sions, the air saturated with grief, desperate to be anywhere else.

"Mary," she said. "Of course. Please try to calm down."

"I'm sorry. I'm so sorry."

"You don't need to be sorry."

"I should have called you sooner. I just didn't . . . Oh God."

*I'm so scared.*

"Tell me what's wrong, Mary."

"My husband."

Dean Price. Amanda remembered how the man had suddenly left the room, unable to accept that his son had been killed because of the story she'd told them both. *Are you saying my son was murdered because of a ghost?* And the threat she'd sensed in him. The barely concealed violence she had felt bubbling below his surface.

"What about him?" she said.

Mary was crying now.

"I think he might have done something bad."

# THIRTY-NINE

The hall light clicked on, and I found myself staring at a pair of combat boots.

They kept swimming in and out of focus. I was lying curled up on the polished floor, trying desperately to breathe through a pain in my lungs that was like nothing I'd ever experienced before. It seemed like the man had barely moved, but he'd somehow hit me in the stomach with such force that he'd knocked the air from me and made it impossible to draw in more.

"Shallow breaths," he told me. "You'll live."

His voice was blank and emotionless: stating the facts without really caring about the outcome. But it turned out he was right. The effect of the impact subsided gradually, and I managed to draw in small mouthfuls of air, the pain flaring less with each one.

The whole time, the man stood there waiting as I recovered, entirely motionless. Somehow I knew better than to attempt to stand up—that he wanted me on the floor, and that I'd simply be knocked down again if I resisted—but after a moment I risked looking up at him. He was standing in the doorway to the front room, dressed in dark combat trousers and a black sweater. His body seemed thin and wiry, and built for violence. His hair was close-cropped. I didn't recognize his face, but the expression there was as implacable as his voice had been.

In one gloved hand he was holding a hunting knife.

Terror began humming in my chest.

"What do you want?" I managed to say, each word making the pain in my chest flare.

The man ignored me, shrugging off a backpack I hadn't even noticed until then. With his free hand, he reached inside and then tossed something in my direction. I flinched as it landed on the floor beside me with a clatter.

Handcuffs.

"Put them on," he said.

Every instinct in my body told me not to. But even if he hadn't had the knife, and I hadn't been lying powerless on the floor, I could tell I was no match for him physically. That he would simply put them on me himself, and it would hurt a lot more if I made him do it.

He took a step closer, turning the knife in his hand.

"I won't tell you again."

"All right."

I picked up the handcuffs. They were solid and professional, with little distance between the cuffs. Police-issue, I thought—or military, perhaps. And there was that air of authority to the man, as though controlling and hurting people came naturally to him.

I slipped one cuff over my left wrist and clicked it shut.

"A bit tighter," he said.

I did as I was told.

"Now the other."

I repeated the action with the other wrist. The action rendered me helpless, but I had been already. Maybe there was even some comfort in the knowledge that he felt the need to restrain me. If he wanted to kill me, I would surely be dead by now.

"What do you want?" I said again.

And again, there was no answer.

Instead, he squatted down and looked me over dispassionately. The knife was much closer now, and I could see it was serrated on one side, thin and wicked on the other. The way the man looked at me, it was like he was examining a carcass he had been given the task of butchering, and a chill ran through me as I realized there might be other reasons to restrain me, and that there were worse fates than simply being dead.

I felt a buzzing against my thigh.

My phone ringing.

The man heard it too and reached into my pocket. He examined the screen for a moment, then placed the phone casually on the floor and sent it spinning away into the dark front room.

He held up the knife.

"Do you see this?" he said.

"Yes."

"This means you and I are going to have a talk."

"About what?"

"Be quiet. The talk will go on for as long as it needs to. If you don't give me the answers I want, I will hurt you very badly until you do. Do you understand?"

"Yes."

"Because I know you have those answers. I know you know what happened to Charlie Crabtree and where he disappeared to."

I blinked.

I wasn't sure what I'd been thinking this was—a robbery, perhaps. But I remembered Billy Roberts now, and how shaken Amanda had seemed after coming from the scene.

*The talk will go on for as long as it needs to.*

The man placed his knee on my side, leaning down and pinning me to the floor, then traced the tip of the knife over my shoulder.

"I have no idea what happened to Charlie," I said.

"Really? Why were you planning to burn the evidence, then?"

I tried to think.

"I just wanted to be done with it all. That's all I've ever wanted."

That seemed to anger him. The pressure of his knee on my side increased, and he moved the knife to my cheek. I felt the tip of it pierce the skin there, a fingertip away from my right eye.

"You know what happened to him," he said.

I could tell him the truth, but I didn't want to, and from the expression on his face I thought he was planning to hurt me whatever I said. Despite the situation, I felt anger flaring up inside me. Fury that, even after all these years, Charlie still had the capacity to get to me, and determination that it was going to stop.

"Tell me where Charlie is."

The tip of the knife suddenly went in deeper, and I winced as the man turned his hand, needling the blade against my cheekbone. The pain wasn't terrible, not yet, but the glinting metal filled my right eye, and the anticipation was worse.

*You need to tell him a story.*

"Hague," I said.

The name came from nowhere, arriving in my head as suddenly and violently as the van that had taken Hague's life.

The beginning of a story.

Now I just needed to find the rest.

But for now, the blade stopped turning as the man considered my answer. It was taking him a second to place the name, but I could tell it was familiar to him. He must have read through the same online forums as I had.

A moment later, the knife moved away from my face.

"The boy who was killed in the accident," he said.

"No," I said. "Not him. His older brother. Rob Hague—that was his name."

I had no idea if that was true.

"What about him?"

"He was in prison, but he got out that year. There were rumors circulating about what Charlie had said on the rugby field that day. Some people thought that

Charlie really had caused the accident, and Rob Hague was one of them. He blamed Charlie for killing his brother."

It was a complete fabrication, of course, but now that I'd started to tell it, I realized I could see it unfolding in my head, the way I had on rare occasions as a teenager when I sat and planned out my stories. Rob Hague and his friends cruising around in their car. Looking for an opportunity to deal with Charlie, and finding him wandering alone near Gritten Wood after he woke up and abandoned Billy among the trees.

Dragging him into the car.

A beating that got out of hand.

"There were three of them," I said. "I can't remember the other names. After Charlie died, they panicked. They kept his body wrapped up in a roll of carpet in the trunk of the car. Later on, they got rid of the body in the woods and burned the car."

"Where in the woods?"

"There's an old well."

"The wells were all searched."

"Beforehand. So where better to hide a body?"

I held my breath as the man thought about that. I needed him to believe the story enough to buy me some time. I had no idea what I was going to do with that time, but I did know I didn't want him to start hurting me. That whatever happened, it was going to be on my terms.

Eventually he moved the knife.

"How do you know about that?"

"Hague showed me."

"Why would he do that?"

A good question.

"This was a couple of months later," I said. "He knew I hated Charlie, and he thought I might want to know that justice had been done. Maybe he figured he could trust me not to tell. And he was right about that."

The man looked at me.

Not quite believing yet. But nearly.

"Hague gave me something," I said.

I nodded toward Charlie's dream diary, which I'd dropped by the door when I was first hit. The man stared at it for a moment, then reached out and picked it up, flicking through the pages. Whoever he was, he had clearly learned enough about the case to understand what he was seeing.

"And I'm glad," I said. "I'm fucking *glad* he told me."

Even if the rest of what I'd said was fiction, there was nothing pretend about the venom in my voice then. If my story had been true—if Hague's brother really had turned up on my doorstep—I'd have gone into those woods with him in a heartbeat. And when he looked at me, the man could see I was telling the truth.

A few seconds later, he tossed the diary into the front room.

"You're going to take me there," he said.

# FORTY

--·-·--·-·--

I stood outside the back door on the edge of the yard, the coils and swirls of grass before me a frozen, dark blue sea. The pitch-black trees at the bottom might as well have been the end of the world. Behind me, the man flicked on a flashlight. The beam turned the undergrowth ahead into a colorless carpet of texture and shadow.

"We go in this way?" he said.

"We're less likely to be seen this way."

"How far is it?"

I thought about it. "A mile or so."

"You'd better not be lying to me." He pressed the knife against the base of my spine. "You know what will happen if you are."

"I'm not lying."

I breathed in the night air. It was cool now. And it was strange how calm I felt, especially as I had no idea how the minutes ahead were going to pan out. In all likelihood this man was going to kill me, and all I was really achieving here was to stretch out whatever time I had left. But there was an off-kilter edge to the world, and an unreal quality to the silence. It felt as though the man and I had stepped out of time and found ourselves in a place where the past and present mingled more freely than usual.

A place where anything might happen.

I lifted my cuffed hands, pinched my nose shut, and tried to breathe.

"What are you doing?" he said.

I lowered my hands.

"Nothing. Come on."

And then I set off down the yard, hardly aware of him following aside from the bobbing light that kept quiet, methodical pace. At the bottom of the yard, I pulled the old chicken wire away from the posts and trampled it down. The man shone the flashlight into the woods, revealing a route so overgrown at the sides and overhead that it was more like a tunnel than a path.

I looked behind me. With the light shining so brightly, it was impossible to see the man, but I had the impression that he was as uneasy as I was—or as I should have been. And then I turned and stepped over the remains of the fence, and began pushing my way through the branches and foliage that were already scratching at my arms.

Heading off into the Shadows for one last time.

It was easy enough to find one of the handful of rough paths that snaked through the woods. Once I had, I led the man along it for a while.

He kept a little way behind but shone the flashlight ahead, and the light made the woods seem eerie and otherworldly. The nearest trees on either side were brightly illuminated, every detail of the pitted bark revealed, and I could see a carpet of tangled grass and broken sticks stretching a little way in front. But the light only penetrated so far. The view just feet in front of me was like a black iris, or a hole into which I was leading the two of us.

As we walked, I began to lose track of the direction we were heading. Not that it mattered. After a few minutes, I spotted a convenient break between the trees on the left-hand side—not a path, but manageable—and that was where I decided to take us off-grid.

"We need to go this way."

"You're sure?"

At hip-height on the nearest trunk, there was a spread of thin branches hanging down from a larger one, like skeletal fingers poised over a piano. I gestured to them as though they were a landmark I recognized.

"I'm sure."

I stepped confidently through, hoping it didn't lead to a dead end. Luck was on my side. A little way along, there was another break between the trees, this time to the right, and I took that, leading us deeper into the woods.

A branch snapped off against my upper arm. With my hands cuffed, I tried awkwardly to bend others out of the way as I went. The deeper into the woods we walked, the less well the flashlight seemed to work, and the trees cast shadows across each other, lending everything a shattered feel. All I could hear in the hush was the twigs snapping beneath our feet as we moved farther and farther away from the rest of the world.

*A mile or so*, I'd told him.

Of course, I had no actual destination in mind. No real idea of where I was taking this man or what would happen when we reached it.

Suddenly there was a break in the land.

I teetered and almost fell. An enormous stretch of earth had been hacked and gouged out a footstep ahead of us.

*Keep calm.*

There was no way forward, so I stepped to the left, carefully lifting my foot over a tangle of undergrowth.

"Watch yourself here," I said.

I just had to hope. I remembered what these woods were like—how it often felt that you weren't moving through them so much as them shifting around you—and I sent a silent plea to the forest to slide a piece into place that would help me now.

Luck was with me again. A little way along, the ground closed up, and I could lead us off to the right again. The town felt a long way behind us now.

"How much farther?" the man said.

"Still a ways."

But I could tell from the silence that followed that his patience was running out. I needed to distract him as I took us deeper.

"Why are you doing this?" I said.

No reply.

"Who are you? A soldier, I'm guessing."

Again, he said nothing. But this time I thought the man was at least considering the question.

"I was a soldier once," he said finally. "For a long time. And I did some very bad things when I was. Things I'm ashamed of. Afterward, I was a father, and everything started to feel right again."

His voice sounded so blank, so empty, and I thought I understood now. He was a parent—presumably of the victim in Featherbank that Amanda had told me about. Charlie had never been found, and therefore his child was dead, and it had broken him. That was why he was here, doing what he was doing. He was trying to rectify that.

"I'm sorry," I said.

"Be quiet."

"I was just a kid. I tried to do the best I could. I had no idea it would lead to other kids copying what Charlie did. I genuinely thought it would all just be forgotten."

And then time ran out.

I stepped between the trees and was faced by a dead end. There was another enormous dip in the land here, the edge ridged with tree roots that looked like black veins coiling out of the crumbling earth. There was no way forward. The ground to the left was overgrown and impassable. To the right, there was a small stretch of earth that ended in a thick wall of trees, the grass and brambles between them as impenetrable as barbed wire.

This was as far as we went.

"There," I said.

The man stepped out beside me. My heart was beating hard as I pointed at the area of ground to the right of the ravine ahead. He angled the flashlight toward it, flicking the beam back and forth, searching for an old well that wasn't there.

"Where?"

*You used to be so decisive.*

I reached out quickly and knocked the flashlight upward toward his face, then shouldered him away from me as hard as I could, as hard as I remembered once going through a boy on a rugby field. He went sprawling—not over the edge as I'd wanted, but at least far enough away for me to spin back the way we'd come.

And then run for my life into the darkness.

# FORTY-ONE

------------

*Are you saying my son was murdered because of a ghost?*

That was what Dean Price had asked her. But as Amanda rocketed along the dark main road toward the town of Gritten Wood, it was Mary Price's words the same day that returned to her.

*Dean used to be in the army.*

*It's only since Dean left the army that the two of them started to bond.*

*Dean's always been practical. A problem-solver.*

At the time Amanda had said this wasn't a problem anyone could solve, but now she wondered if that was true. Michael Price had been murdered because Charlie Crabtree had never been found. The mystery of his disappearance had cast a shadow over everything and caused so much pain. And that was a problem that could be solved, couldn't it?

If you had the training and the will.

If you had nothing left to live for.

Back at the department, Mary had told her Dean had walked out of the house three days ago, and she hadn't heard from him since. His phone was switched off. The man had gone dark.

*Everything is fine,* Amanda told herself.

She had already checked, and Paul wasn't in his room at the hotel. But that just meant he was probably at his mother's house. And, while he wasn't answering his phone, the most likely explanation was surely that, after the events of the day, he didn't want to speak to her.

So there was nothing to worry about.

But that was logic speaking, and she was hearing other, louder voices right now. The dark landscape outside the car reminded her of the nightmare she often had, and she was beginning to feel the same panic and urgency it always brought. Someone was in trouble and she was not going to reach them in time.

Her phone was attached to the dashboard. She dialed Dwyer.

"Where the hell did you disappear to?" he said.

"I'm on my way to Gritten Wood."

She explained what she'd learned from Mary Price.

"Jesus fucking Christ," he said. "You didn't think to wait for me?"

"No time. I'm sure everything is okay, but I wanted to get out here as quickly as possible. Stay on the line and I'll let you know if I need you."

"I'm sending someone anyway."

She thought about it. "Fine by me."

The car in front of her was driving too slowly. Amanda

pulled out and overtook it, accelerating away and ignoring the horn blaring behind her—but then the turn-off for Gritten Wood came up suddenly on the left, and she swerved off the main road, hardly slowing as the street narrowed. The car juddered and bounced around her, the tires bumping over the rough ground. The husk of the town appeared ahead of her, as dark and apparently deserted as before.

And beyond it, the black mass of trees.

Her heart started beating more quickly.

She reached the house a minute later. Paul Adams's car was parked outside. She pulled in behind it, cricking on the hand brake and grabbing her cell phone from the dashboard.

"I'm there," she said.

"Anything?"

"The car's here." She got out and looked at the house. "The hall light's on."

"Just stay on the line."

"Will do."

"And don't do anything stupid."

Amanda remembered the savagery that had been done to Billy Roberts, and the terror she'd felt afterward at having come so close to such a monster.

"Don't worry, I won't."

She kept the phone pressed to her ear as she headed up the path to the front door. She knocked, but didn't wait for a reply—just turned the handle and found it unlocked. Inside, the brightly lit hallway was empty.

"Paul?" she shouted.

There was no reply.

"What's going on?" Dwyer said.

"Hang on."

Amanda stared down the hallway toward the kitchen at the far end. The light wasn't on in there, but she could feel a breeze coming from that direction. She headed down. The back door was open onto the black, overgrown sea of the yard.

"Back door's open."

She stepped out. It was difficult to make out much detail, but she could see the trees at the bottom. The darkness there was absolute.

"Officers en route," Dwyer told her.

Which was excellent news, Amanda thought. Because she was aware she needed help here—that she couldn't do this by herself. There was absolutely no way she was setting foot into those woods on her own. But at the same time, a different thought was gnawing at the back of her mind, and while there was no way she could know it for certain, somehow she did.

The backup wasn't going to get here in time.

For a few seconds she found herself frozen on the back step, unable to head down through the grass toward the implacable blackness at the end. She was shivering. Even though she was willing her body to move, it wouldn't respond.

Then:

*Calm down,* she told herself.

The voice came like a slap. For a moment, she thought it was her father's, but it wasn't.

It was just hers.

*Someone needs you.*

Yes, she realized. That was what it came down to. She wasn't that little girl anymore, lying in bed in the middle of the night, afraid of the dark and waiting for someone to save her. She was the person who came when someone else called.

"Are you there?" Dwyer said.

"I'm here," Amanda said.

And then she lowered the phone and headed quickly down the yard toward the woods.

# FORTY-TWO

I crouched down between two trees, out of breath and trying to fight the panic that was filling me. The invisible undergrowth was thick and tangled around me. I could hardly see a thing.

And I was lost.

When I'd first run from the man, I'd been sure I was heading back the way we'd come. But I must have taken a wrong turn somewhere, because I had no idea where I was now. The woods were disorienting even in daylight, never mind the almost absolute blackness I found myself in now. I wasn't even sure whether I'd headed back toward the town or burrowed myself deeper into the forest.

I held still and listened.

Branches cracked off to my right—not too close, but not far enough away either. I glanced that way and saw light flickering dimly between the trees. He was over there, scanning the woods for me. And he seemed like a man who would search methodically. If I stayed where I was, he was going to find me.

But if I moved, where would I go?

A bramble was digging into my arm. I shifted ever so slightly, trying to think.

*Go left—away from the light, for a start.*

I started to get up, but then heard a voice—

"You can't hide."

—and my head jerked around. The words had come from somewhere off to the left. I could see light flashing between the trees in that direction now: closer than it had been before. But it was impossible for him to have covered that much ground so quickly.

Was it me turning or was it the world?

"I used to hunt people like this for a living."

I turned away from the voice and the light and felt my way slowly between the trees, my hands against the rough trunks, moving slowly and quietly, and praying I didn't end up cornered.

Everything was silent for a time, apart from the rustling of the leaves against my arms and the soft snap of tangled grass giving way around my ankles.

Then suddenly the world opened up ahead. One second the back of my hand was against a branch, the next it felt like the tree had rotated away from me. And somehow the light was directly in front of me now, slashing brightly between the black trunks.

"There you are."

The light clicked off and the woods were plunged into darkness.

And then I heard an awful, angry snapping sound

as the man came straight at me. I turned and ran to one side, plunging blindly through the woods now, shouldering my way wildly into the trees, rebounding from them, heading in any direction that became open to me. And yet wherever I went, it felt like I was actually moving toward *him*: that the woods were spiraling the two of us ever closer together. The noise seemed to be coming from everywhere.

Whichever way I looked, I saw only indistinguishable gray shapes, and every time I turned, the vague path before me was identical to the last. And I was surrounded on all sides by the snap and crunch of the man hunting me here.

I couldn't find the way out of here by myself.

I needed—

"Paul!"

The voice pulled me up short. It came from behind me, and was so far away in the distance that I wondered if I had imagined it. But in its own way it was as heavy as an anchor. It was a woman's voice. For a moment, I thought it was Jenny—but, of course, that was impossible.

"Paul, are you in there?"

I hesitated, then began to head back the way I'd come. But the man had heard the woman's voice too. I could sense him somewhere away between the trees to my right. There was the rasp of heavy breathing coming from there.

And as I moved, I felt it coming closer.

"Paul?"

I crept along at first, following the voice like a thread

through a maze. Twigs cracked off to the side as the man tracked me, but at least it was *only* one side now. Then the trees thinned before me and I found myself on a path. I moved more quickly now, still expecting the man to emerge at any moment.

And then, from somewhere just behind me, I heard a different sound. The man's voice again, not words this time but a primal scream of frustration and pain.

I started to run.

"Paul!"

The screams behind me faded. For some reason, he wasn't following me. And the woman's voice, whoever she was, grew louder, leading me out of here. I ran faster and faster, as hard as I could, back toward Gritten, toward her, toward the even more distant sound of approaching sirens, and out of the Shadows.

# FORTY-THREE

--------

## AFTER

Early morning.

The day was bright and crisp as Amanda left her home and started the half-hour drive to Rosewood Gardens. The sky was clear and the roads were quiet. She left the radio off and drove slowly, appreciating the silence. As usual at this hour, she was the only visitor to the cemetery. When she arrived, she parked on the gravel, and then made her way along the path she always took between the graves here.

Perhaps it was just her imagination, but things felt different today. She passed the usual familiar plots: the ones adorned with flowers; the one with the old whiskey bottle; the grave with the stuffed toys resting against the stone. On the surface, they looked the same as always, but it felt like she was seeing them with fresh eyes this morning. The bottle had been there for a long time, and whoever had left it—presumably an old drinking buddy—had not returned since. The vibrant flowers seemed less like gestures of grief than of gratitude and love. And as sad as the child's toys were, there was at least a kind of acknowledgment in their presence. Better they were here, surely, than gathering dust in some small, untouched bedroom maintained like a museum.

And all of that spoke a basic truth to her. In the past, she had thought of coming here as visiting her father, but she realized now that had never been the case. Her father was gone. Graveyards might have housed the dead below the ground, but what lay above was always for the living; they were the places where people came to deal with the break between what their lives had once been and what they now were. All the times she had come here, she had only really been visiting herself, and her relationship with the past.

And how she did that was up to her to decide.

She reached her father's grave. That solid, dependable square of granite, with its careful lack of emotion.

"Hi, Dad," she said. "I know you said you didn't want me to talk to you, or any of that nonsense, but I'm afraid that's tough. Because I miss you."

There was no response from the stone, of course, and the cemetery around her remained silent. But the relief she felt was so overwhelming that she actually started to laugh. It turned into tears halfway through, and she put her hand to her nose.

"Oh fuck. But I do, you know. I miss you. And I'm sorry I didn't turn out to be like you, but I guess that's tough as well. Because the thing is, I think you'd be proud of me anyway."

She paused.

"Yeah, I really think you would."

That was enough for now. She stood there for a time, crying. Following another of her father's instructions, she had never allowed herself to do that here before. But, as with everything else, she figured he would understand. Maybe he would even have quietly nodded his approval. Because he had raised his daughter to be strong, hadn't he? To stand on her own two feet and make her own decisions rather than taking orders. If she wanted to cry, she would. Her choice.

In the same way, the answer to what kind of police officer she had turned out to be did not need to be judged against the kind her father had been. She was the kind *she* was. And if that was sometimes too involved, too haunted, too unable to box things up and keep the work separate from her life—so fucking be it.

But it felt like even that had changed, at least a little. It was nearly a week since the events in Gritten, and she had had the nightmare only once, two days after helping Paul escape from the woods. The dream had been superficially the same as always, but it too had felt different. She had been standing in the darkness, knowing someone was lost nearby, but this time she had recognized the dream for what it was, and the realization had calmed her.

Apparently, you could do anything you wanted in a lucid dream. But rather than attempting to create anything elaborate, Amanda had simply started walking in the blackness. She had never done that before. And while she had no idea if she was heading in the right direction, at least she was moving.

The nightmare hadn't returned since.

She looked down at her father's grave.

"I'll only do this once," she said. "I promise."

She balanced the flowers she'd brought with her against the headstone, then turned around and went to work.

But not to Featherbank.

Instead, close to midday, she drove through the idyllic countryside surrounding Gritten, and then into the gray, beaten-down heart of its center. She passed the hotel she had stayed in last week, then pulled into the parking lot of the pub Paul had brought her to the first time they'd met. Inside, she found him sitting in the same seat as then. He looked different, though. His hair was cut neatly, and he was wearing a smart black suit. There was a half-finished beer on the table in front of him. She got herself a wine and joined him, making a show of checking her watch.

"Should you really be drinking yet?" she said.

"Absolutely. I'm not a fan of public speaking."

"You're a lecturer, for God's sake."

"I know. For now, at least." He gestured at the beer. "And you didn't even buy me a drink."

She smiled. It was strange, given the bare handful of times they'd met, that she felt as relaxed in his company as she did. Perhaps it was simply a case of being bonded by events, but she liked him. Or, at least, she liked him well enough not to want to press him about everything that had really happened here in Gritten.

On one level, that was simple enough—messy in its own way, but still relatively straightforward. Forensics had tied Dean Price to the murders of William Roberts and Eileen and James Dawson. Bereft at the killing of his son, it seemed that Price had set out to discover the truth about Charlie Crabtree's disappearance. To *solve the problem* in his own way. Amanda knew a little more about Price's history in the army now: the things he had done; the dishonorable discharge; the way he'd struggled to find a purpose once back in civilian life. His son Michael had helped to provide that. When he lost that, something inside him had snapped.

Price's body had been found deep in the woods the morning after he abducted Paul. While chasing him through the trees, Price had twisted an ankle. It appeared he had then attempted to move farther away between the trees, before eventually giving up hope of escape. Amanda had seen photographs of the scene officers discovered after the sun rose that next morning. A man like Price was never going to allow himself to be captured. He had been found sitting on the ground, his back against the base of a tree, his wrists cut, and the undergrowth around him soaked with blood.

Case closed.

Except there were so many questions that still lingered. She still didn't know why Carl Dawson had returned to Gritten, or what he and Paul had really spoken about in the old playground that day. And Dean Price's methods certainly did not fit with the marks that had been left on Paul's mother's door, or the doll that had been delivered to the house. And while the CC666 account had been traced to James Dawson's computer, she didn't understand why he would have sent the messages he had, or how he'd had a photo of Charlie Crabtree's dream diary.

All of which meant she was quite sure there was something else going on here that she was missing. But neither Carl nor Paul were prepared to discuss it. They had kept their silences, leaving her with pieces of a mystery she couldn't fit into place.

But which perhaps, she decided as she sipped her wine now, did not necessarily matter. After all, she had answers to the questions she needed. And while she was not her father, she had a feeling that whatever was being hidden from her here was something that might be better for everyone's sake to leave alone.

"Why did you want to meet me today?" Paul said.

"Moral support," she said. "Didn't you know? Once you save someone's life, you're responsible for them forever."

He raised an eyebrow at her.

"Okay," she said. "I admit, that's a level of responsibility I'm probably not up to. I actually had another reason too."

She reached down and took a thin file out of her bag.

"The story you told Dean Price that night," she said. "About Hague's brother being responsible for killing Charlie Crabtree."

"I made that up."

"Yeah, you said. And honestly, no offense intended, but we checked. His brother was called Liam, and he was still in prison at the time."

"I was just trying to think of anything I could."

"And I believe you."

Amanda put the file on the table between them and slid it across to him.

"What's this?" he said.

"I got it yesterday. Go on. Knock yourself out."

He looked at her for a moment, then down at the file. When he opened it, she saw the single photograph inside. It was upside down from her perspective, but she had already stared at it enough to make sense of it from any angle. The tattered clothes; the spread of old bones half wrapped in undergrowth; the bare skull that had rolled to one side.

The photograph had been taken on the same morning Dean Price's body was found, only a short distance from where he was lying. The official identification had been confirmed late yesterday, and Dwyer had sent it to her as a courtesy. Amanda, in turn, had texted Paul to arrange to meet today for the exact same reason.

He was still looking at the photo.

"Is this . . . ?"

"Charlie Crabtree," she said. "Yes."

He continued staring down, and she wondered what he was thinking. How must it feel, to see that after all this time? To know a nightmare that had lasted for a quarter of a century was finally over? It was difficult to imagine what must be going through his head.

"I shouldn't be showing you that, by the way," she said. "But I figured you might want to know. That you deserved to know."

Finally, he looked up at her, and she saw so many

emotions on his face that it was impossible to untangle most of them.

All except one.

The relief she saw there reminded her of how she'd felt at the cemetery first thing that morning.

"Thank you," he said.

# FORTY-FOUR

------------

It was my mother who took me to the train station.

It was actually my father who drove, but he had become little more than a distant presence in my life by then, and this last journey was undertaken on my behalf almost begrudgingly. He stayed in the car when we got there. It was supposedly because he wanted to watch for traffic cops, but we both knew the real reason was that we had nothing to say to each other, and it was easier to forget a goodbye at a car than on a train station platform. It was my mother who accompanied me inside and waited with me, and so it's her I always think of as taking me there that day.

I had a crammed duffel bag and a heavy suitcase. The latter was on wheels that made a *tricking* noise on the concourse as we made our way through the crowds of commuters. I remember the departures boards whirring and flickering as they updated overhead, and the loudspeaker blaring out intermittent garbled messages. Everywhere, the mingled thrum of conversation echoed off the tiled walls. At that point in my life, I had never been on a train before, and I found the sensations almost overwhelming. I remember being nervous. Scared, even.

Which I didn't say.

My mother and I didn't speak until we reached the platform. The train was due in a few minutes, and we found a place in the shade to wait.

"Do you have your ticket?" she said.

I wanted to give her a look that conveyed I was eighteen years old now and not an idiot. But in that moment, I found myself remembering a different journey we had made together, when I was starting at a new school and she had asked me something similar. The question had not been for my benefit back then, and a part of me understood it wasn't now either—that she was asking the question to reassure herself.

"Yes," I said.

"Of course you have," she said. "I'm sorry."

She sounded genuinely apologetic, but I could tell she was also distracted: full of nervous energy. It was the way people get when they're fretting about something important that's outside their control.

*You don't need to be sorry,* I thought.

And did not say.

I remember being scared, yes, but the honest truth is that I was also excited. The last couple of years had been very difficult for me. It's important not to overplay that, of course, and on the few occasions I've thought about Gritten over the years—in those brief moments when I forgot to forget—it's always been in these very specific terms: what happened, never what happened *to me*. Because I knew then, and know better now, that other people suffered far worse than I did, and the tragedy belongs more appropriately to them. And most of all, of course, to Jenny Chambers.

Nevertheless, like so many of us, I was part of that story, and I was haunted by the role I played, however unwittingly, in *what happened*. The knowledge of the things I had and had not done had overshadowed my life ever since. Waiting on the platform that day, I had no idea what lay in store for me in the future, only that I was leaving far more behind me than Gritten itself.

"It will be Christmas before you know it," my mother said.

"I know."

I had spent the last couple of years saving up. I worked at the bookshop, and took whatever odd jobs in the area I could fit in between my studies. My focus, barely acknowledged even to myself, had been laser-like. And while it would indeed be Christmas before I knew it, I also knew that I had no intention of coming home when it was.

Which I did not say.

I looked up to see the train arriving: two rickety train cars rolling slowly toward us, blue at the top, stained with black muck at the bottom, as though they had trudged here through muddy fields. Farther up the platform, people were already shouldering their bags. I moved forward, feeling as though I needed to get on immediately or else I might miss my chance and the train would leave without me. But then my mother put her hand on my arm. When I looked at her, I could tell from the expression on her face she already knew what I hadn't said out loud. That she wasn't going to see me again for a long time. And that she had reconciled herself to that.

"I love you, Paul," she said quietly. "Look after yourself."

"I will."

"And for God's sake, give your mom a hug."

I shrugged my bag off and did. I don't know how many years it had been since I had embraced my mother by that point, but I remember being surprised by how small and fragile she felt. When we separated again, she put both her hands on the sides of my arms and appraised me.

"You've got so tall."

I didn't know what to say to that, so I didn't say anything. Behind me, the train *chuffed,* and my mother patted my arms and then let go.

"Just promise me you'll take care," she said.

"I'll be fine, Mom."

She smiled.

"I know you will."

Once on the train, I found my seat, and she waited on the platform to wave goodbye. I didn't understand at the time what was going through her head, and obviously I still don't know for certain, but at least now I have an idea.

She was thinking that I was going to be a writer.

Because there was a story of mine that I had never shown to her, but which she had found and read anyway. And while she was sad to see me leave, I think she was also happy that I was heading out into the world, escaping the past and moving forward into a different present without even glancing behind me. Because, however painful it might be, that's what all good parents have to do in the end. I think it was just that *what happened* had raised a curtain of silence between us that made it impossible to say certain things out loud.

I like to think they didn't need to be.

*I'm proud of you,* she didn't say. *And I understand.*

*Thank you,* I didn't reply. *And I love you.*

I paused and looked up from my notes.

With Sally's help, I had managed to speak to many of my mother's friends in the days since her death, and I had discovered that the casual religious belief she'd nurtured throughout her life had flourished in later years. So the decision had been made for me: it had to be a church funeral. The space before me now seemed cavernous, and yet every aisle was full. Rows and rows of people were crammed in shoulder to shoulder, as though everyone within miles of Gritten had been summoned here by some sense of duty to gather together and say goodbye.

When I had been sitting there earlier, waiting for the service to begin, every shuffle and cough behind me had echoed. The words I'd just spoken did the same now.

*Thank you. And I love you.*

I glanced around. It was dark in the church, the crowd before me illuminated by the sunlight streaming weakly in through the stained-glass windows above. But I caught sight of a few familiar faces among the strangers. Sally was sitting near the front, along with some of the friends I'd subsequently met. Carl was here. He was seated at the end of an aisle toward the front, and despite everything that had happened he was formally dressed, the pain he was feeling held back for the moment, his focus on the struggle that lay before him right now. Saying farewell to someone I knew he had loved.

Amanda was here, close to the back of the church.

My gaze moved from her and again to Carl as I thought about what she'd told me an hour earlier. Charlie had been found, and so that part of the story was over. Whether there would be questions still to answer on that score, I didn't know yet. I would deal with them if it came to it. But after the fire I'd finally lit two days ago, I knew there was nothing now to connect my mother to what had happened. And in the meantime I thought I saw on Carl's face the same conviction that I felt in my heart right now. There was no need to talk about such things unless we had to. Everyone had lost enough already.

And finally, I saw Marie.

She had found a seat at the end of one of the middle rows of the church, and she smiled when she saw me notice her. I had gone into the bookshop yesterday, taking an old book with me. *The Nightmare People*. It had taken its place on the shelves opposite the counter, but without a price written in pencil on the inside. I'd suggested to Marie that if someone found it and wanted it, they should just take it, and she had agreed with me.

Then I'd helped her with a delivery just like old times, and she had said something else, a little pointedly.

*You know . . . I won't be up to doing this much longer, Paul.*

I was still thinking about that. When I'd spoken to Amanda earlier I'd said I was a lecturer for now, because even though I'd never have imagined it a week ago, a part of me was already picturing a different sign above that shop. JOHNSON & ROSS still, of course—it was important to remember where you came from—but it didn't seem impossible that a new sign might add a different name as well. After all, it had always felt like home.

It was something to think about.

But for now, I looked back down.

"The story I wrote," I said. "The one my mother read. It was a stupid one. It was about someone returning to his home for one last time. It stopped before he actually got there, because I didn't know how to end it. I still don't. All I know is what happened when I did."

And then I spoke a little of what I'd learned about my mother since returning to Gritten. There wasn't much, but there was at least a little. The friends I hadn't known about until now. The love of reading she'd discovered later in life. The people she had cared about, and who had in turn cared about her.

When I was done, I looked at the coffin beside me, remembering all the photographs I'd seen. The ones where she was young, unguarded, and laughing with joy, the life ahead of her full of possibility. And even though I wasn't a religious man, I found myself wondering if she might be dreaming anything now.

"Sleep well," I said.

# ACKNOWLEDGMENTS

As with the writing of any novel, I owe a large debt of gratitude to a vast number of people—in this case, especially, my editors, Joel Richardson and Ryan Doherty, without whom this would be a very different book. Their expertise and patience are second to none and massively appreciated. Thanks are also due to Cecily van Buren-Freedman, Emma Henderson, Grace Long, Ellie Hughes, the rights team at Michael Joseph, and literally everybody else in publishing I've had the good fortune to meet and work with on this book and the last. Some writers get lucky on that level; I feel utterly blessed.

A huge thank-you to my awesome agent, Sandra Sawicka, and to Leah Middleton, Guy Herbert, and everybody else at Marjacq.

Thank you also to the reviewers, bloggers, and readers who have picked up my work and taken the time to say kind things about it—you're all hugely appreciated. To the wonderful staff at The Packhorse, Briggate, and the Bower's Tap in Leeds for putting up with me typing away in the corners. To my friends and family.

And to the crime-fiction community as a whole, especially Colin Scott for keeping me sane and being ridiculously ace.

Last of all, thank you so much to Lynn and Zack. I couldn't do any of it without you, and so this book is dedicated to you once more, with so much love.

**Read on for an excerpt from**
**THE ANGEL MAKER—**
**The next electrifying novel by Alex North,**
**Available soon in trade paperback from**
**Celadon Books!**

# PROLOGUE

"If you could see the future," Sam asked her, "would you want to?"

It was the end of the day, and they were sitting outside the school building. There was a roundabout there with a stone edge and a circle of flower beds in the center, and Sam and Katie met there every afternoon at the end of lessons. They were seventeen years old. As teenagers do, they sat and gossiped. They complained about her parents.

They asked each other questions.

*If you could see the future, would you want to?*

Katie thought about that. It was exactly the kind of question that had made her fall in love with Sam in the first place, but in that moment it made her uneasy. Sam was handsome and charismatic—full of talent and ambition—and for some unfathomable reason, he seemed to be in love with her as well. That made her happy, of course, but she was also frightened of losing him. Next year they would both be going away to different universities, and that upcoming separation felt like a threat looming on the horizon.

What was going to happen to them then?

"Katie?" Sam prompted.

"I don't know."

"Why not?"

"Because what if you saw something you didn't like?"

"Then you'd be able to change it."

"Maybe."

It was a warm afternoon with only the slightest of breezes. She watched as a group of kids drifted past them, hitching their bags up on their shoulders, talking and laughing. They were heading down the sunlit drive that led to the nearby village, while others were wandering away toward the bus stop. It was a reminder that she and Sam would have to part ways shortly. Katie lived close to the school, whereas his house was a bus journey away.

For a long time, Katie had felt like a spare tire in her family; it was her younger brother, Chris, whom her parents doted on. But over the last year, Sam had made her parents a *lot* more interested in her life than they had been previously. Her mother, especially, was suspicious of him and overly keen to monitor their relationship and keep it from going too far. If Katie was not home on time after school, there would be questions. At weekends, she and Sam were not allowed to be alone together. If Katie went to his house, her mother was always careful to ensure his parents were home too.

The resentment that caused had been growing steadily,

simmering away inside her, a little hotter every day. What she *wanted* to do was to spend as much time as possible with Sam before they were separated, and it seemed desperately unfair that her mother believed she was entitled to intervene.

"*Could* you change it though?" Katie wondered.

"What do you mean?"

"Well—if you just saw the future, you wouldn't know how you got there. So anything you did to avoid it might actually be what led you to it all along."

Sam considered that.

"You're so clever," he said.

"That's why you love me, right?"

"No. It's just *one* of the reasons."

She leaned her head on his shoulder, and he kissed her hair.

They sat like that in comfortable silence for a few seconds, and she closed her eyes, enjoying the sunlight on her face.

But then Sam started to say something and stopped.

She opened her eyes.

"What?"

He hesitated, which made the familiar anxiety flare up inside her. They hadn't spoken about what was going to happen next year, but she was sure university must have been on his mind as well—that he might be worrying about what was going to happen too. Perhaps that had been what had prompted his question. Maybe he'd decided it was better to end things now.

Katie leaned away and looked at him.

"Sam?"

"I was just thinking."

"Yeah, about what?"

"That my parents won't be home for an hour or so."

Her chest tightened for a second, and then her anxiety evaporated. He'd said it so casually, as though the words meant nothing at all—just an observation, really—but the weight of his suggestion hung in the air, and despite the warmth of the afternoon, she shivered a little.

She wanted to go back with him so badly.

"I can't," she said.

"Yeah, I know."

"I mean . . . I want to. I just can't."

He nodded. Katie wondered what was going through his mind. Was he losing patience with her? Had he already? There had been no pressure from Sam on that level at all, but she couldn't help feeling she'd just failed a test of some kind. And she supposed that she had. Because even though her parents didn't seem to care very much about her, she was still being good, wasn't she?

Still doing what she'd been told.

"One day though," she said.

"One day."

She looked to her right—and there was Chris, walking slowly along the road toward them. As always, he was alone; she didn't think he had any friends. His hands were tucked in his pockets, and his head was bowed. He was fifteen but looked younger and smaller than his age, and Katie had to wait for him every day and walk home with him. Her mother insisted. Katie supposed it made sense. They were at the same high school, after all, and were both going to the same place at the same time.

But while she loved her brother very much, she was not his keeper, and the sight of him now caused the resentment inside her to blaze even brighter. God— he even *carried* himself like he didn't belong. Why couldn't he look after himself instead of her being expected to do it? Why didn't her life matter to her parents as much as his?

Sam saw Chris approaching them.

He sighed and stood up, hitching his bag onto his shoulder.

"I'll see you tomorrow," he said quietly. "I love you."

"I love you too."

Then he stood in front of her, waiting for her to stand up and kiss him goodbye as she always did. But she was still looking to her right, watching Chris walking toward them, and the feeling of resentment that had been building inside her finally spilled over.

She looked back at Sam.

"No," she said. "Wait."

*If you could see the future, would you want to?*

You can't, of course. A life is lived forward. The present is a vantage point from which every moment in the past is inevitable and every moment in the future invisible. Most of those moments won't be important, but a handful will turn out to be pivotal—shattering, even—and you never know which until it's too late.

As Katie boarded the bus with Sam that day, she didn't know that a local man named Michael Hyde was leaving his house right then.

That he was walking toward his car with a knife in his hand.

She spent an hour at Sam's house that afternoon. She had made a decision to do what *she* wanted to do for once, and it was thrilling. She would deal with the consequences later—and really, how bad could they be? Sam walked her to the bus stop afterward, their hands clasped tightly together and their upper arms pressed against each other. He kissed her goodbye. When the bus set off, Katie smiled at him through the window until he was out of sight, and then she looked straight ahead, smiling to herself instead, her body full of warmth and light. It felt as though she hadn't just discovered a secret but somehow become one.

After getting off the bus, she walked home slowly. She was more than ready to have whatever argument awaited her there, but she also wanted to hold on to that feeling inside her for as long as possible. And besides, it was a beautiful afternoon. The sun was still bright and warm, and there was a lovely cast to the light that brought out fresh colors in the world around her. Everywhere she looked, it was like she was seeing things for the first time. As though everything had changed.

And, of course, it had. She just didn't know it yet.

Katie reached their road.

As she turned the corner, the scene before her made no sense. They lived in a quiet area, but the street ahead was crowded with police cars and vans. Everywhere she looked, she saw red and blue lights flashing around. The sight of it all stopped her in her tracks. Her gaze moved to the yellow cordon that had been set up across the street, with what seemed like crowds of police officers moving around behind. A part of her was aware there should have been a great deal of noise, but for a few seconds it was like being underwater, and all she could hear was her heartbeat thudding dully in her ears.

*Something terrible has happened.*

She would always remember the sickening, sinking feeling inside herself. And she would remember what came along with it: the desperate urge to go back in time and change things.

*Please*, she would remember thinking.

*Oh God, please.*

Because right then, she would have given up Sam for that chance.

She would have given up herself.

She would have given up anything.

Katie took a few faltering steps forward, unsure at first whether her body would work properly—and then she began to run. One of the police officers saw her coming and intercepted her at the tape. She didn't know it at the time, but he had been expecting her. Her parents had called Sam's house while she'd been on the bus and learned she was on her way.

"Hey," the officer said gently. "Hey."

Katie ignored him. He was tall and solid, and she had to step to one side in order to stare past him at the scene beyond the cordon.

She didn't understand what she was seeing—not right then. But she took it in anyway, and even seventeen years later she could still see it all so clearly whenever she closed her eyes.

The old red car, abandoned at an angle across the pavement, where it had swerved in to block Chris's path.

The blood spatters from where he had been stabbed repeatedly.

And the larger pool of blood, in the gutter, where Michael Hyde had begun his desperate attempt to cut off her brother's face.

# ONE

--------

*You can't do this.*
  *It's not allowed.*

Alan Hobbes looks up from the book on his desk. He listens carefully, but the only thing he can hear is the silence ringing in the room. There is nobody else here. He sent everyone home earlier and is alone in the house. Or, at least, he is for the moment.

And yet the voice of his brother, Edward, echoes in the air from across the years.

Hobbes stares at his bookshelves for a few seconds and then shakes his head. He is old now; that is all it is. Everything is swimming together as the end approaches. And really, that is fine. They say that people's lives flash before their eyes as they die, and what else can that mean except that the nature of time changes as death approaches? Or rather—he corrects himself—that our *perception* of it does, so that we finally begin to see time for what it was all along. A journey seems to take place step by step while you're on it, but if you could look down from above you would see the whole route laid out below you. You would understand that the beginning, middle, and end all exist at once, and that they always had and always would.

It is not something to be afraid of.

Hobbes looks back down at the notebook on the desk. The time he has left is limited, and he needs to concentrate. Because death is coming for him. He can feel it approaching steadily and inexorably. It will be arriving at the house in just a few short hours, where-upon it will open the door downstairs and creep up one of the twinned staircases that lead to his rooms.

And then it will all be over.

Except that isn't true. His *own* journey will end to-night, but others will continue. Has he been careful enough? Is everything in place? It is difficult to be sure, especially as there are other drifts than the perception of time that come with old age. But he has done his best.

He thinks of those people he has never met and never will, but whom it feels he knows so well.

Right now, Katie Shaw is at home, making dinner. She is worrying about her daughter, her marriage, and one of the children she teaches. She is blissfully un-aware of the turn her journey will take tomorrow and where it will lead her.

Detective Laurence Page is listening to classical music at home. He doesn't know Hobbes's name yet.

And Christopher Shaw, of course.

Christopher will be here soon, which reminds Hobbes that time is short. He can see death edging ever closer in his mind's eye—a knife in its hand—and the thought of what is going to happen spurs him on.

It is October 4, 2017.

Hobbes picks up the old pen.

*You can't do this*, he remembers.

*It's not allowed.*

Even so, he begins to write.

# TWO

------

"Holy shit," Pettifer said. "Would you look at this?"

Laurence was doing exactly that.

He had his shirtsleeves rolled up and his arm resting on the sill of the open passenger window. He had been staring idly out for some time, watching as they left the old factories and office blocks of the city center behind them and then the suburbs full of crammed houses. Now they were passing through the more affluent neighborhoods to the north. It was aspirational here: a world of sprawling bungalows, detached mansions, and enormous gardens.

But there were even richer locales ahead.

"How the other half live," Pettifer said.

"And yet die like the rest of us."

"Yes, well. Let's try not to upset anyone at the scene, shall we?"

"Don't worry." Laurence closed his eyes, enjoying the sensation of the fresh air rushing over his face. "I will behave."

"Do you need to have the window open?"

"I like the wind."

"Could you close it?"

"I could," he said happily. "It is within my power. But I'm not going to."

Pettifer sighed. She had fallen into that trap before.

But she did have a point, Laurence thought. Not about the window, or him behaving (although, of course, there was that), but about the divisions of wealth within the city. Although it was *also* interesting that it seemed a fresh observation to her. Laurence had come to this city—this country—as an infant, shortly after his mother's death, and one of the many things he had inherited from his father was an immigrant's sense of curiosity. Many of the other officers seemed to take the city for granted, whereas Laurence had never quite shaken away the sensation of being an outsider here. Of not quite belonging. Of seeing the city as something that needed to be understood. The way he thought about it was this: his colleagues were excellent at telling the time on the clockface, but it often seemed to surprise them to discover there were cogs behind it that made the hands turn.

A short time later, he opened his eyes.

They were driving through countryside now. Fields sprawled away into the distance on either side. Some were dotted with cattle or crops, but most seemed empty. Perhaps they were simply being left fallow? Laurence wasn't sure; his knowledge of the agricultural industry was cursory. But it was difficult to shake the sensation that the land here belonged to people who owned so much of it that they could afford to leave acres barren and untended, forgotten afterthoughts in their vast inventories.

Laurence yawned.

"How much farther?" he asked.

"I'm afraid I can't hear you because the window is open."

"I don't believe you."

She didn't reply—this time avoiding another familiar trap. Laurence smiled to himself. He liked Pettifer a lot. They had been working together as partners for more than three years. They complemented each other well in that they annoyed each other in precisely the right ways unless it was important that they did not.

A minute or so later, she slowed down and flicked the blinker. They turned right onto what seemed to Laurence little more than a narrow dirt road leading off between the trees that were packed in tightly on either side. The muddy ground beneath the car had hardened into an undulating wave, and the tires rolled from one side to the other as Pettifer navigated the twists and turns.

"Mr. Hobbes liked his privacy," Laurence said.

"I guess so. But if you had as much money as that, wouldn't you?"

"I honestly don't know how much money he had."

"No, well." Pettifer ducked her head slightly, peering out of the windshield at the winding track ahead. "Clearly enough to get away from other people. Which I have to say has always been an enduring dream of mine."

"And of all the people who know you."

The world suddenly brightened as the dark trees fell away, curling off to either side to form a black perimeter around a large, sunlit clearing. The dirt track beneath the car became an immaculately maintained driveway of pale gravel that led in a straight line across an expanse of neatly trimmed grass.

The house was about three hundred feet ahead—although, Laurence thought, leaning forward himself now, *house* barely did the structure justice. There was a three-story building at the center, and taller wings stretching out on either side, every visible edifice topped with towers and turrets. His gaze moved over the face of the property. There were almost too many windows to count. Some were aligned in neat rows, while others appeared to be just randomly placed dark squares. Taken as a whole, the building looked like a curve of jawbone, inverted and pressed into the land.

Two police vans were parked out front.

A few officers dotted around.

The *house*—he needed to think of it as something—loomed ever larger as they approached. Looking up, Laurence noticed that a part of the roof in the middle was more jagged than the rest. Whatever room had once been up there was now partially exposed to the air, and he could see a few blackened struts of wood sticking up. An old fire. The bricks below were scorched, and the window directly beneath had shattered and not been repaired.

The tires crackled as Pettifer brought the car to a halt behind one of the vans at the entrance. One of the uniformed officers approached the vehicle.

Laurence held out his ID.

"Detective Laurence Page," he said. "Detective Caroline Pettifer."

"Yes, sir. Ma'am."

They got out of the car. Laurence looked at the entrance before them: two enormous wooden doors beneath a stone arch. They were far wider and taller than any human would require.

"Good Lord," he said. "You could ride a horse through there."

Pettifer walked around the car and stood beside him, hands on her hips, looking up.

"Told you so," she said. "The other half."

A sergeant led them inside to the scene.

Through the doors, there was a large reception area, the floor made of cracked black and white tiles. Laurence looked up as they walked; the ceiling was two stories above. Ahead of them, separated by a vast mirror, two wooden staircases curled upward. There were no windows, and dust hung visibly in the air, and yet there was the hint of a breeze coming from somewhere.

He and Pettifer followed the officer up one of the staircases—which joined the other on a small landing. Another pair led up from there, curving around each other like a figure eight, so that they turned back on themselves again as they ascended. The arrangement seemed pointless to Laurence—whichever route they chose, they ended up in the same place—but eventually they emerged into a large area he estimated must have been above the entrance hall. Despite the solid floor beneath his feet, he was aware of a vast distance stretching away below him, and it felt like if he fell he would be falling forever.

"This way, sir."

"And ma'am," Pettifer said.

"Yes, ma'am. Sorry."

A thin corridor led away to the left with an open door at the far end. As they approached it, Laurence could see officers moving in the room beyond. He was expecting another grand, ornate space, but his expectations were confounded. He and Pettifer followed the officer into a small area that, in some ways, reminded him of the modest confines of his own apartment. Looking around, he saw little in the way of furnishings: a single bed against one wall, on which the victim was still lying; a cart of medical equipment beside it; an old television on a stand, angled toward the bed. He looked to his left. There was a small, open-plan kitchen area there, and a closed door next to it that he assumed led to a bathroom.

And at the far end of the room, an archway.

He stared at that for a moment. It clearly led away into some deeper chamber of the house, but the blackness there was impenetrable. Laurence could hear the faintest rush of air emerging from it, and the sound reminded him of something breathing.

He stepped over to the bed and looked down at the victim.

*Breathing* was clearly not a sound Alan Hobbes would be making again. The old man's lower body was still beneath the covers, but he was exposed from the waist up. His head was tilted at an unnatural angle, all but severed by a vicious knife wound.

The cause of death, at least, was clear.

But Laurence also scanned the man's exposed, scrawny torso, taking in the additional stab wounds there. The bedsheets below the body had once been white but were now saturated with blood. Whoever had murdered Alan Hobbes had taken their time in doing so, and the old man had clearly been too weak and feeble even to begin to fight them off. . . .